JUSTICE LEAGUE UNLIMITED

CHAMPIONS OF JUSTICE

Written by:
Adam Beechen

Colored by:
Heroic Age

Illustrated by:
Carlo Barberi
Walden Wong

Lettered by:
Pat Brosseau
Travis Lanham

Superman created by **Jerry Siegel** and **Joe Shuster**

Batman created by **Bob Kane**

Wonder Woman created by **William Moulton Marston**

JUSTICE LEAGUE UNLIMITED VOL. 3: CHAMPIONS OF JUSTICE
Published by DC Comics. Cover and compilation copyright © 2006 DC Comics. All Rights
Reserved. Originally published in single magazine form as JUSTICE LEAGUE UNLIMITED
11-15. Copyright © 2005 DC Comics. All Rights Reserved. All characters, their distinctive
likenesses and related elements featured in this publication are trademarks of DC Comics.
The stories, characters and incidents featured in this publication are entirely fictional.
DC Comics does not read or accept unsolicited submissions of ideas, stories or artwork.

CARTOON NETWORK and its logo are trademarks of Cartoon Network.

DC Comics, 1700 Broadway, New York, NY 10019
A Warner Bros. Entertainment Company.
Printed in Canada. First Printing.
ISBN: 1-4012-1015-5   ISBN 13: 978-1-4012-1015-1
Cover illustration by Ben Caldwell.
Publication design by John J. Hill.

WB SHIELD ™ & © Warner Bros. Entertainment Inc.
(s06)

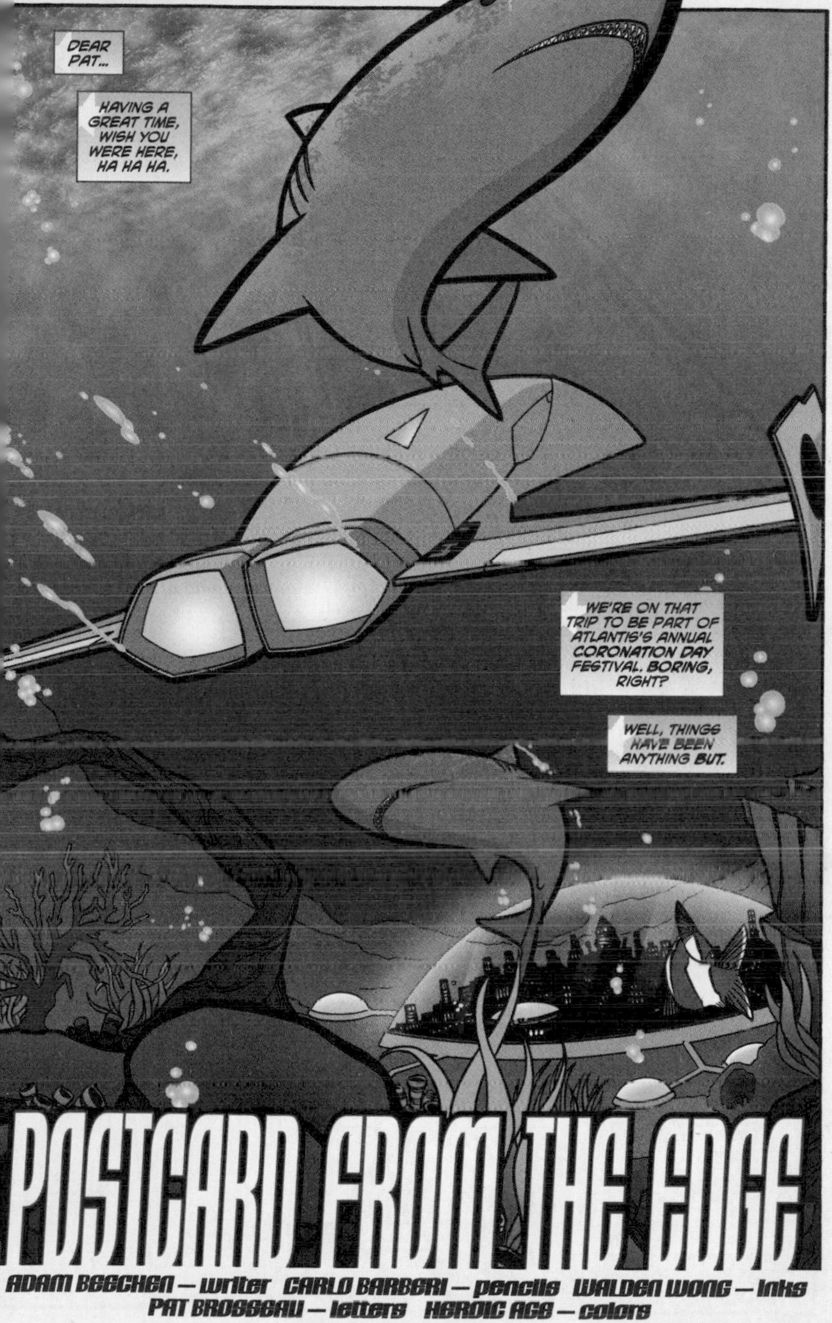
DEAR PAT...
HAVING A GREAT TIME, WISH YOU WERE HERE, HA HA HA.
WE'RE ON THAT TRIP TO BE PART OF ATLANTIS'S ANNUAL CORONATION DAY FESTIVAL. BORING, RIGHT?
WELL, THINGS HAVE BEEN ANYTHING BUT.
POSTCARD FROM THE EDGE
ADAM BEECHEN — writer CARLO BARBERI — pencils WALDEN WONG — inks
PAT BROSSEAU — letters HEROIC AGE — colors

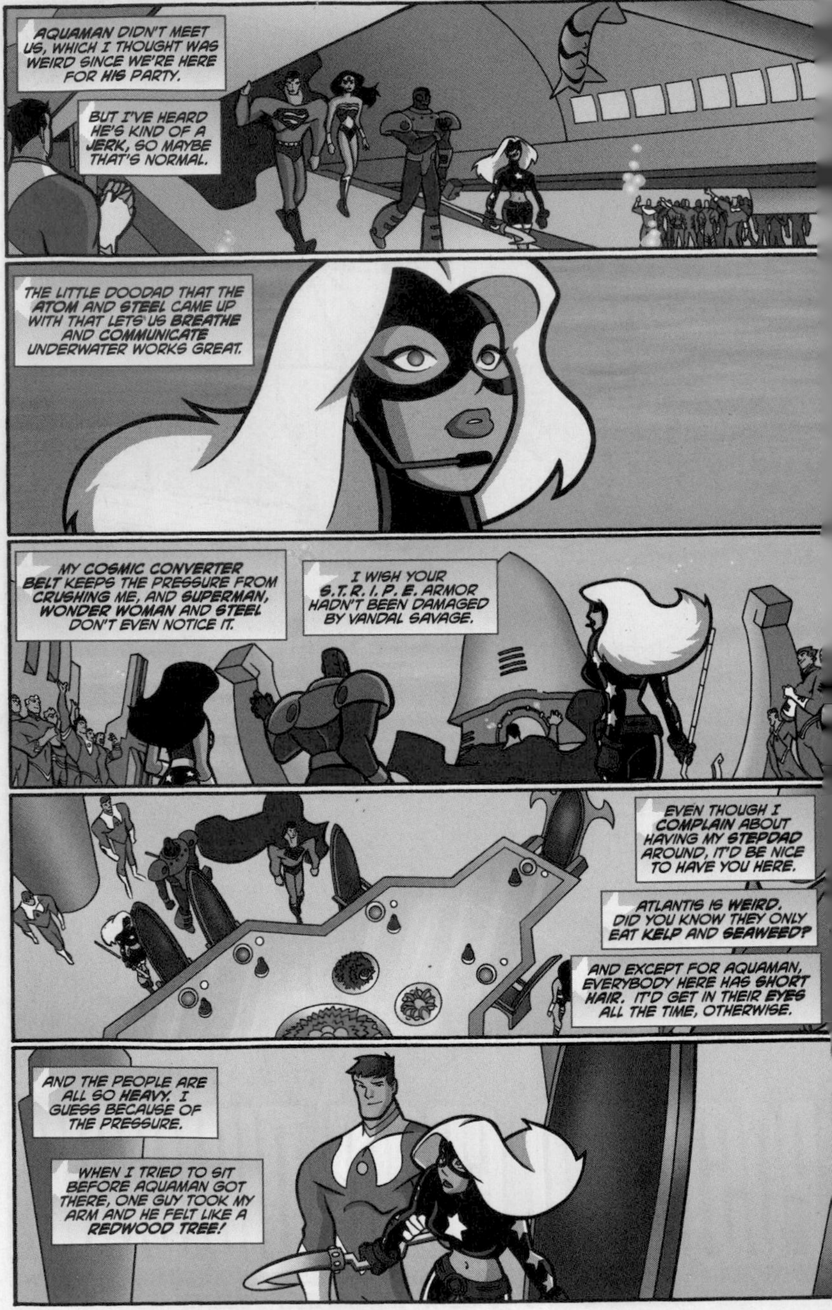
AQUAMAN DIDN'T MEET US, WHICH I THOUGHT WAS WEIRD SINCE WE'RE HERE FOR HIS PARTY.
BUT I'VE HEARD HE'S KIND OF A JERK, SO MAYBE THAT'S NORMAL.
THE LITTLE DOODAD THAT THE ATOM AND STEEL CAME UP WITH THAT LETS US BREATHE AND COMMUNICATE UNDERWATER WORKS GREAT.
MY COSMIC CONVERTER BELT KEEPS THE PRESSURE FROM CRUSHING ME, AND SUPERMAN, WONDER WOMAN AND STEEL DON'T EVEN NOTICE IT.
I WISH YOUR S.T.R.I.P.E. ARMOR HADN'T BEEN DAMAGED BY VANDAL SAVAGE.
EVEN THOUGH I COMPLAIN ABOUT HAVING MY STEPDAD AROUND, IT'D BE NICE TO HAVE YOU HERE.
ATLANTIS IS WEIRD. DID YOU KNOW THEY ONLY EAT KELP AND SEAWEED?
AND EXCEPT FOR AQUAMAN, EVERYBODY HERE HAS SHORT HAIR. IT'D GET IN THEIR EYES ALL THE TIME, OTHERWISE.
AND THE PEOPLE ARE ALL SO HEAVY. I GUESS BECAUSE OF THE PRESSURE.
WHEN I TRIED TO SIT BEFORE AQUAMAN GOT THERE, ONE GUY TOOK MY ARM AND HE FELT LIKE A REDWOOD TREE!

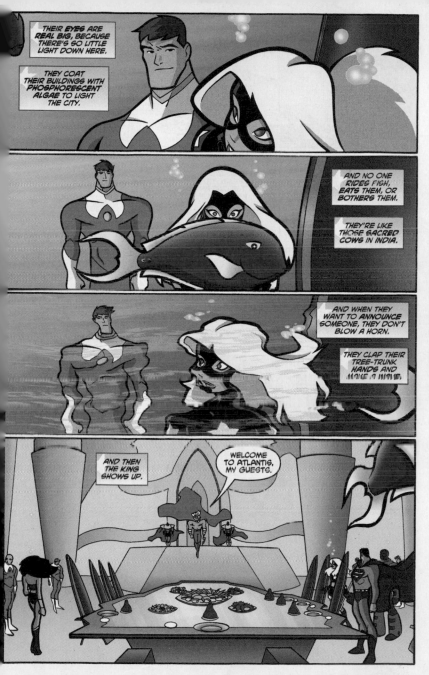

THEIR EYES ARE REAL BIG, BECAUSE THERE'S SO LITTLE LIGHT DOWN HERE.

THEY COAT THEIR BUILDINGS WITH PHOSPHORESCENT ALGAE TO LIGHT THE CITY.

AND NO ONE RIDES FISH, EATS THEM, OR BOTHERS THEM.

THEY'RE LIKE THOSE SACRED COWS IN INDIA.

AND WHEN THEY WANT TO ANNOUNCE SOMEONE, THEY DON'T BLOW A HORN.

THEY CLAP THEIR TREE-TRUNK HANDS AND MAKE A NOISE.

AND THEN THE KING SHOWS UP.

WELCOME TO ATLANTIS, MY GUESTS.

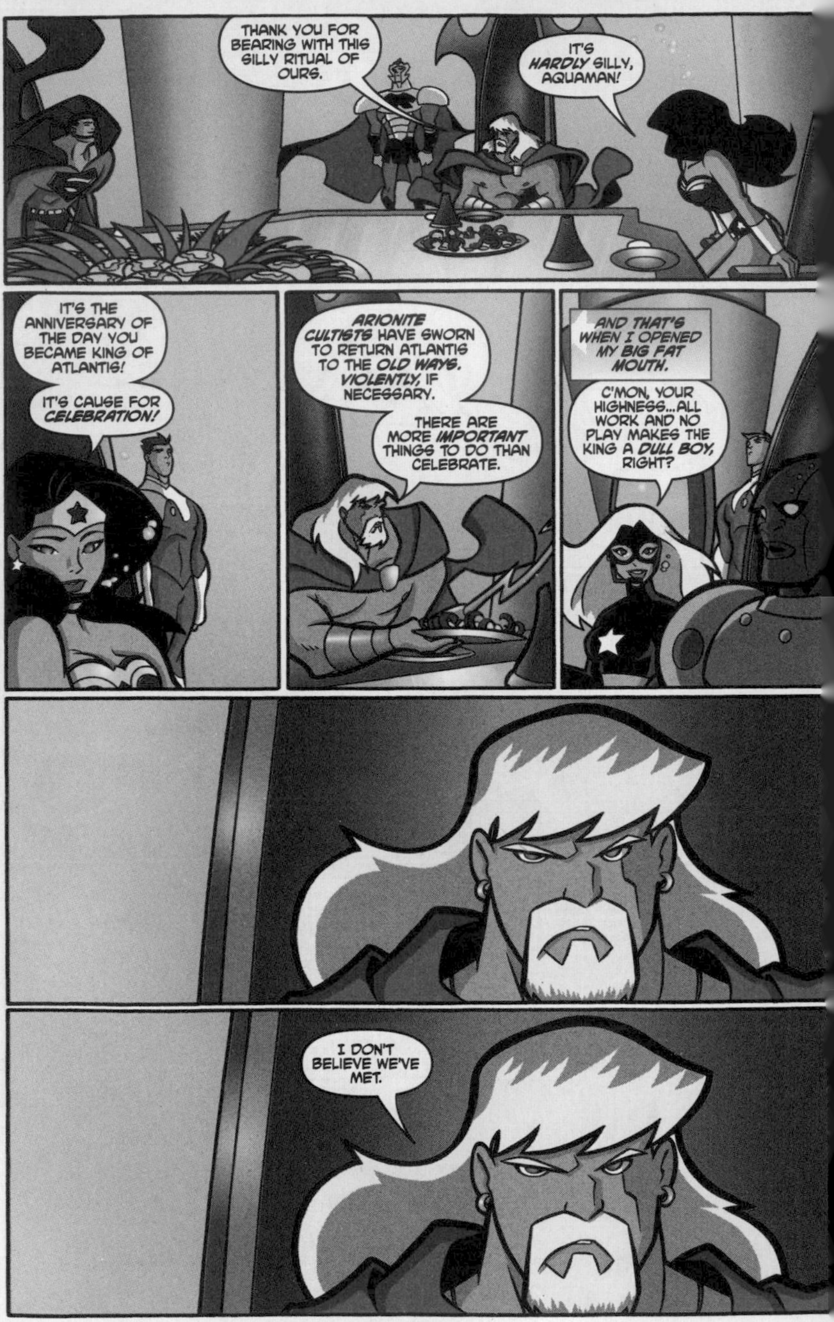
THANK YOU FOR BEARING WITH THIS SILLY RITUAL OF OURS.
IT'S HARDLY SILLY, AQUAMAN!
IT'S THE ANNIVERSARY OF THE DAY YOU BECAME KING OF ATLANTIS!
IT'S CAUSE FOR CELEBRATION!
ARIONITE CULTISTS HAVE SWORN TO RETURN ATLANTIS TO THE OLD WAYS. VIOLENTLY, IF NECESSARY.
THERE ARE MORE IMPORTANT THINGS TO DO THAN CELEBRATE.
AND THAT'S WHEN I OPENED MY BIG FAT MOUTH.
C'MON, YOUR HIGHNESS...ALL WORK AND NO PLAY MAKES THE KING A DULL BOY, RIGHT?
I DON'T BELIEVE WE'VE MET.

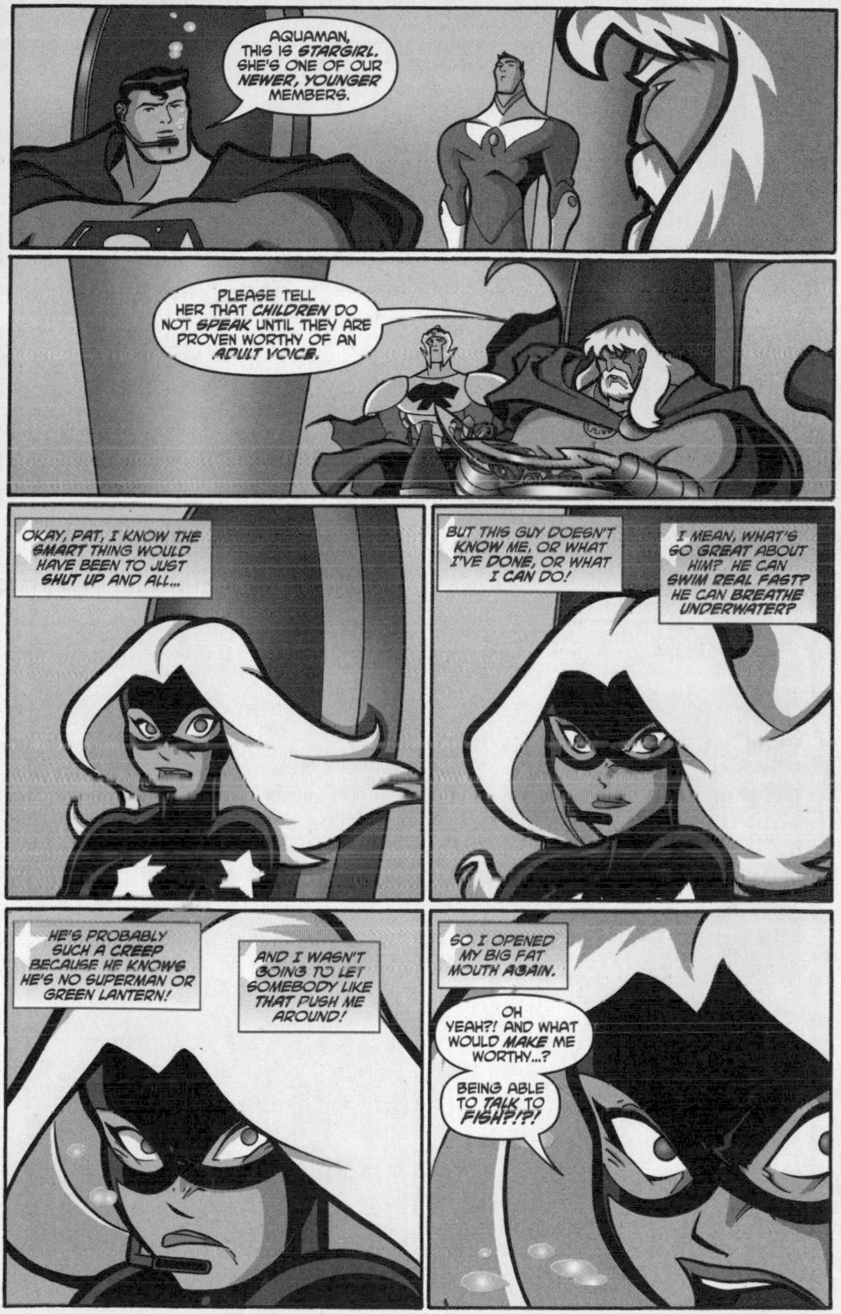
AQUAMAN, THIS IS STARGIRL. SHE'S ONE OF OUR NEWER, YOUNGER MEMBERS.
PLEASE TELL HER THAT CHILDREN DO NOT SPEAK UNTIL THEY ARE PROVEN WORTHY OF AN ADULT VOICE.
OKAY, PAT, I KNOW THE SMART THING WOULD HAVE BEEN TO JUST SHUT UP AND ALL...
BUT THIS GUY DOESN'T KNOW ME, OR WHAT I'VE DONE, OR WHAT I CAN DO!
I MEAN, WHAT'S SO GREAT ABOUT HIM? HE CAN SWIM REAL FAST? HE CAN BREATHE UNDERWATER?
HE'S PROBABLY SUCH A CREEP BECAUSE HE KNOWS HE'S NO SUPERMAN OR GREEN LANTERN!
AND I WASN'T GOING TO LET SOMEBODY LIKE THAT PUSH ME AROUND!
SO I OPENED MY BIG FAT MOUTH AGAIN.
OH YEAH?! AND WHAT WOULD MAKE ME WORTHY...?
BEING ABLE TO TALK TO FISH?!?!

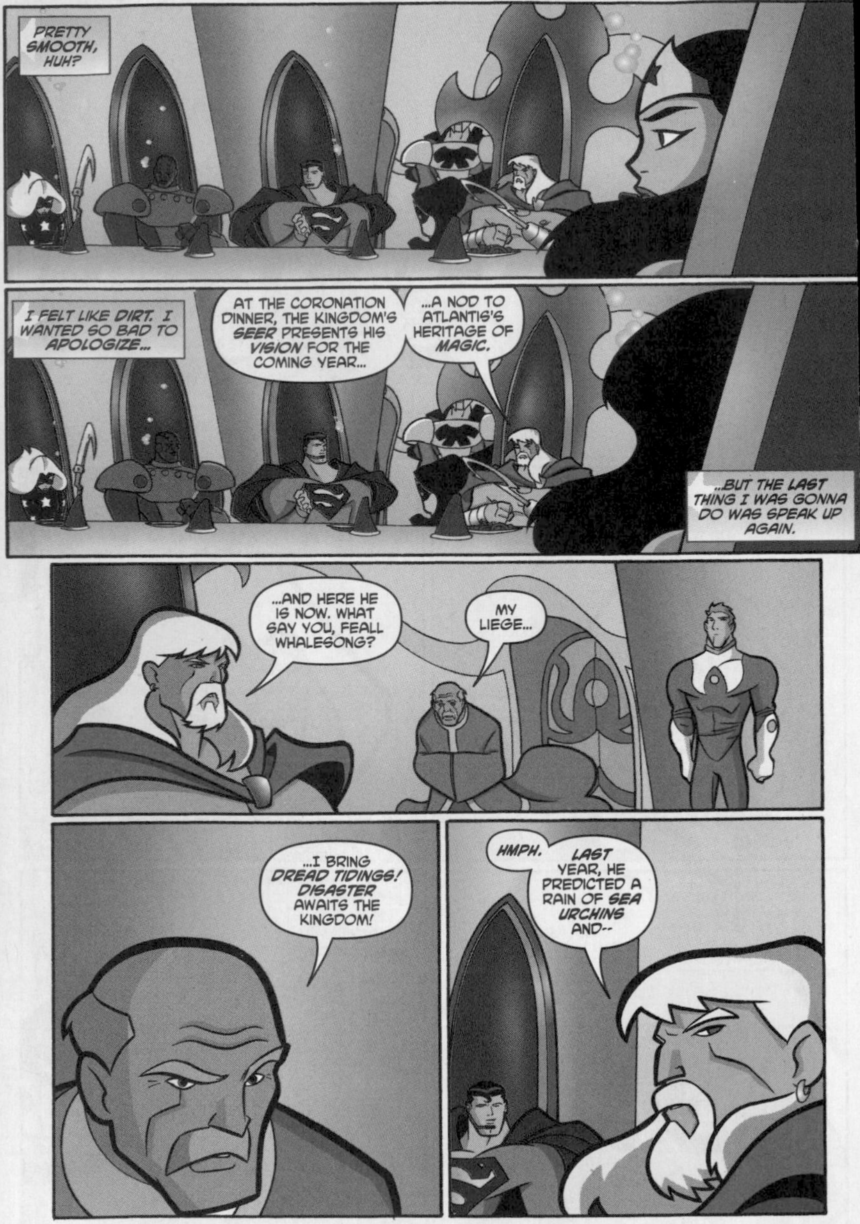
PRETTY SMOOTH, HUH?
I FELT LIKE DIRT. I WANTED SO BAD TO APOLOGIZE...
AT THE CORONATION DINNER, THE KINGDOM'S SEER PRESENTS HIS VISION FOR THE COMING YEAR...
...A NOD TO ATLANTIS'S HERITAGE OF MAGIC.
...BUT THE LAST THING I WAS GONNA DO WAS SPEAK UP AGAIN.
...AND HERE HE IS NOW. WHAT SAY YOU, FEALL WHALESONG?
MY LIEGE...
...I BRING DREAD TIDINGS! DISASTER AWAITS THE KINGDOM!
HMPH.
LAST YEAR, HE PREDICTED A RAIN OF SEA URCHINS AND--

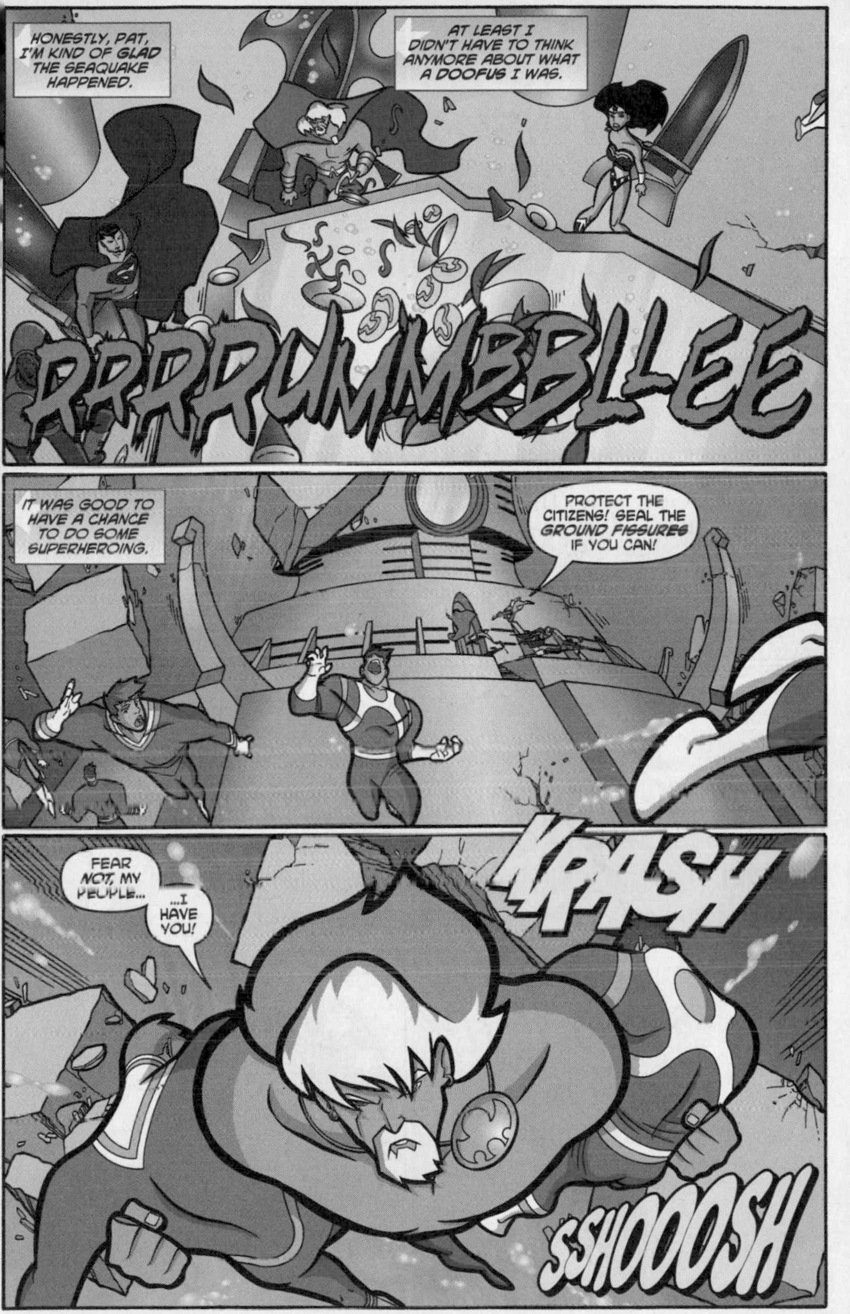
HONESTLY, PAT, I'M KIND OF GLAD THE SEAQUAKE HAPPENED.
AT LEAST I DIDN'T HAVE TO THINK ANYMORE ABOUT WHAT A DOOFUS I WAS.
RRRRUMMBBLLEE
IT WAS GOOD TO HAVE A CHANCE TO DO SOME SUPERHEROING.
PROTECT THE CITIZENS! SEAL THE GROUND FISSURES IF YOU CAN!
FEAR NOT, MY PEOPLE...
...I HAVE YOU!
KRASH
SSHOOOSH

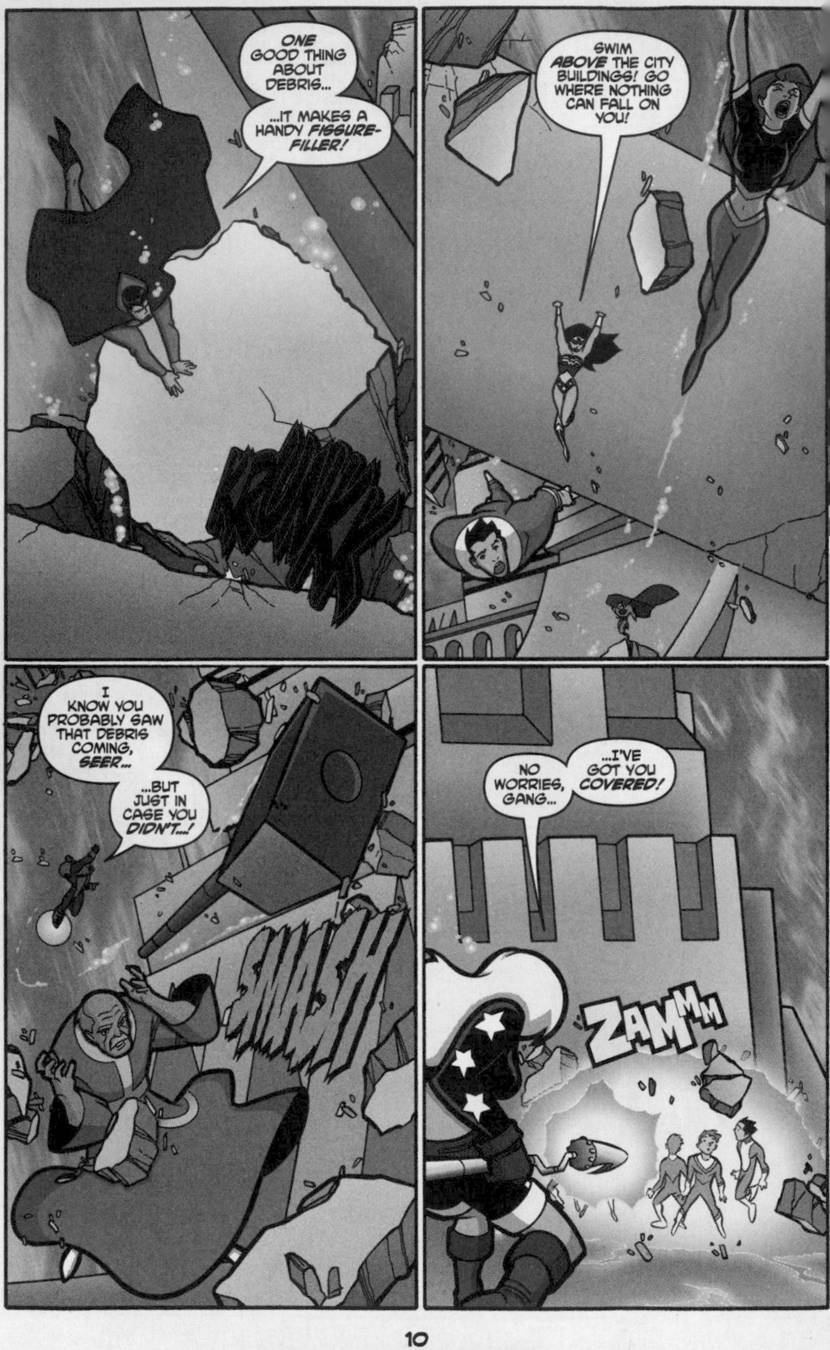

ONE GOOD THING ABOUT DEBRIS...
...IT MAKES A HANDY FISSURE-FILLER!
SWIM ABOVE THE CITY BUILDINGS! GO WHERE NOTHING CAN FALL ON YOU!
I KNOW YOU PROBABLY SAW THAT DEBRIS COMING, SEER...
...BUT JUST IN CASE YOU DIDN'T...!
SMASH
NO WORRIES, GANG...
...I'VE GOT YOU COVERED!
ZAMMM

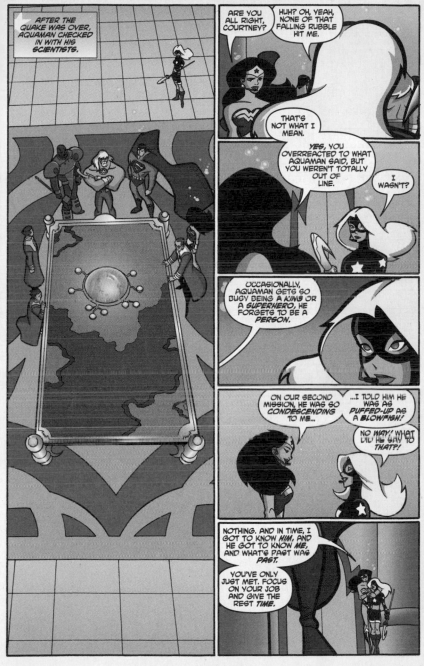

AFTER THE QUAKE WAS OVER, AQUAMAN CHECKED IN WITH HIS SCIENTISTS.

ARE YOU ALL RIGHT, COURTNEY?

HUH? OH, YEAH, NONE OF THAT FALLING RUBBLE HIT ME.

THAT'S NOT WHAT I MEAN.

YES, YOU OVERREACTED TO WHAT AQUAMAN SAID, BUT YOU WEREN'T TOTALLY OUT OF LINE.

I WASN'T?

OCCASIONALLY, AQUAMAN GETS SO BUSY BEING A *KING* OR A *SUPERHERO*, HE FORGETS TO BE A *PERSON*.

ON OUR SECOND MISSION, HE WAS SO CONDESCENDING TO ME...

...I TOLD HIM HE WAS AS *PUFFED-UP* AS A *BLOWFISH!*

NO *WAY!* WHAT DID HE SAY TO *THAT?!*

NOTHING. AND IN TIME, I GOT TO KNOW *HIM*, AND HE GOT TO KNOW *ME*, AND WHAT'S PAST WAS *PAST*.

YOU'VE ONLY JUST MET. FOCUS ON YOUR JOB AND GIVE THE REST *TIME*.

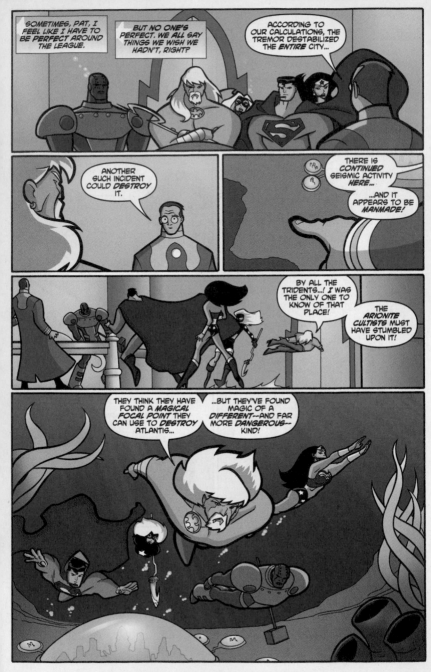

SOMETIMES, PAT, I FEEL LIKE I HAVE TO BE *PERFECT* AROUND THE LEAGUE.

BUT NO ONE'S *PERFECT*. WE ALL SAY THINGS WE WISH WE HADN'T, RIGHT?

ACCORDING TO OUR CALCULATIONS, THE TREMOR DESTABILIZED THE *ENTIRE* CITY...

ANOTHER SUCH INCIDENT COULD *DESTROY* IT.

THERE IS *CONTINUED* SEISMIC ACTIVITY *HERE*...

...AND IT APPEARS TO BE *MANMADE!*

BY ALL THE *TRIDENTS...! I* WAS THE ONLY ONE TO KNOW OF THAT PLACE!

THE *ARIONITE CULTISTS* MUST HAVE STUMBLED UPON IT!

THEY THINK THEY HAVE FOUND A *MAGICAL FOCAL POINT* THEY CAN USE TO *DESTROY* ATLANTIS...

...BUT THEY'VE FOUND MAGIC OF A *DIFFERENT*--AND FAR MORE *DANGEROUS*-- KIND!

12

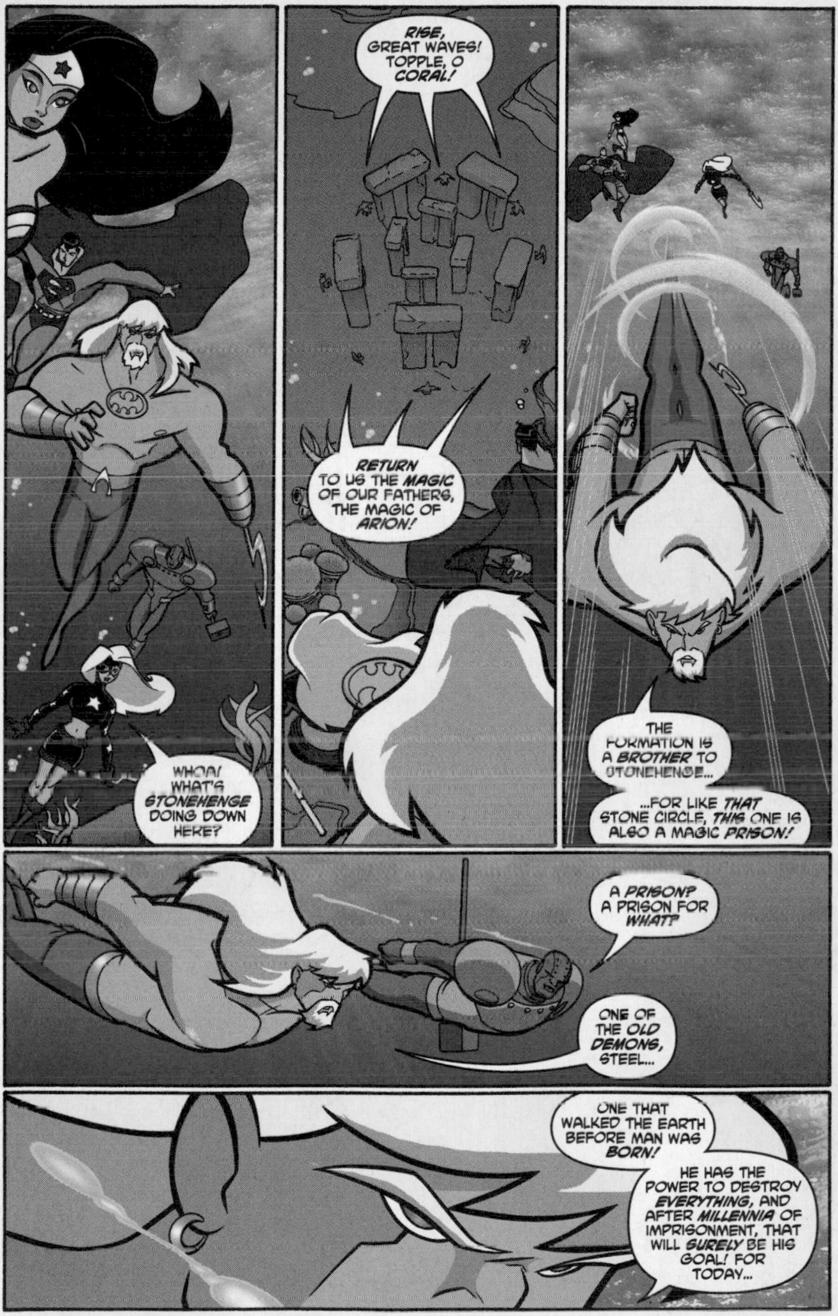
WHOA! WHAT'S STONEHENGE DOING DOWN HERE?
RISE, GREAT WAVES! TOPPLE, O CORAL!
RETURN TO US THE MAGIC OF OUR FATHERS, THE MAGIC OF ARION!
THE FORMATION IS A BROTHER TO STONEHENGE...
...FOR LIKE THAT STONE CIRCLE, THIS ONE IS ALSO A MAGIC PRISON!
A PRISON? A PRISON FOR WHAT?
ONE OF THE OLD DEMONS, STEEL...
ONE THAT WALKED THE EARTH BEFORE MAN WAS BORN!
HE HAS THE POWER TO DESTROY EVERYTHING, AND AFTER MILLENNIA OF IMPRISONMENT, THAT WILL SURELY BE HIS GOAL! FOR TODAY...

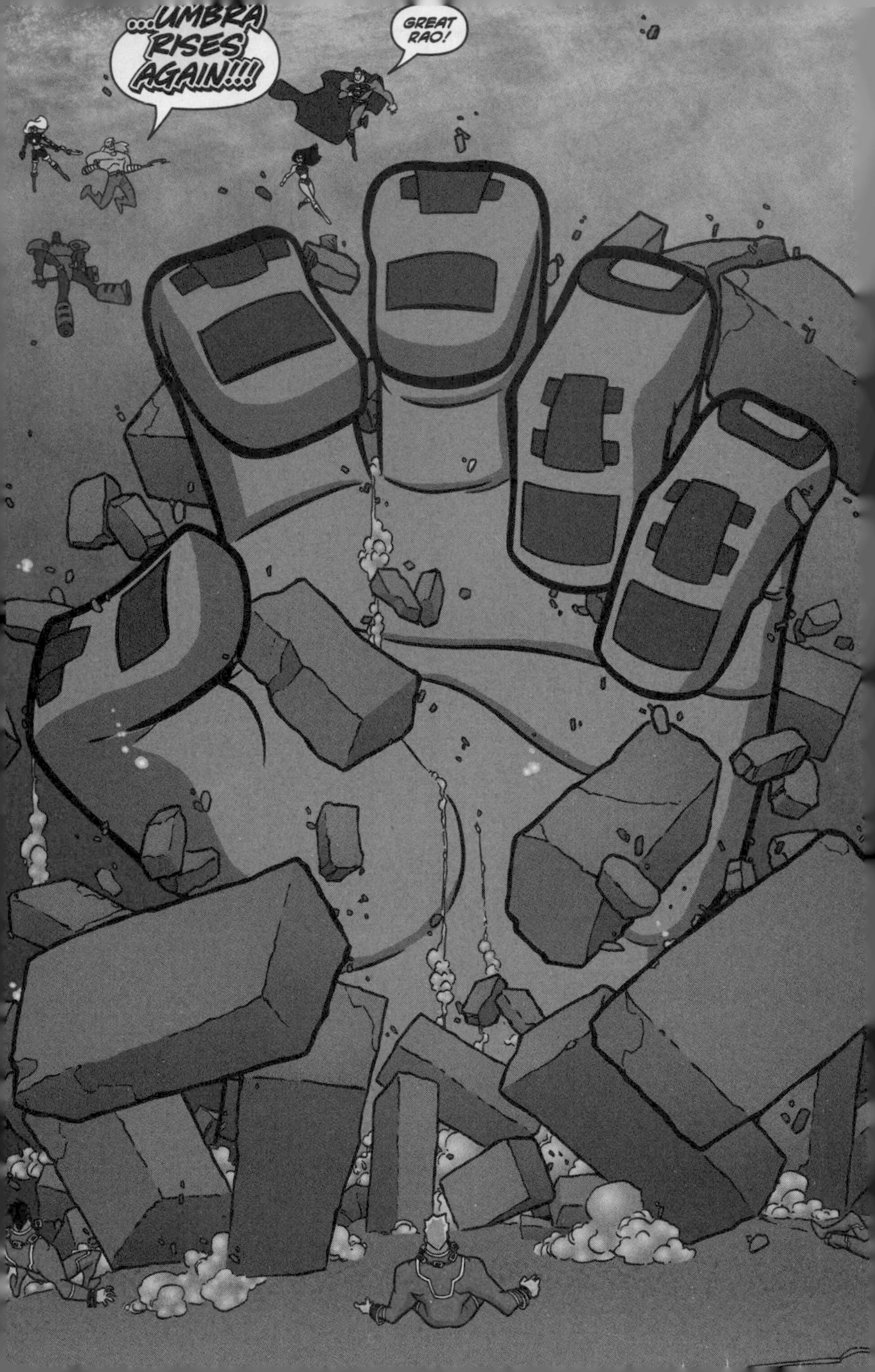
...UMBRA RISES AGAIN!!!
GREAT RAO!

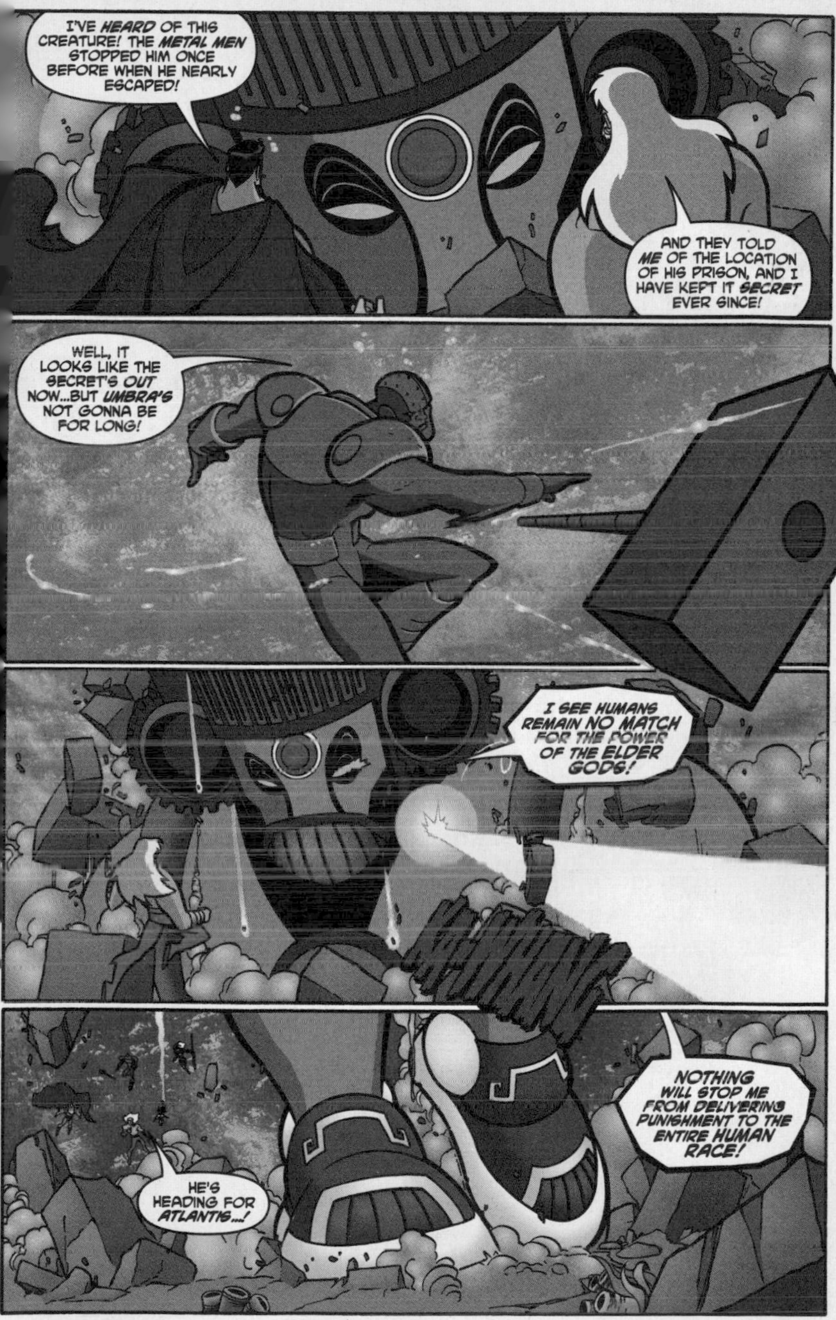
I'VE HEARD OF THIS CREATURE! THE METAL MEN STOPPED HIM ONCE BEFORE WHEN HE NEARLY ESCAPED!
AND THEY TOLD ME OF THE LOCATION OF HIS PRISON, AND I HAVE KEPT IT SECRET EVER SINCE!
WELL, IT LOOKS LIKE THE SECRET'S OUT NOW...BUT UMBRA'S NOT GONNA BE FOR LONG!
I SEE HUMANS REMAIN NO MATCH FOR THE POWER OF THE ELDER GODS!
NOTHING WILL STOP ME FROM DELIVERING PUNISHMENT TO THE ENTIRE HUMAN RACE!
HE'S HEADING FOR ATLANTIS...!

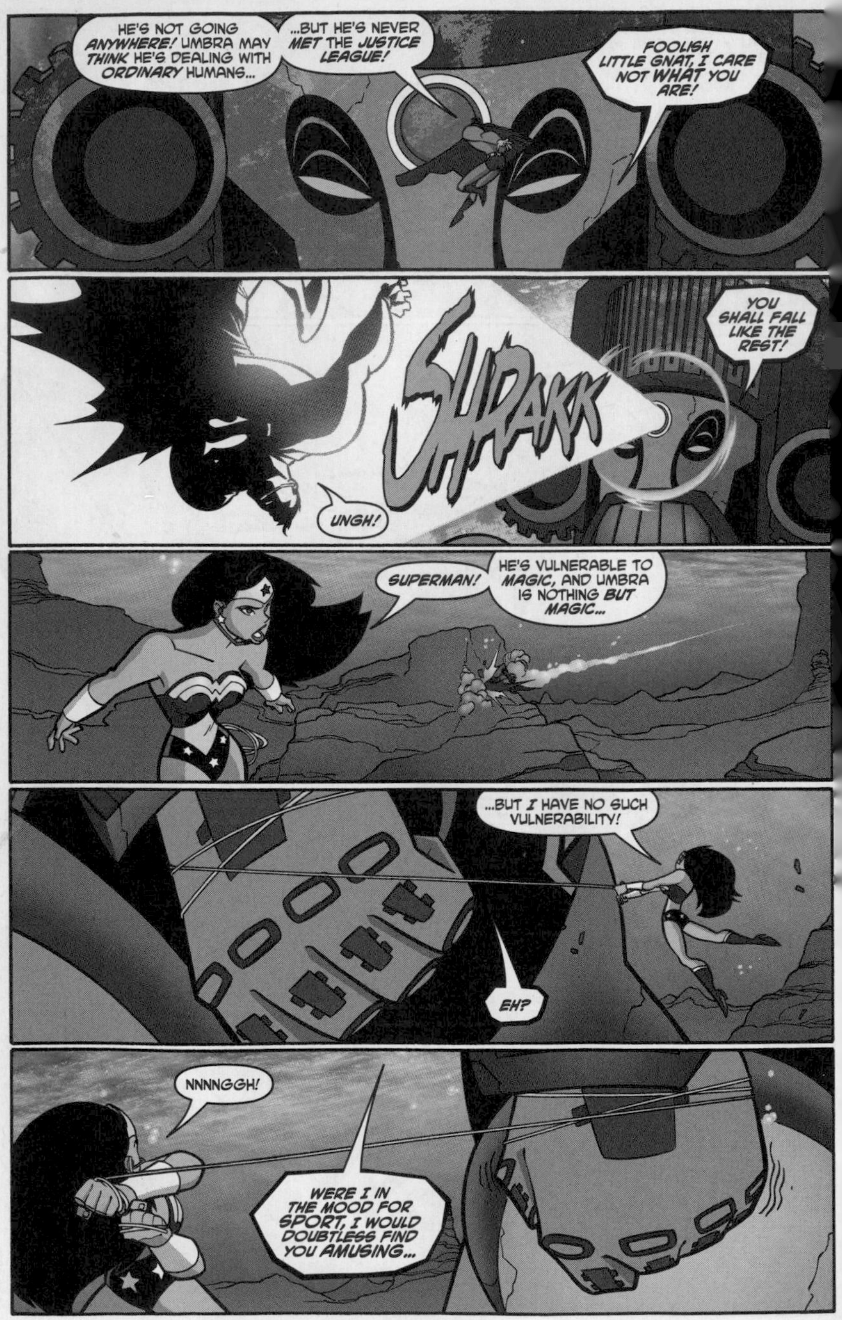
HE'S NOT GOING ANYWHERE! UMBRA MAY THINK HE'S DEALING WITH ORDINARY HUMANS...
...BUT HE'S NEVER MET THE JUSTICE LEAGUE!
FOOLISH LITTLE GNAT, I CARE NOT WHAT YOU ARE!
SHRAKK
YOU SHALL FALL LIKE THE REST!
UNGH!
SUPERMAN!
HE'S VULNERABLE TO MAGIC, AND UMBRA IS NOTHING BUT MAGIC...
...BUT I HAVE NO SUCH VULNERABILITY!
EH?
NNNNGGH!
WERE I IN THE MOOD FOR SPORT, I WOULD DOUBTLESS FIND YOU AMUSING...

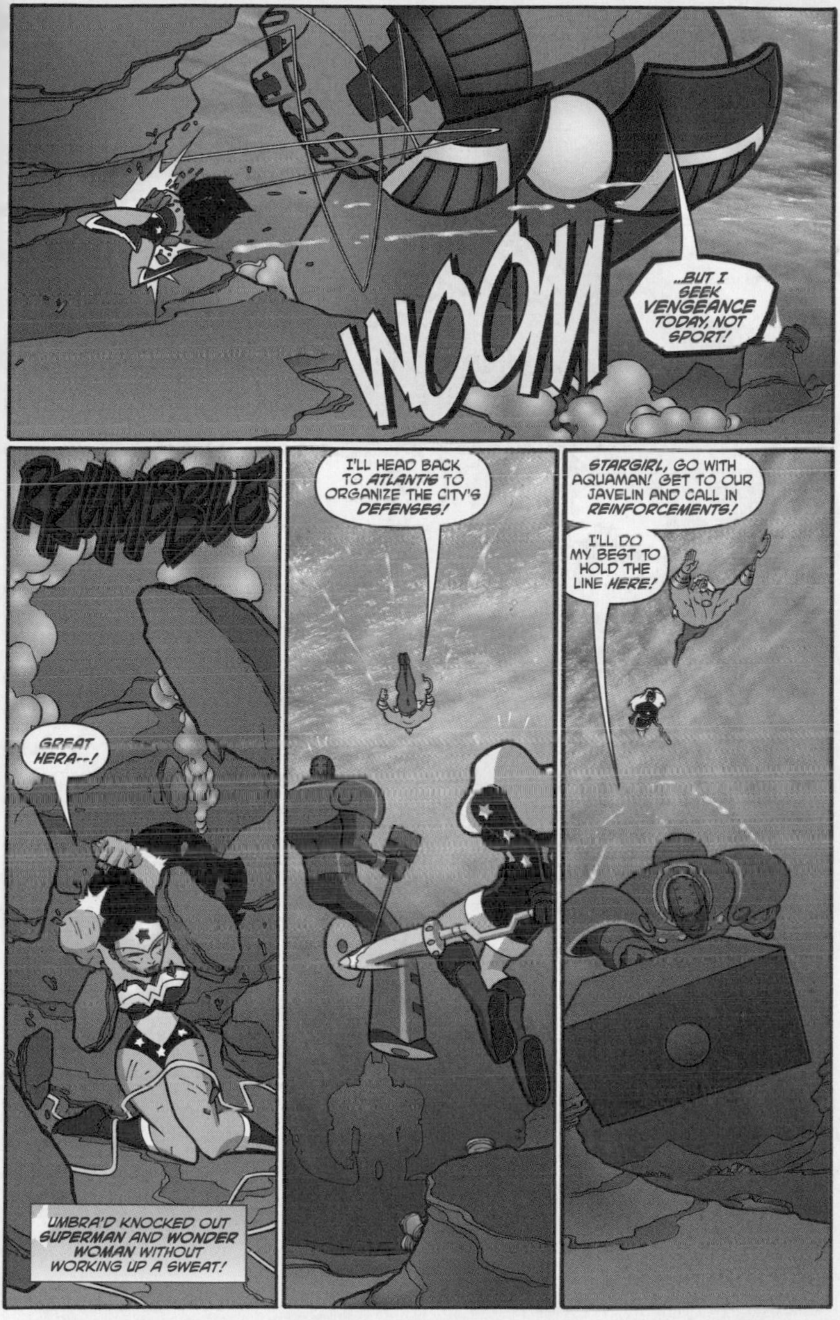
WOOM
...BUT I SEEK VENGEANCE TODAY, NOT SPORT!
RRUMBBLE
GREAT HERA--!
UMBRA'D KNOCKED OUT SUPERMAN AND WONDER WOMAN WITHOUT WORKING UP A SWEAT!
I'LL HEAD BACK TO ATLANTIS TO ORGANIZE THE CITY'S DEFENSES!
STARGIRL, GO WITH AQUAMAN! GET TO OUR JAVELIN AND CALL IN REINFORCEMENTS!
I'LL DO MY BEST TO HOLD THE LINE HERE!

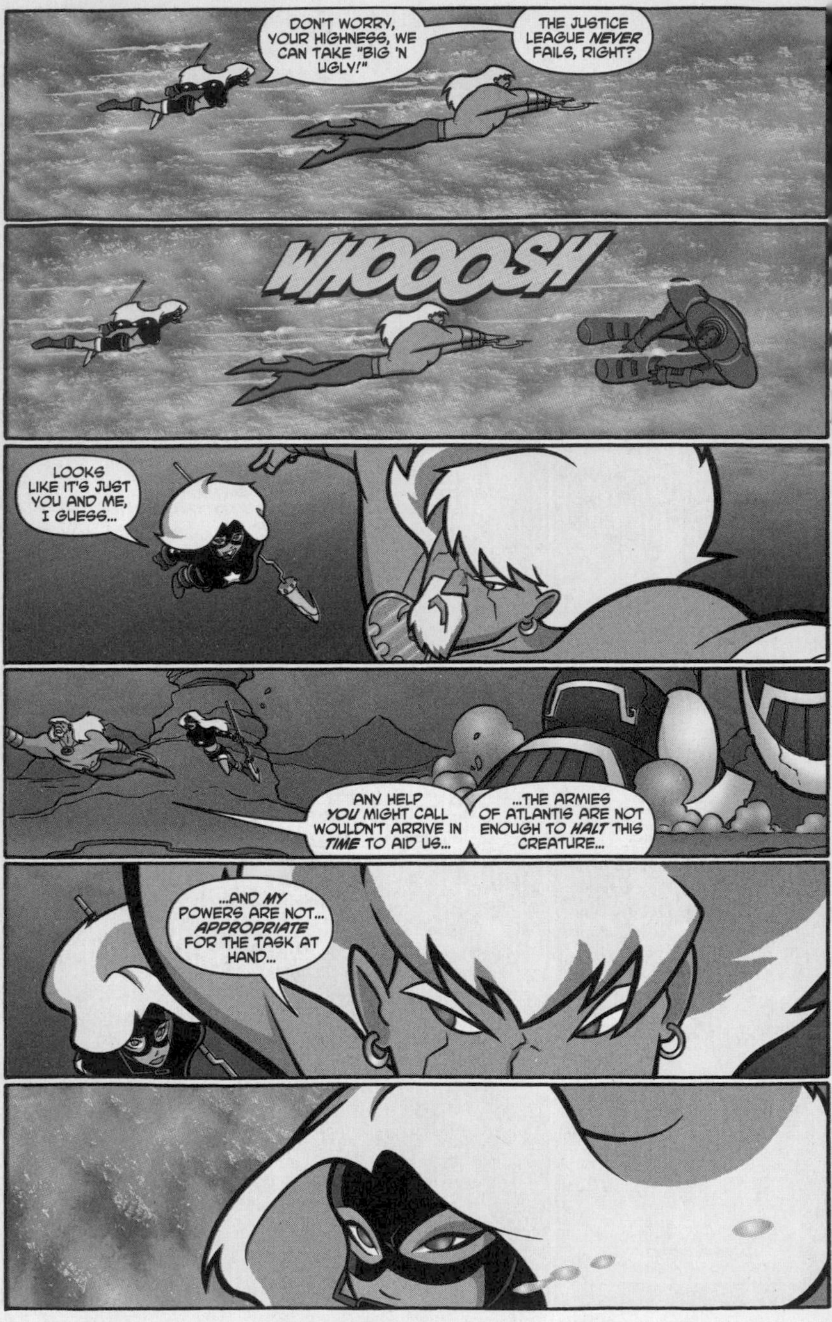
DON'T WORRY, YOUR HIGHNESS, WE CAN TAKE "BIG 'N UGLY!"
THE JUSTICE LEAGUE *NEVER* FAILS, RIGHT?
WHOOOSH
LOOKS LIKE IT'S JUST YOU AND ME, I GUESS...
ANY HELP *YOU* MIGHT CALL WOULDN'T ARRIVE IN *TIME* TO AID US...
...THE ARMIES OF ATLANTIS ARE NOT ENOUGH TO *HALT* THIS CREATURE...
...AND *MY* POWERS ARE NOT... *APPROPRIATE* FOR THE TASK AT HAND...

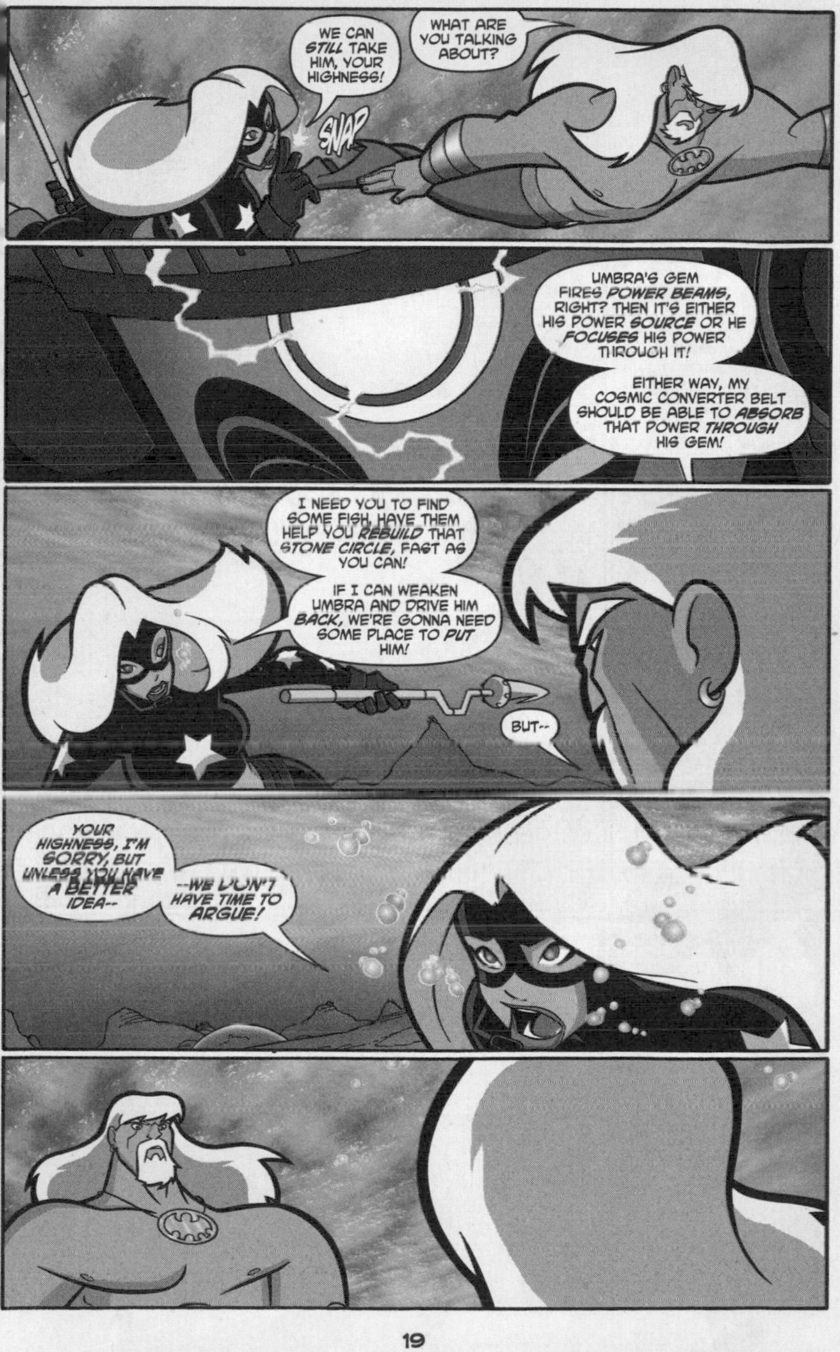
WE CAN STILL TAKE HIM, YOUR HIGHNESS!
WHAT ARE YOU TALKING ABOUT?
SNAP
UMBRA'S GEM FIRES POWER BEAMS, RIGHT? THEN IT'S EITHER HIS POWER SOURCE OR HE FOCUSES HIS POWER THROUGH IT!
EITHER WAY, MY COSMIC CONVERTER BELT SHOULD BE ABLE TO ABSORB THAT POWER THROUGH HIS GEM!
I NEED YOU TO FIND SOME FISH, HAVE THEM HELP YOU REBUILD THAT STONE CIRCLE, FAST AS YOU CAN!
IF I CAN WEAKEN UMBRA AND DRIVE HIM BACK, WE'RE GONNA NEED SOME PLACE TO PUT HIM!
BUT--
YOUR HIGHNESS, I'M SORRY, BUT UNLESS YOU HAVE A BETTER IDEA--
--WE DON'T HAVE TIME TO ARGUE!

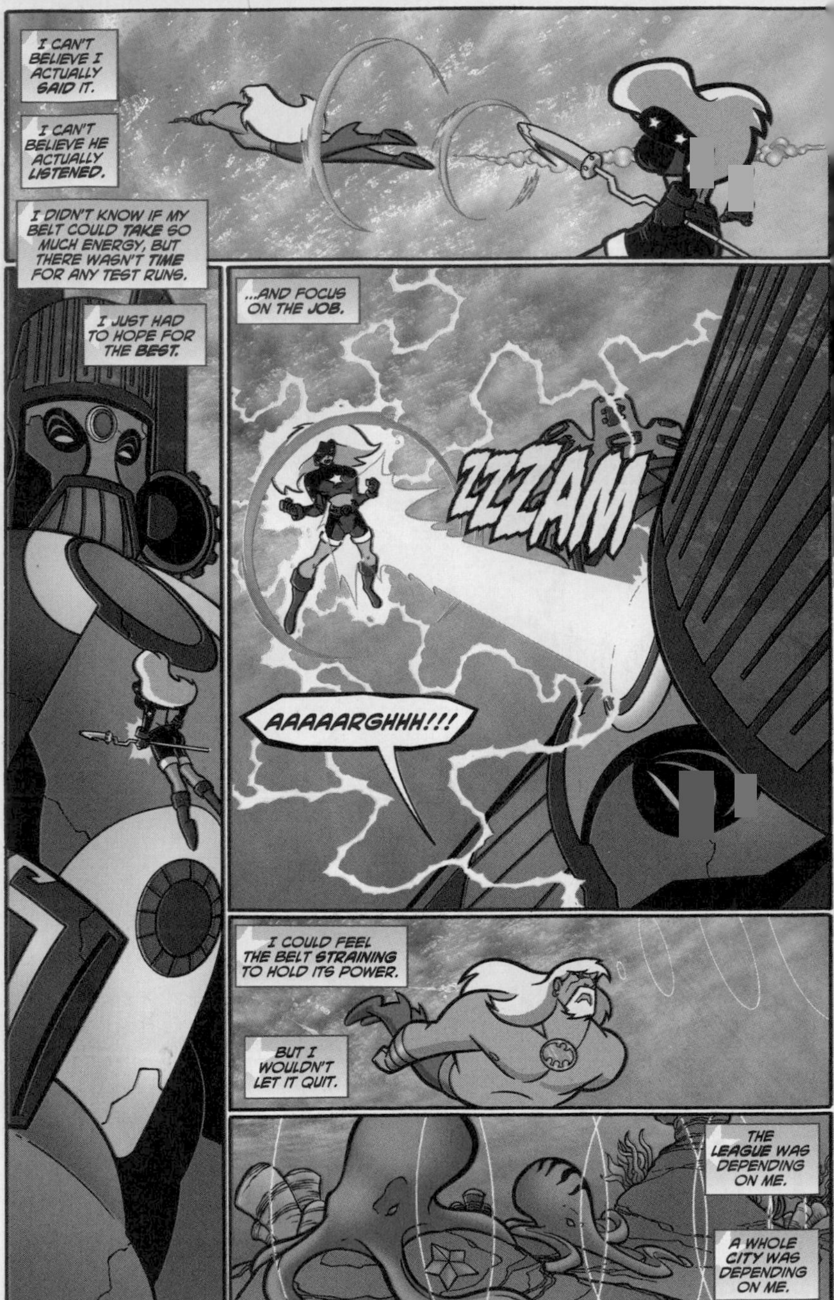
I CAN'T BELIEVE I ACTUALLY SAID IT.
I CAN'T BELIEVE HE ACTUALLY LISTENED.
I DIDN'T KNOW IF MY BELT COULD TAKE SO MUCH ENERGY, BUT THERE WASN'T TIME FOR ANY TEST RUNS.
I JUST HAD TO HOPE FOR THE BEST.
...AND FOCUS ON THE JOB.
ZZZAM
AAAAARGHHH!!!
I COULD FEEL THE BELT STRAINING TO HOLD ITS POWER.
BUT I WOULDN'T LET IT QUIT.
THE LEAGUE WAS DEPENDING ON ME.
A WHOLE CITY WAS DEPENDING ON ME.

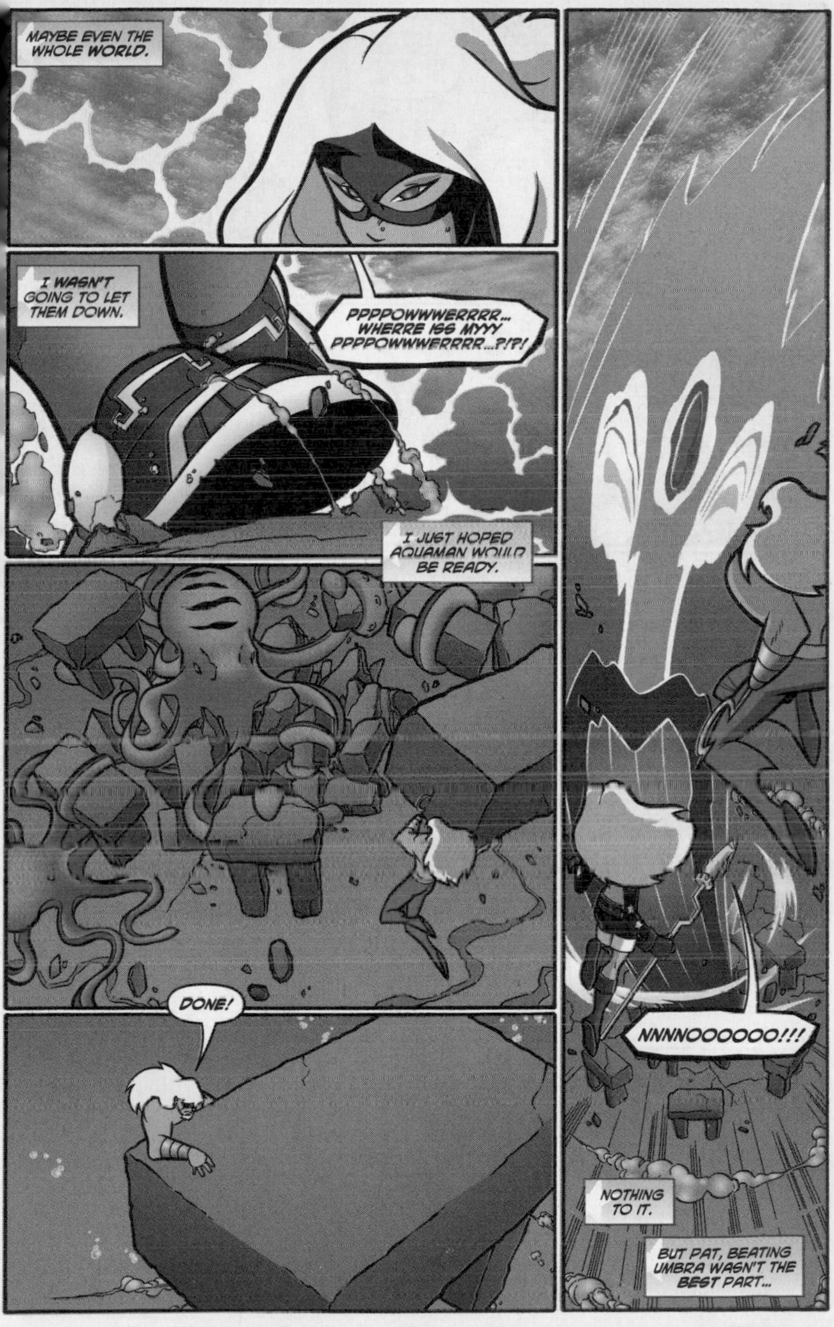
MAYBE EVEN THE WHOLE WORLD.
I WASN'T GOING TO LET THEM DOWN.
PPPPOWWWERRRR... WHERRE ISS MYYY PPPPOWWWERRRR...?!?!
I JUST HOPED AQUAMAN WOULD BE READY.
DONE!
NNNNOOOOOOO!!!
NOTHING TO IT.
BUT PAT, BEATING UMBRA WASN'T THE BEST PART...

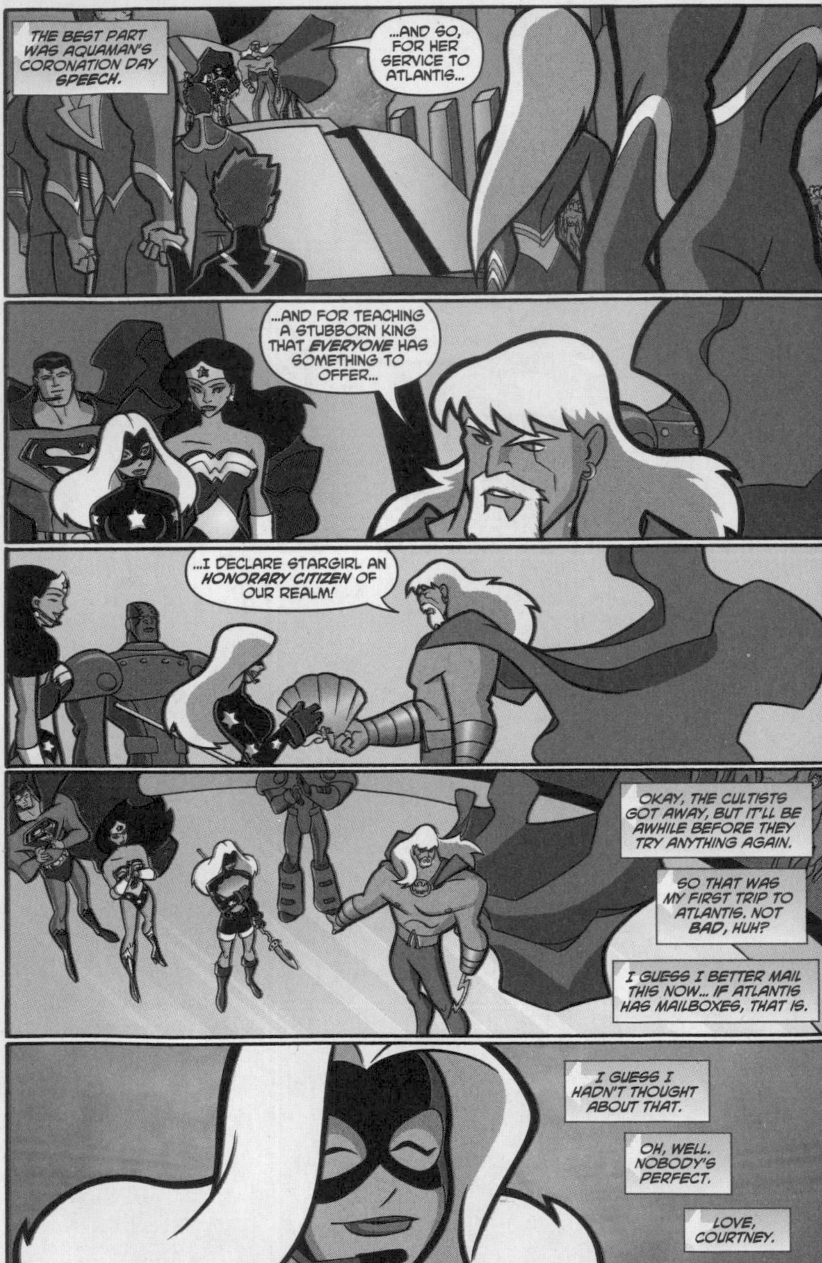
THE BEST PART WAS AQUAMAN'S CORONATION DAY SPEECH.
...AND SO, FOR HER SERVICE TO ATLANTIS...
...AND FOR TEACHING A STUBBORN KING THAT EVERYONE HAS SOMETHING TO OFFER...
...I DECLARE STARGIRL AN HONORARY CITIZEN OF OUR REALM!
OKAY, THE CULTISTS GOT AWAY, BUT IT'LL BE AWHILE BEFORE THEY TRY ANYTHING AGAIN.
SO THAT WAS MY FIRST TRIP TO ATLANTIS. NOT BAD, HUH?
I GUESS I BETTER MAIL THIS NOW... IF ATLANTIS HAS MAILBOXES, THAT IS.
I GUESS I HADN'T THOUGHT ABOUT THAT.
OH, WELL. NOBODY'S PERFECT.
LOVE, COURTNEY.
THE END

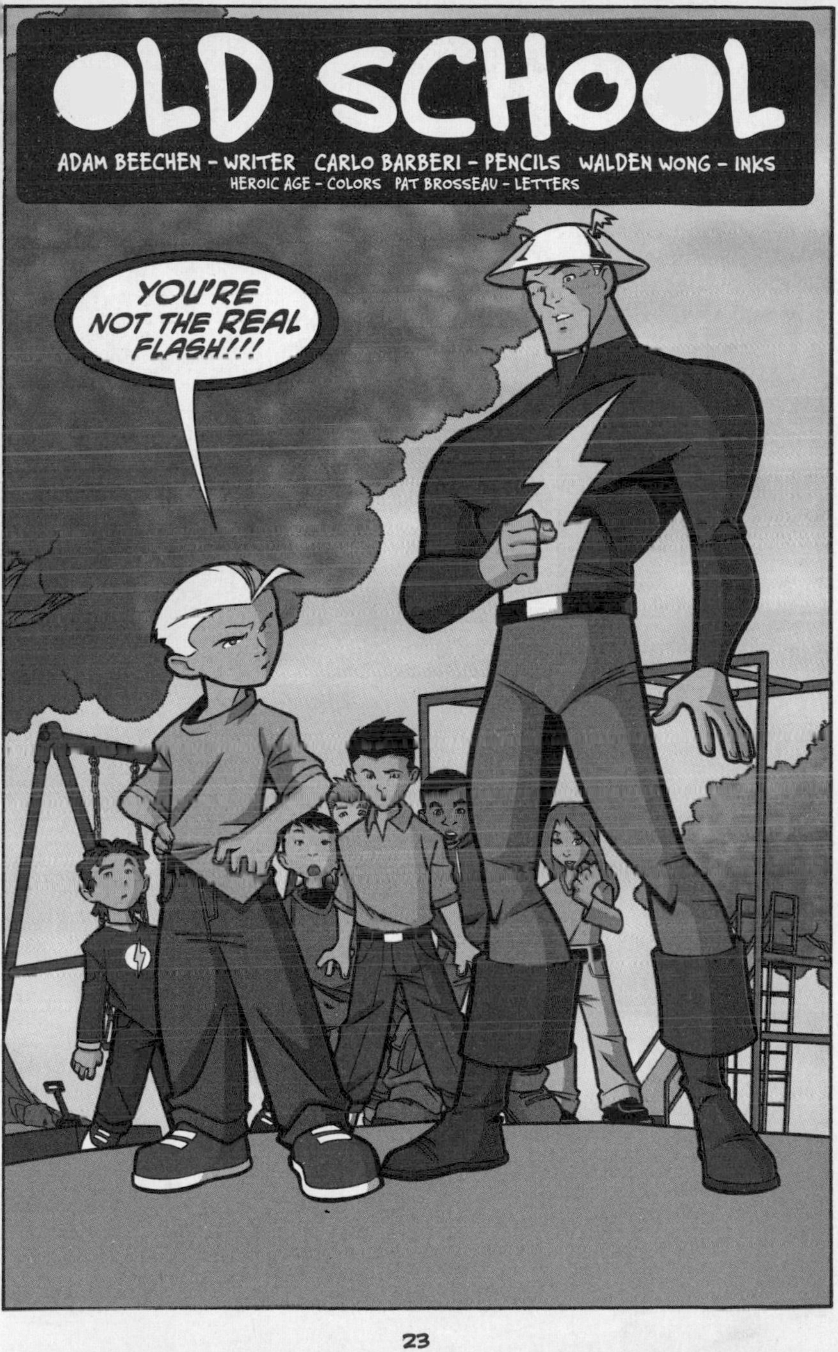
OLD SCHOOL
ADAM BEECHEN - WRITER CARLO BARBERI - PENCILS WALDEN WONG - INKS
HEROIC AGE - COLORS PAT BROSSEAU - LETTERS
YOU'RE NOT THE REAL FLASH!!!

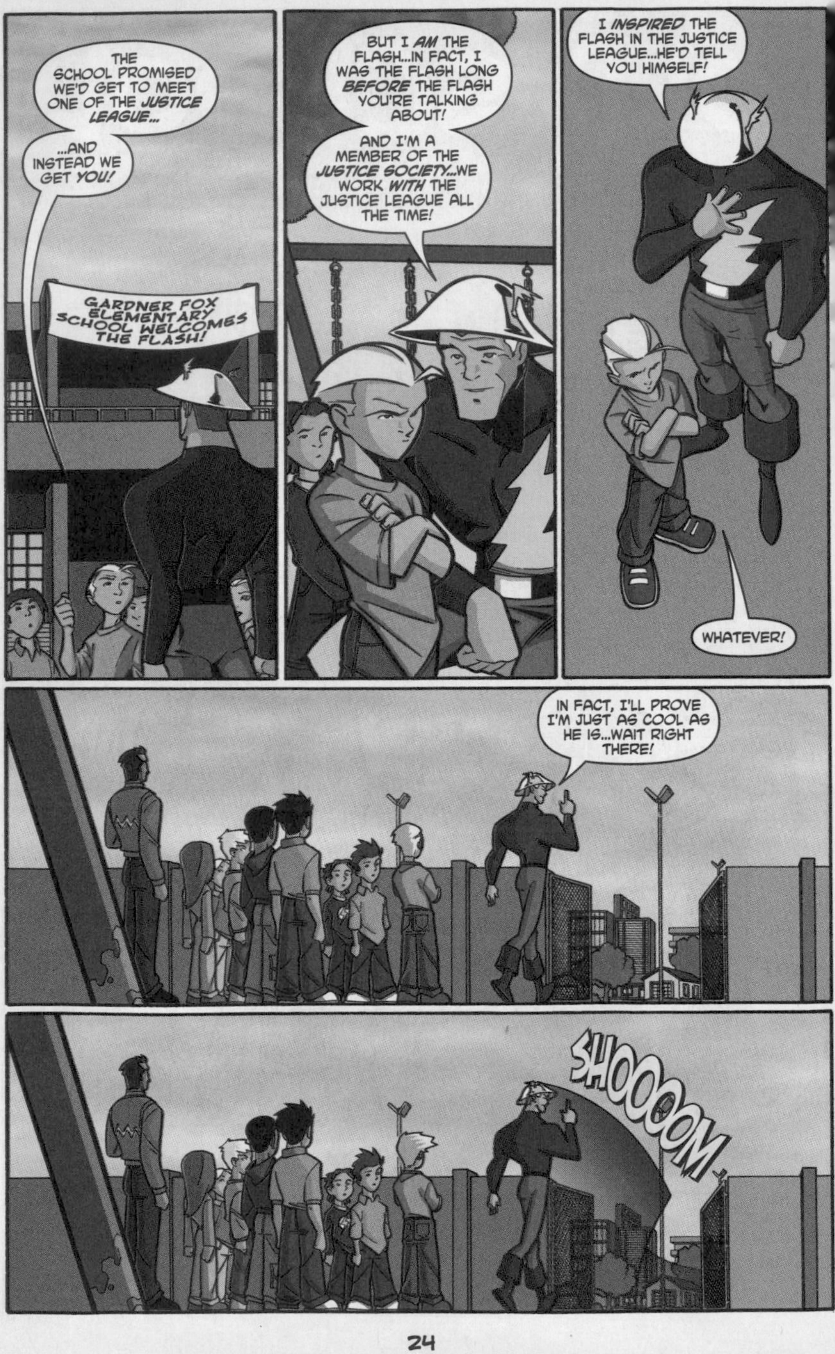
THE SCHOOL PROMISED WE'D GET TO MEET ONE OF THE JUSTICE LEAGUE...
...AND INSTEAD WE GET YOU!
GARDNER FOX ELEMENTARY SCHOOL WELCOMES THE FLASH!
BUT I AM THE FLASH...IN FACT, I WAS THE FLASH LONG BEFORE THE FLASH YOU'RE TALKING ABOUT!
AND I'M A MEMBER OF THE JUSTICE SOCIETY...WE WORK WITH THE JUSTICE LEAGUE ALL THE TIME!
I INSPIRED THE FLASH IN THE JUSTICE LEAGUE...HE'D TELL YOU HIMSELF!
WHATEVER!
IN FACT, I'LL PROVE I'M JUST AS COOL AS HE IS...WAIT RIGHT THERE!
SHOOOOM

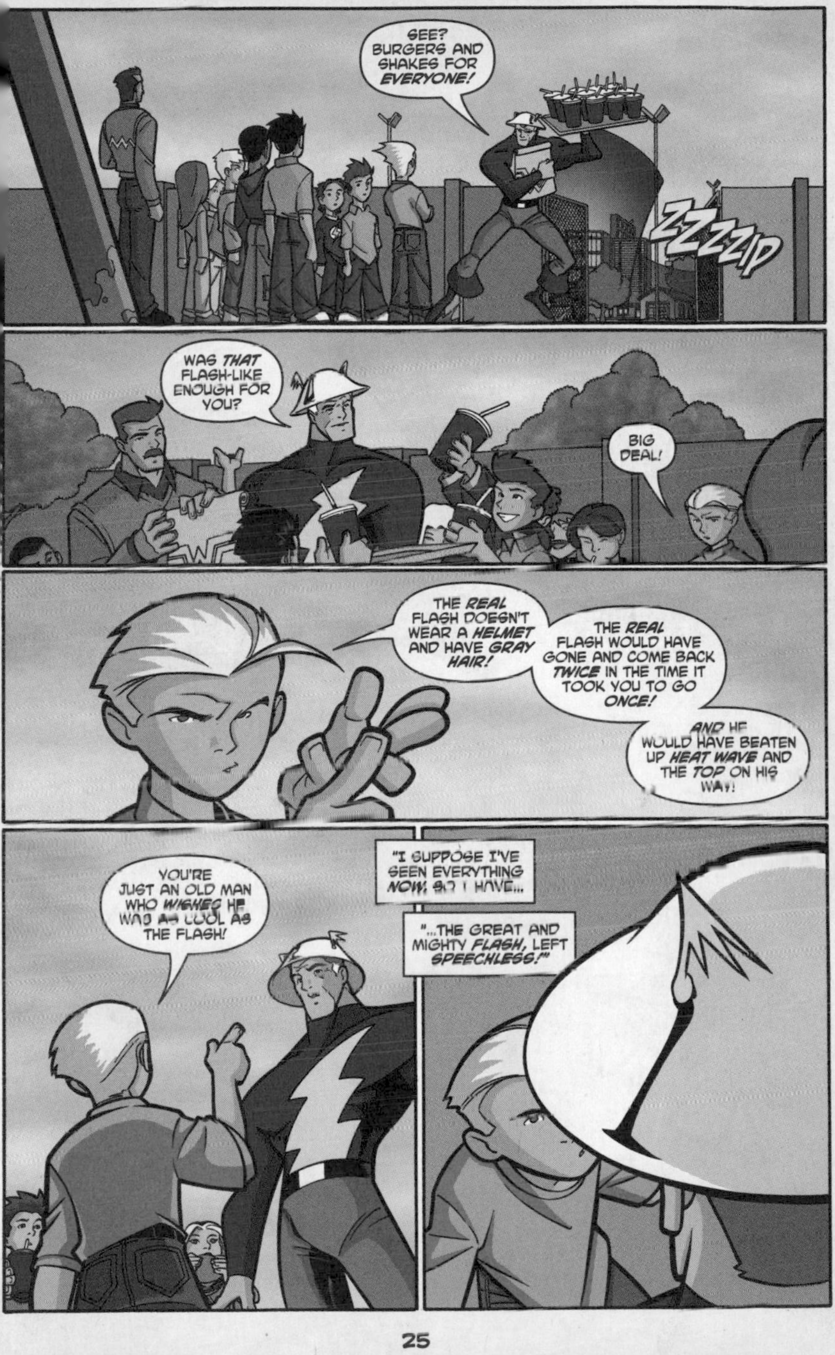
SEE? BURGERS AND SHAKES FOR EVERYONE!
ZZZZIP
WAS THAT FLASH-LIKE ENOUGH FOR YOU?
BIG DEAL!
THE REAL FLASH DOESN'T WEAR A HELMET AND HAVE GRAY HAIR!
THE REAL FLASH WOULD HAVE GONE AND COME BACK TWICE IN THE TIME IT TOOK YOU TO GO ONCE!
AND HE WOULD HAVE BEATEN UP HEAT WAVE AND THE TOP ON HIS WAY!
YOU'RE JUST AN OLD MAN WHO WISHES HE WAS AS COOL AS THE FLASH!
"I SUPPOSE I'VE SEEN EVERYTHING NOW, SO I HAVE...
"...THE GREAT AND MIGHTY FLASH, LEFT SPEECHLESS!"

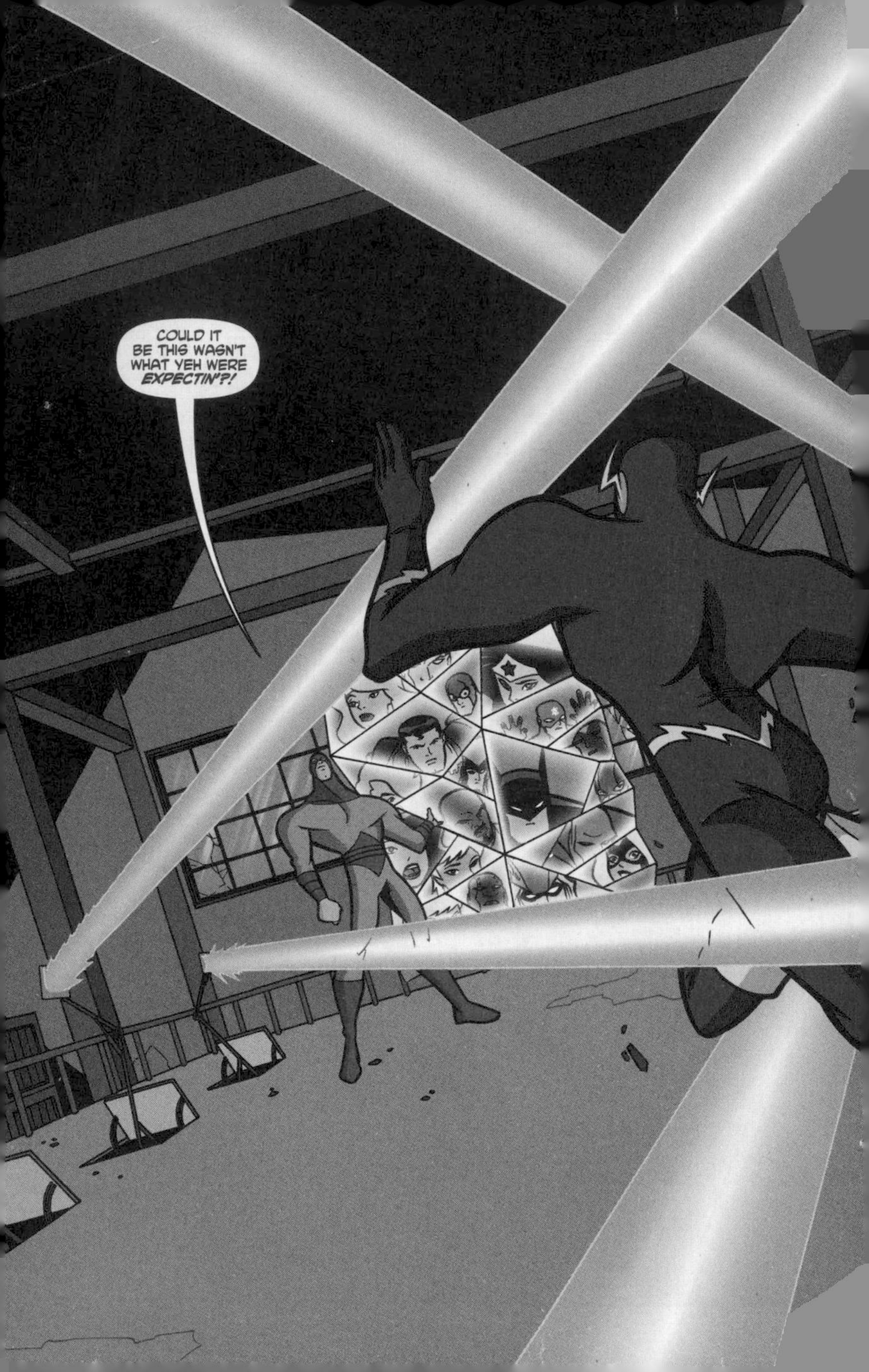
COULD IT BE THIS WASN'T WHAT YEH WERE *EXPECTIN'*?!

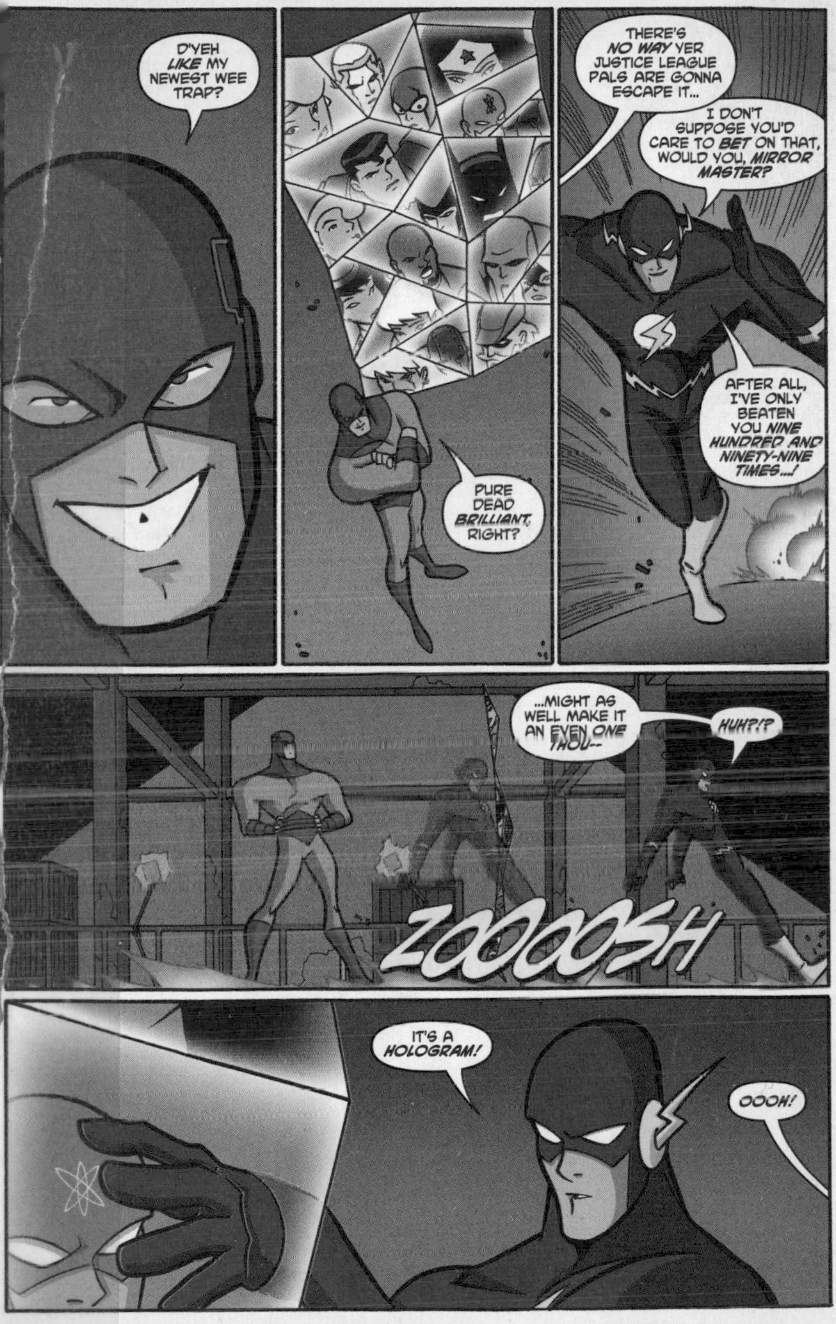
D'YEH LIKE MY NEWEST WEE TRAP?
PURE DEAD BRILLIANT, RIGHT?
THERE'S NO WAY YER JUSTICE LEAGUE PALS ARE GONNA ESCAPE IT...
I DON'T SUPPOSE YOU'D CARE TO BET ON THAT, WOULD YOU, MIRROR MASTER?
AFTER ALL, I'VE ONLY BEATEN YOU NINE HUNDRED AND NINETY-NINE TIMES...!
...MIGHT AS WELL MAKE IT AN EVEN ONE THOU--
HUH?!?
ZOOOOSH
IT'S A HOLOGRAM!
OOOH!

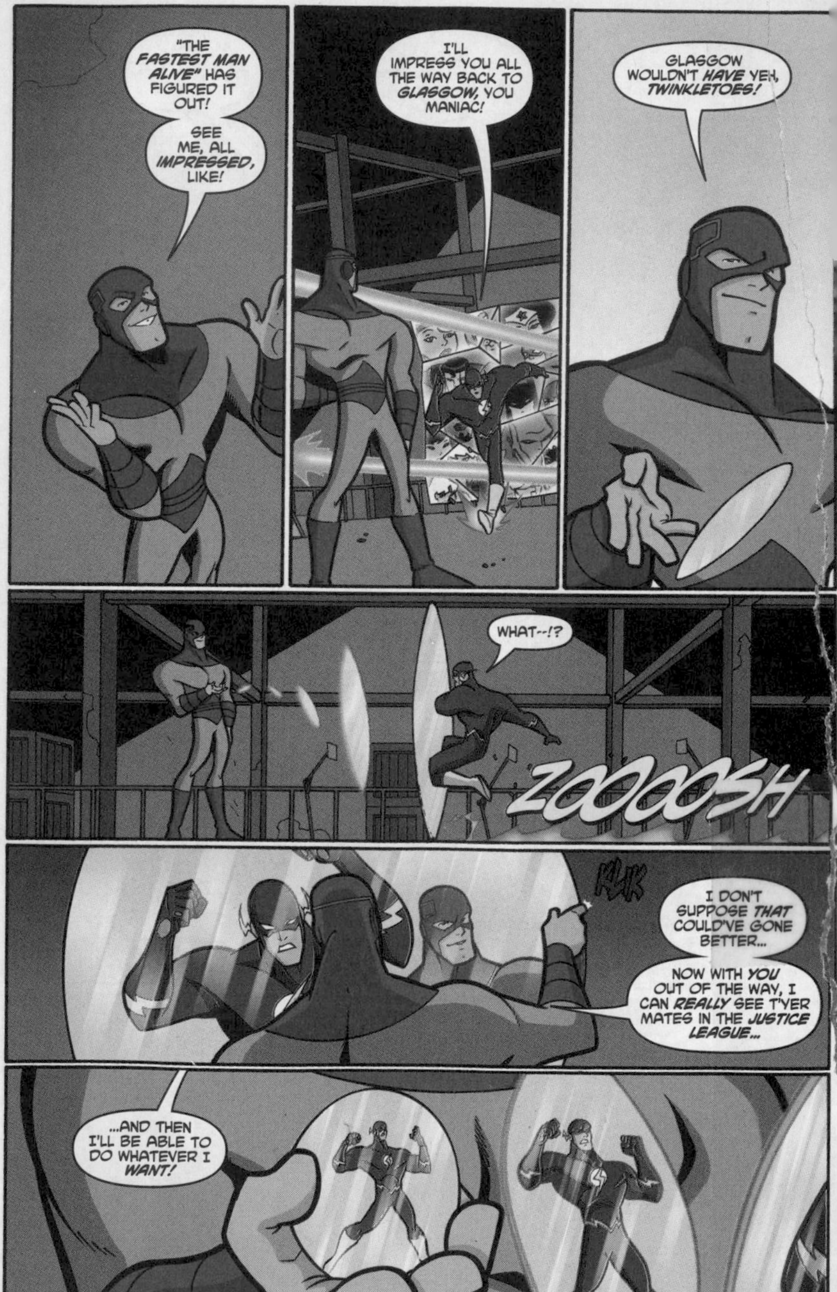
"THE FASTEST MAN ALIVE" HAS FIGURED IT OUT!
SEE ME, ALL IMPRESSED, LIKE!
I'LL IMPRESS YOU ALL THE WAY BACK TO GLASGOW, YOU MANIAC!
GLASGOW WOULDN'T HAVE YEH, TWINKLETOES!
WHAT--!?
ZOOOOSH
KLIK
I DON'T SUPPOSE THAT COULD'VE GONE BETTER...
NOW WITH YOU OUT OF THE WAY, I CAN REALLY SEE T'YER MATES IN THE JUSTICE LEAGUE...
...AND THEN I'LL BE ABLE TO DO WHATEVER I WANT!

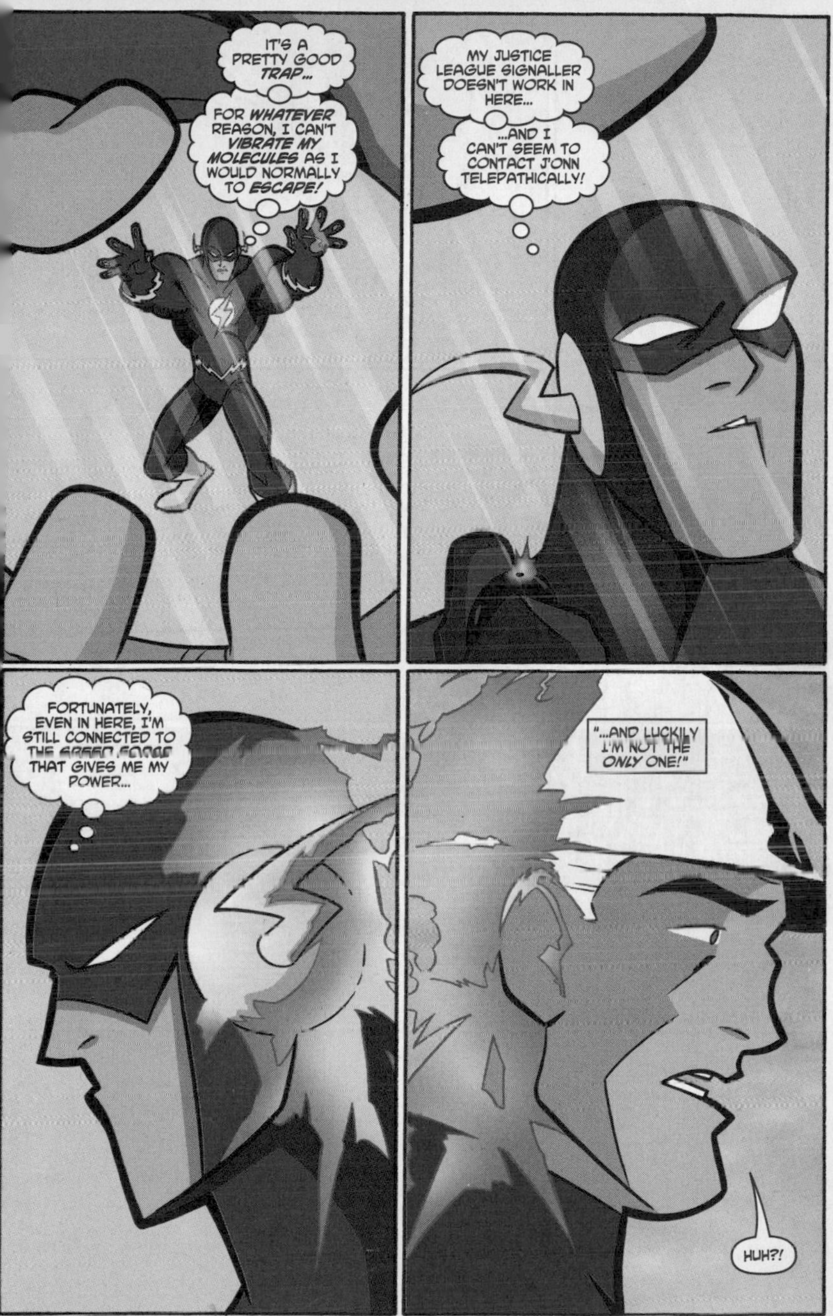
IT'S A PRETTY GOOD *TRAP...*
FOR *WHATEVER* REASON, I CAN'T *VIBRATE MY MOLECULES* AS I WOULD NORMALLY TO *ESCAPE!*
MY JUSTICE LEAGUE SIGNALLER DOESN'T WORK IN HERE...
...AND I CAN'T SEEM TO CONTACT J'ONN TELEPATHICALLY!
FORTUNATELY, EVEN IN HERE, I'M STILL CONNECTED TO THE
THAT GIVES ME MY POWER...
"...AND LUCKILY I'M NOT THE *ONLY* ONE!"
HUH?!

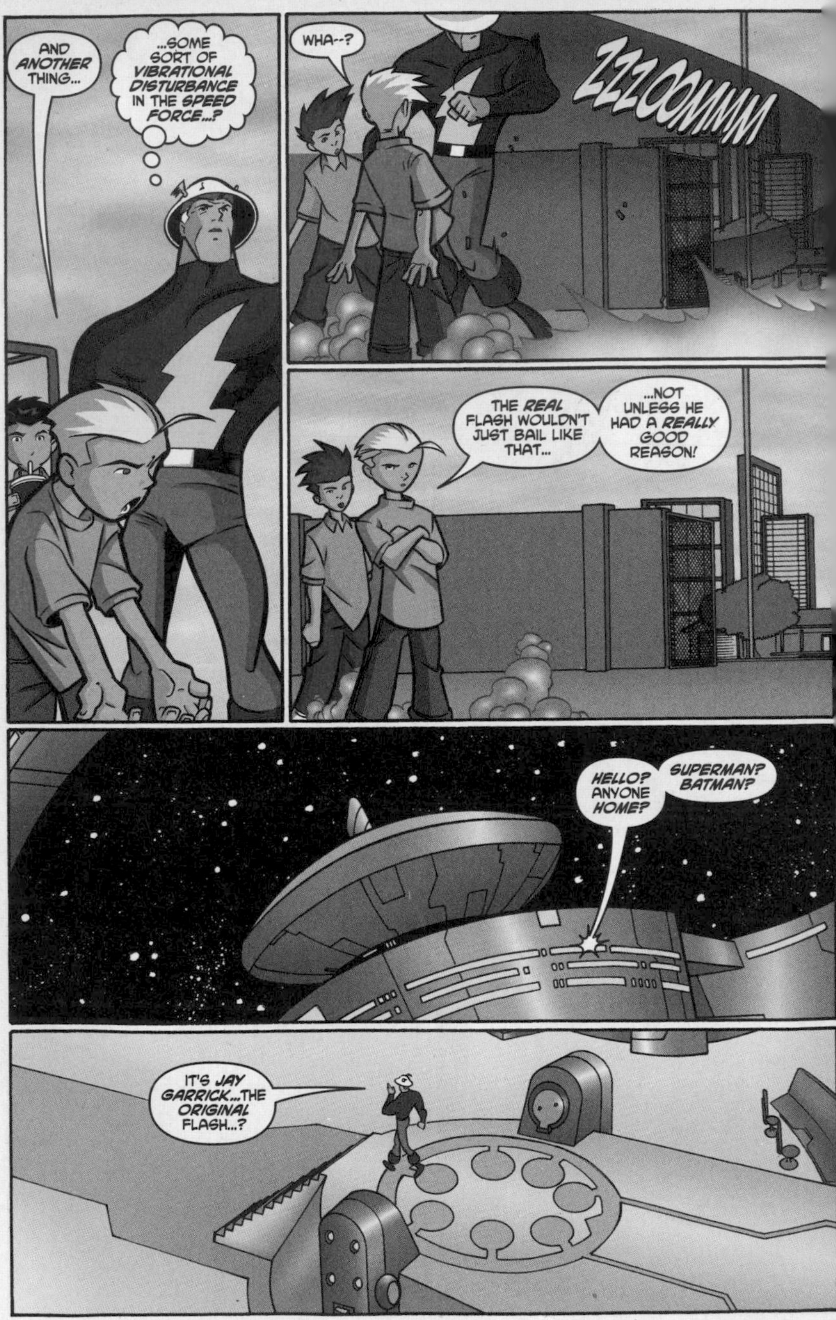
AND ANOTHER THING...
...SOME SORT OF VIBRATIONAL DISTURBANCE IN THE SPEED FORCE...?
WHA--?
ZZZOOMMM
THE REAL FLASH WOULDN'T JUST BAIL LIKE THAT...
...NOT UNLESS HE HAD A REALLY GOOD REASON!
HELLO? ANYONE HOME?
SUPERMAN? BATMAN?
IT'S JAY GARRICK...THE ORIGINAL FLASH...?

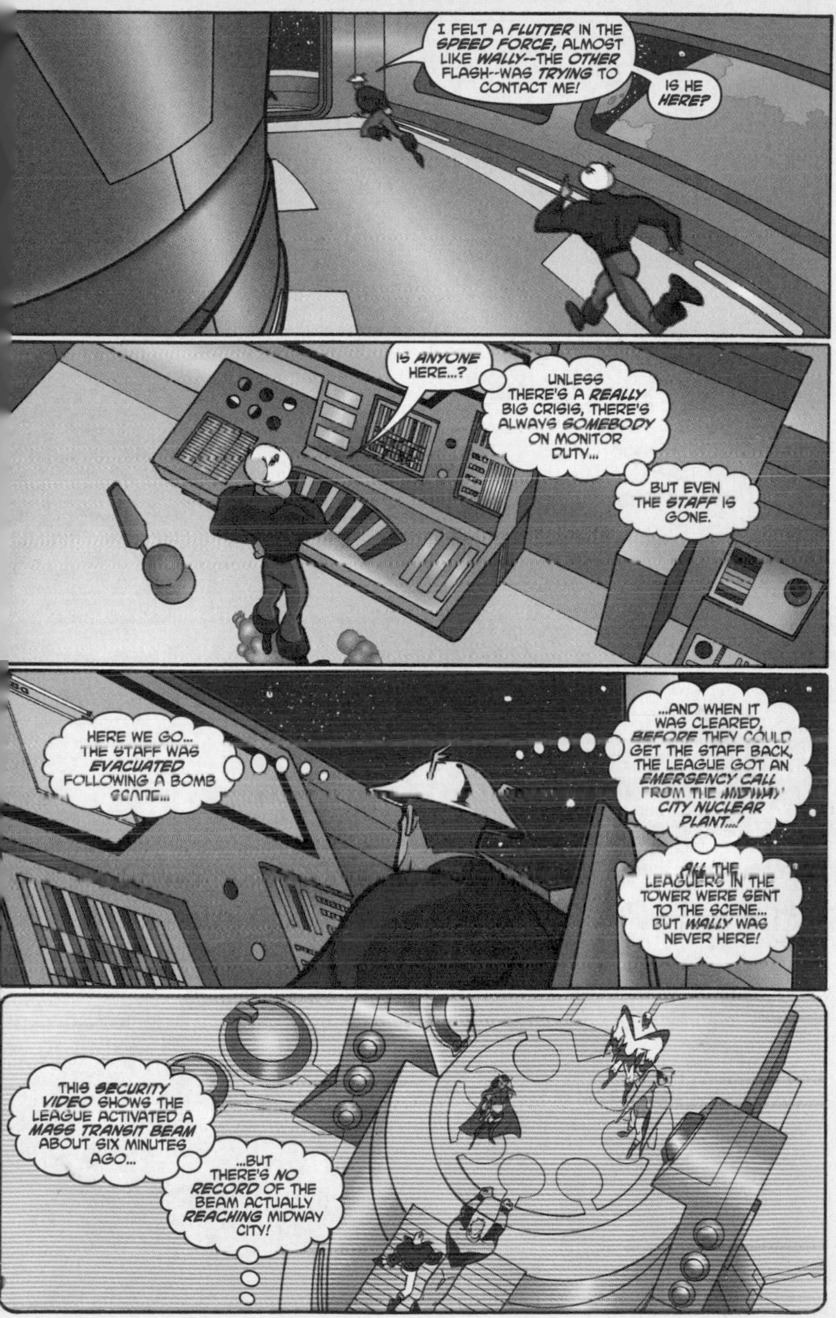
I FELT A FLUTTER IN THE SPEED FORCE, ALMOST LIKE WALLY--THE OTHER FLASH--WAS TRYING TO CONTACT ME!
IS HE HERE?
IS ANYONE HERE...?
UNLESS THERE'S A REALLY BIG CRISIS, THERE'S ALWAYS SOMEBODY ON MONITOR DUTY...
BUT EVEN THE STAFF IS GONE.
HERE WE GO... THE STAFF WAS EVACUATED FOLLOWING A BOMB SCARE...
...AND WHEN IT WAS CLEARED, BEFORE THEY COULD GET THE STAFF BACK, THE LEAGUE GOT AN EMERGENCY CALL FROM THE MIDWAY CITY NUCLEAR PLANT...!
ALL THE LEAGUERS IN THE TOWER WERE SENT TO THE SCENE... BUT WALLY WAS NEVER HERE!
THIS SECURITY VIDEO SHOWS THE LEAGUE ACTIVATED A MASS TRANSIT BEAM ABOUT SIX MINUTES AGO...
...BUT THERE'S NO RECORD OF THE BEAM ACTUALLY REACHING MIDWAY CITY!

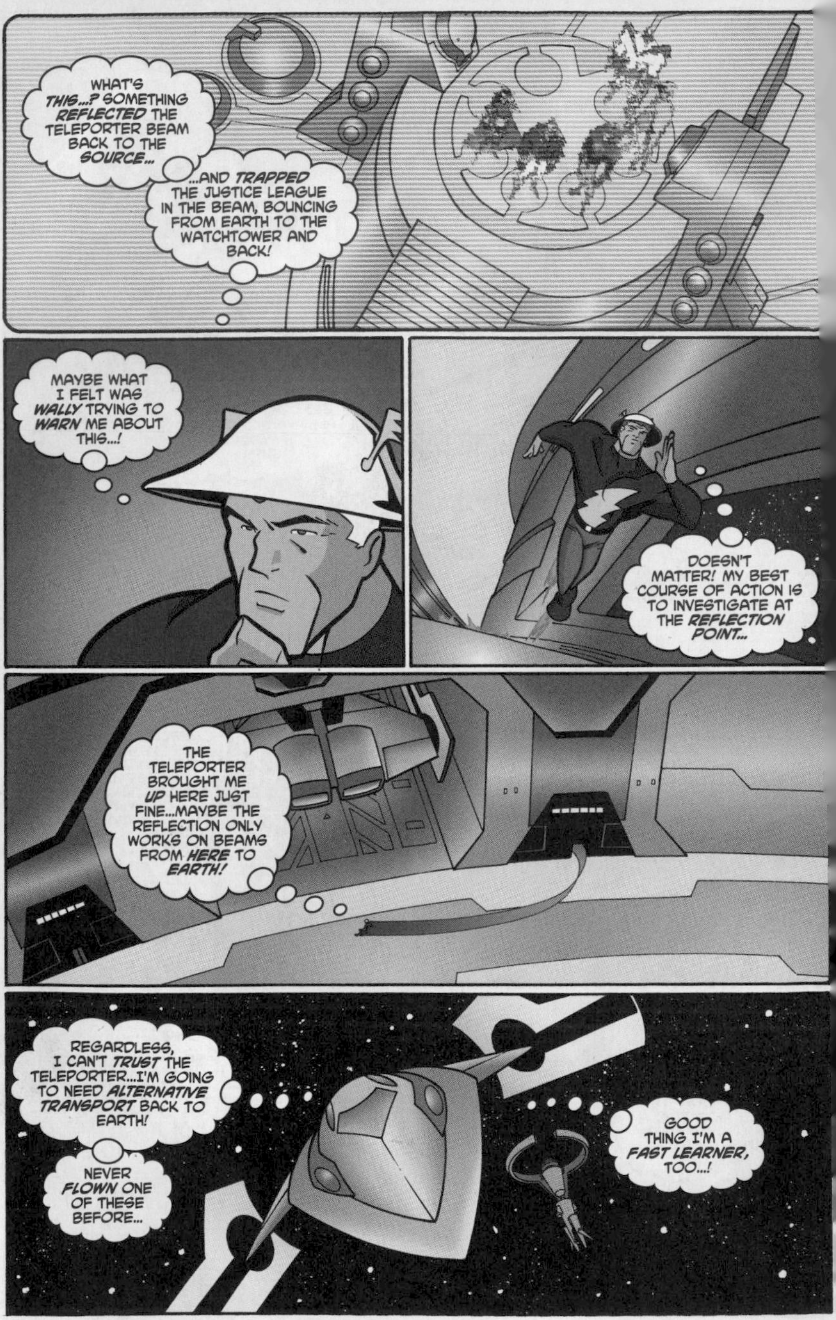
WHAT'S THIS...? SOMETHING REFLECTED THE TELEPORTER BEAM BACK TO THE SOURCE...
...AND TRAPPED THE JUSTICE LEAGUE IN THE BEAM, BOUNCING FROM EARTH TO THE WATCHTOWER AND BACK!
MAYBE WHAT I FELT WAS WALLY TRYING TO WARN ME ABOUT THIS...!
DOESN'T MATTER! MY BEST COURSE OF ACTION IS TO INVESTIGATE AT THE REFLECTION POINT...
THE TELEPORTER BROUGHT ME UP HERE JUST FINE...MAYBE THE REFLECTION ONLY WORKS ON BEAMS FROM HERE TO EARTH!
REGARDLESS, I CAN'T TRUST THE TELEPORTER...I'M GOING TO NEED ALTERNATIVE TRANSPORT BACK TO EARTH!
NEVER FLOWN ONE OF THESE BEFORE...
GOOD THING I'M A FAST LEARNER, TOO...!

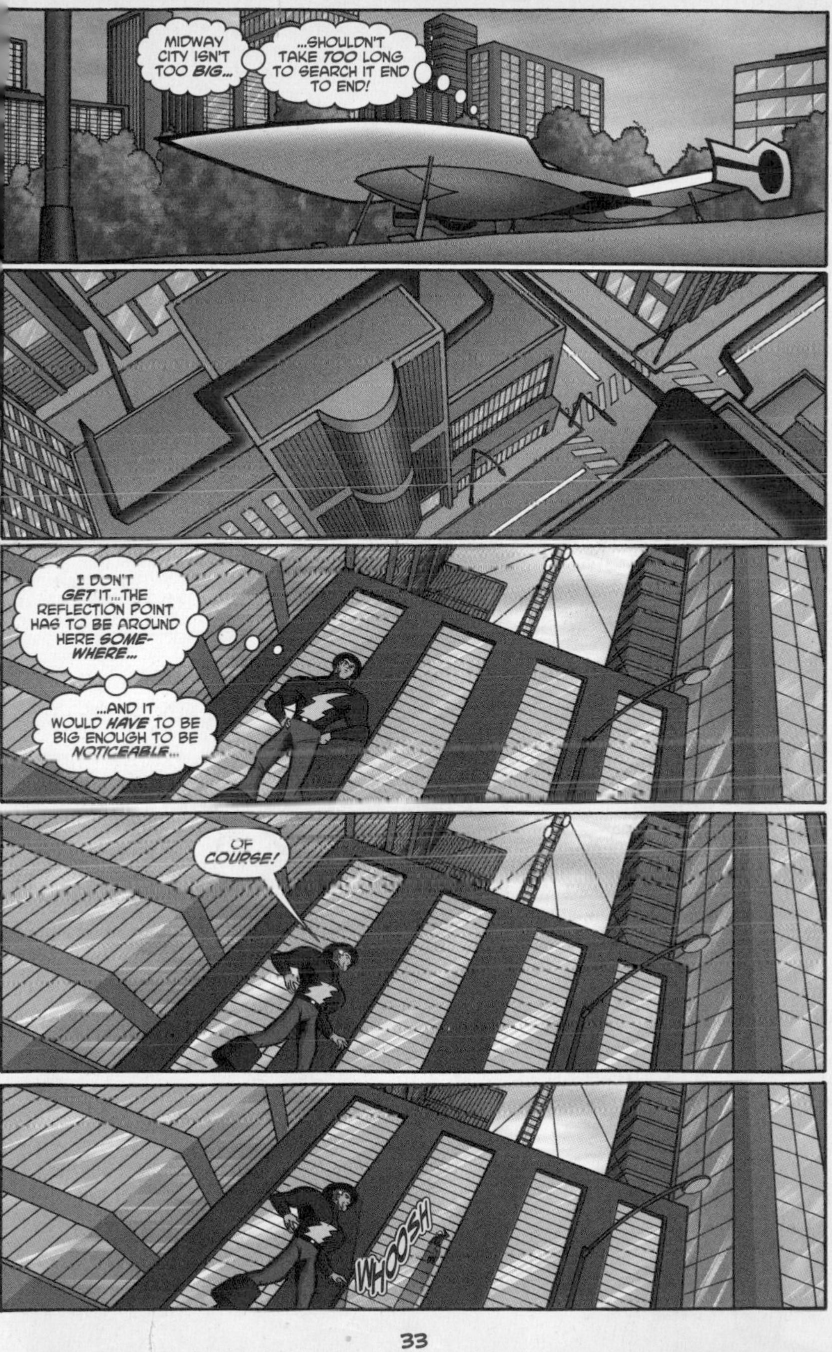
MIDWAY CITY ISN'T TOO BIG...
...SHOULDN'T TAKE TOO LONG TO SEARCH IT END TO END!
I DON'T GET IT...THE REFLECTION POINT HAS TO BE AROUND HERE SOME-WHERE...
...AND IT WOULD HAVE TO BE BIG ENOUGH TO BE NOTICEABLE...
OF COURSE!
WHOOSH

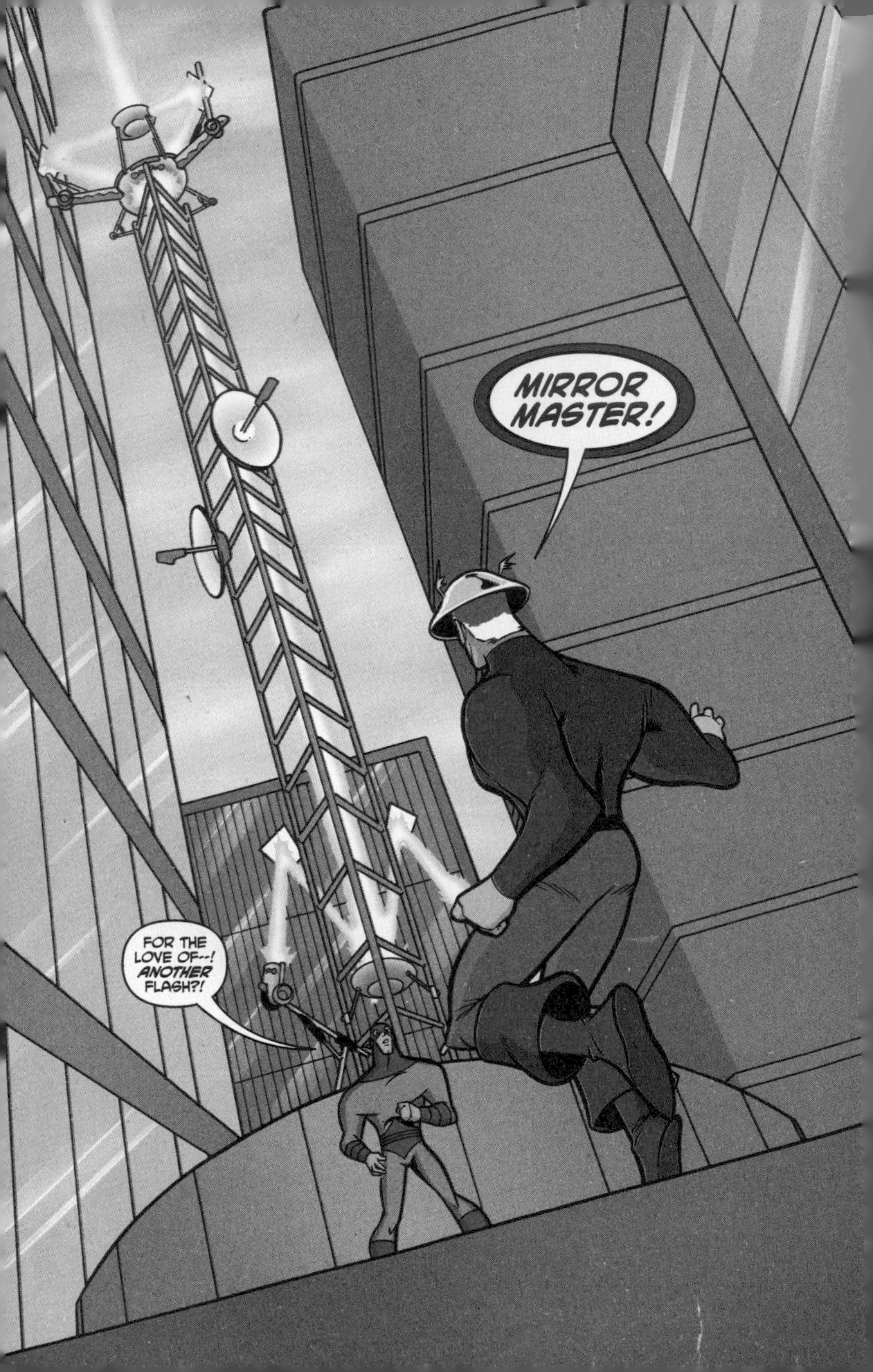
MIRROR MASTER!
FOR THE LOVE OF--! ANOTHER FLASH?!

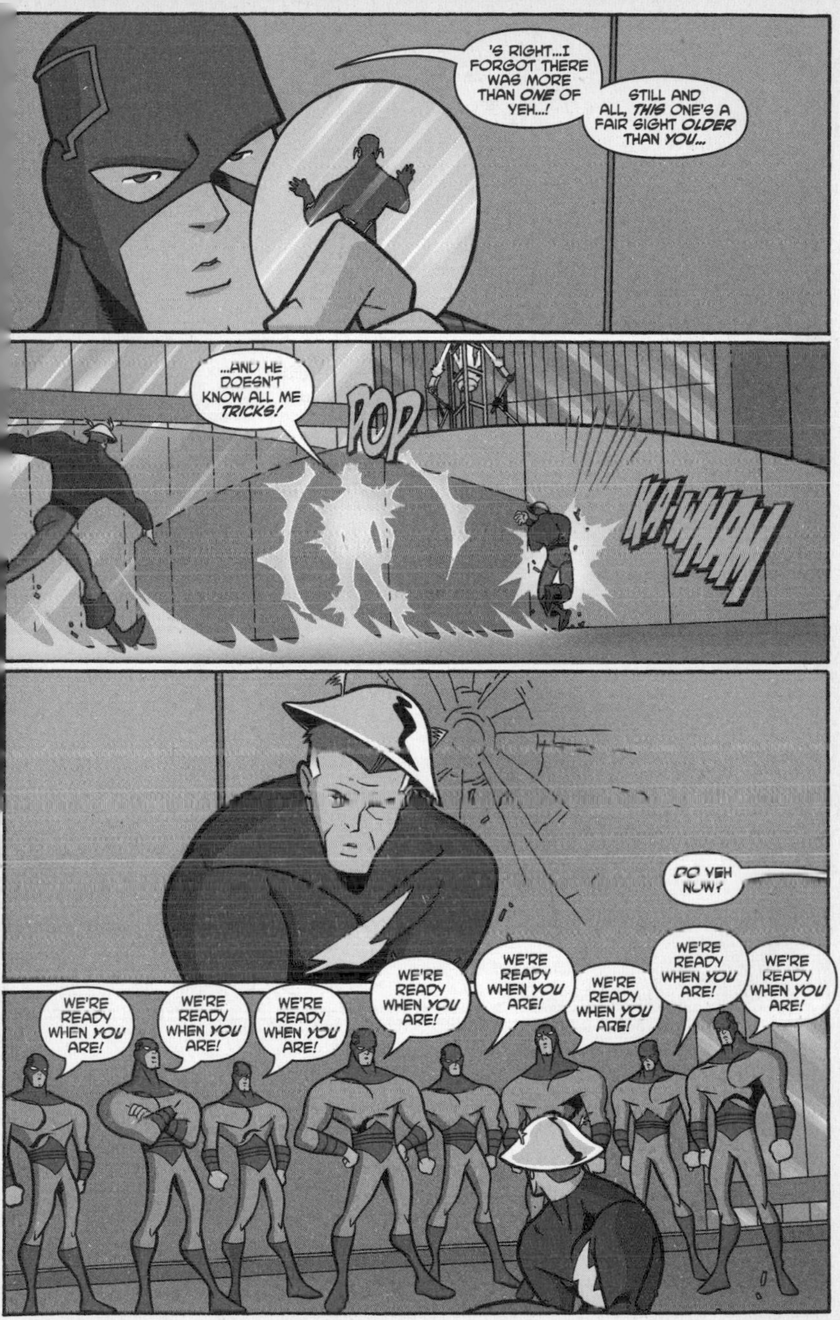
'S RIGHT...I FORGOT THERE WAS MORE THAN *ONE* OF YEH...!
STILL AND ALL, *THIS* ONE'S A FAIR SIGHT *OLDER* THAN *YOU*...
...AND HE DOESN'T KNOW ALL ME *TRICKS!*
POP
KA-WHAM
DO YEH NOW?
WE'RE READY WHEN *YOU* ARE!
WE'RE READY WHEN *YOU* ARE!
WE'RE READY WHEN *YOU* ARE!
WE'RE READY WHEN *YOU* ARE!
WE'RE READY WHEN *YOU* ARE!
WE'RE READY WHEN *YOU* ARE!
WE'RE READY WHEN *YOU* ARE!
WE'RE READY WHEN *YOU* ARE!

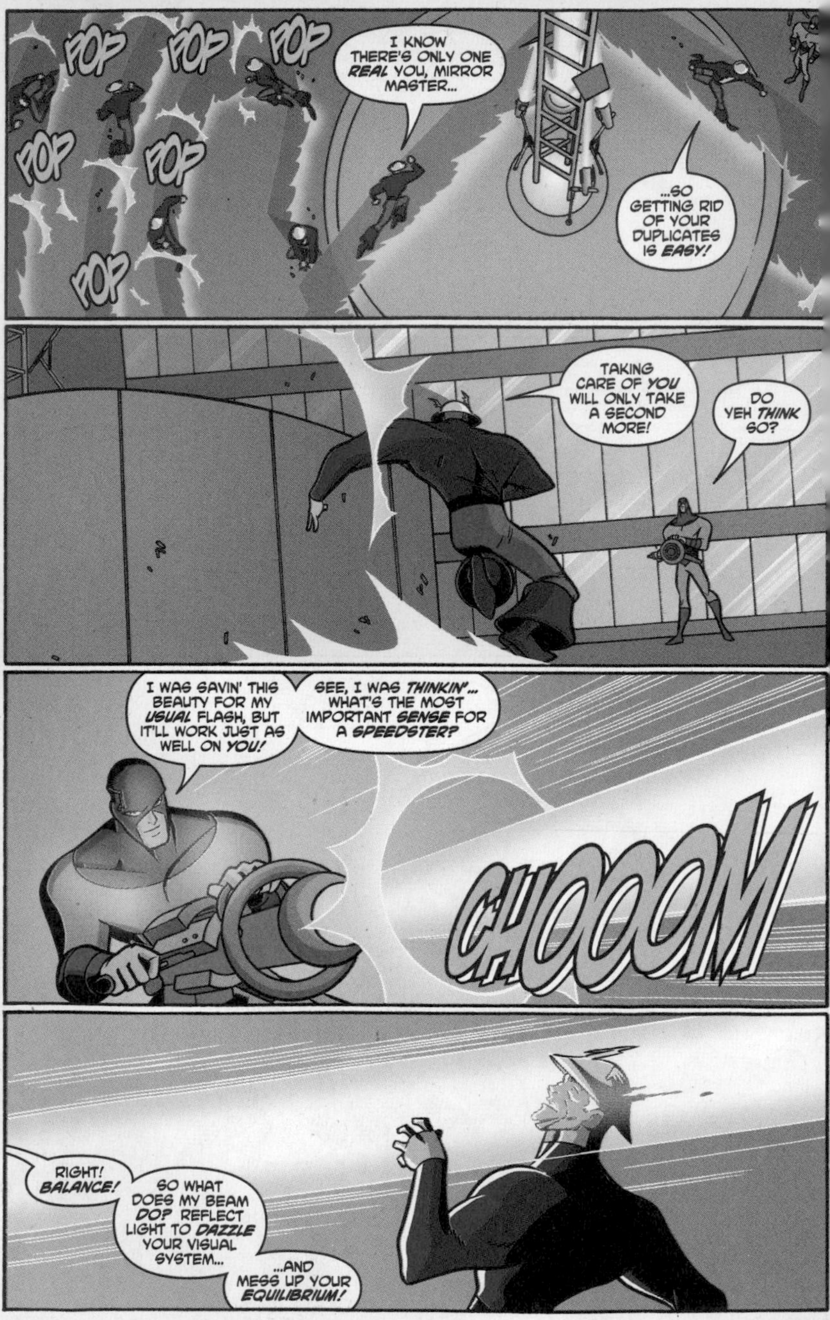
POP
POP
POP
POP
POP
POP
I KNOW THERE'S ONLY ONE REAL YOU, MIRROR MASTER...
...SO GETTING RID OF YOUR DUPLICATES IS EASY!
TAKING CARE OF YOU WILL ONLY TAKE A SECOND MORE!
DO YEH THINK SO?
I WAS SAVIN' THIS BEAUTY FOR MY USUAL FLASH, BUT IT'LL WORK JUST AS WELL ON YOU!
SEE, I WAS THINKIN'... WHAT'S THE MOST IMPORTANT SENSE FOR A SPEEDSTER?
CHOOOM
RIGHT! BALANCE!
SO WHAT DOES MY BEAM DO? REFLECT LIGHT TO DAZZLE YOUR VISUAL SYSTEM...
...AND MESS UP YOUR EQUILIBRIUM!

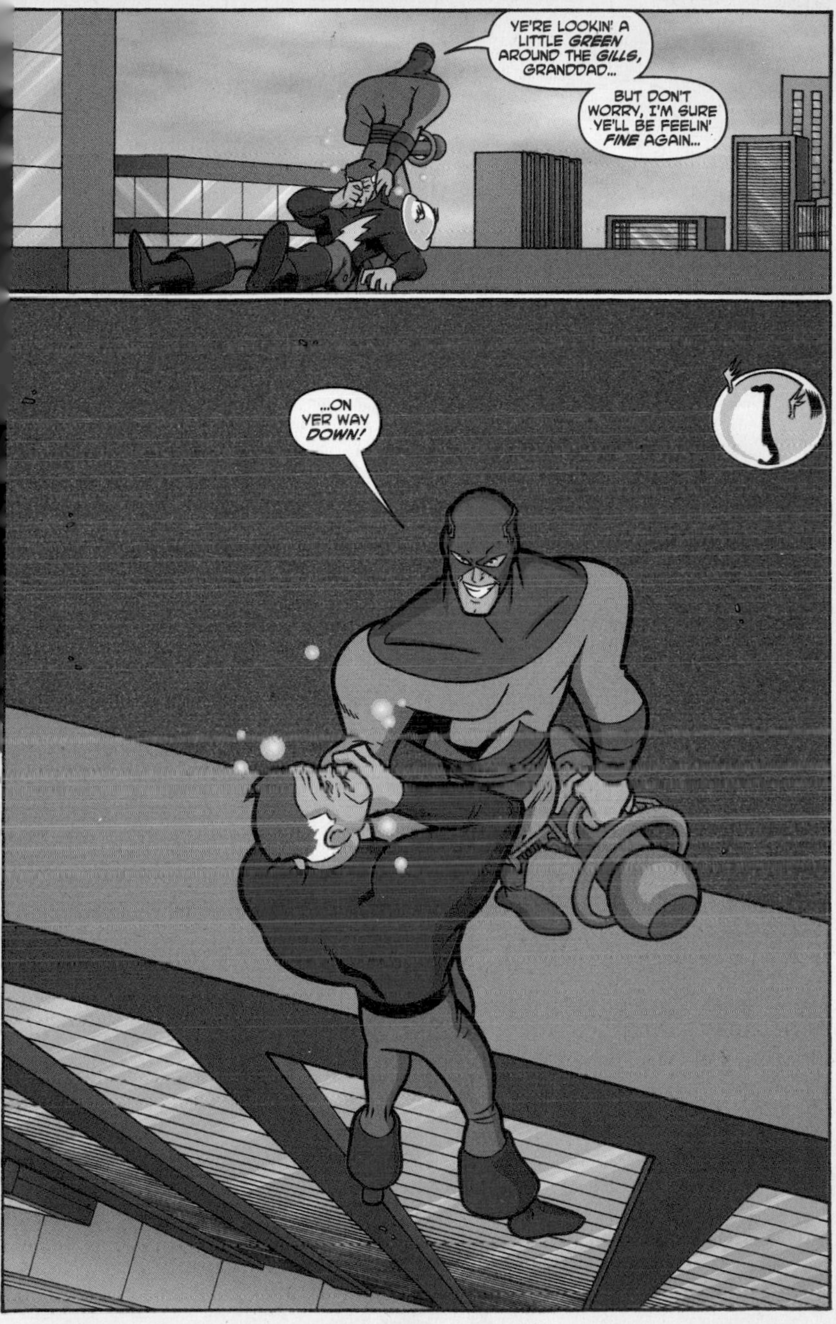
YE'RE LOOKIN' A LITTLE GREEN AROUND THE GILLS, GRANDDAD...
BUT DON'T WORRY, I'M SURE YE'LL BE FEELIN' FINE AGAIN...
...ON YER WAY DOWN!

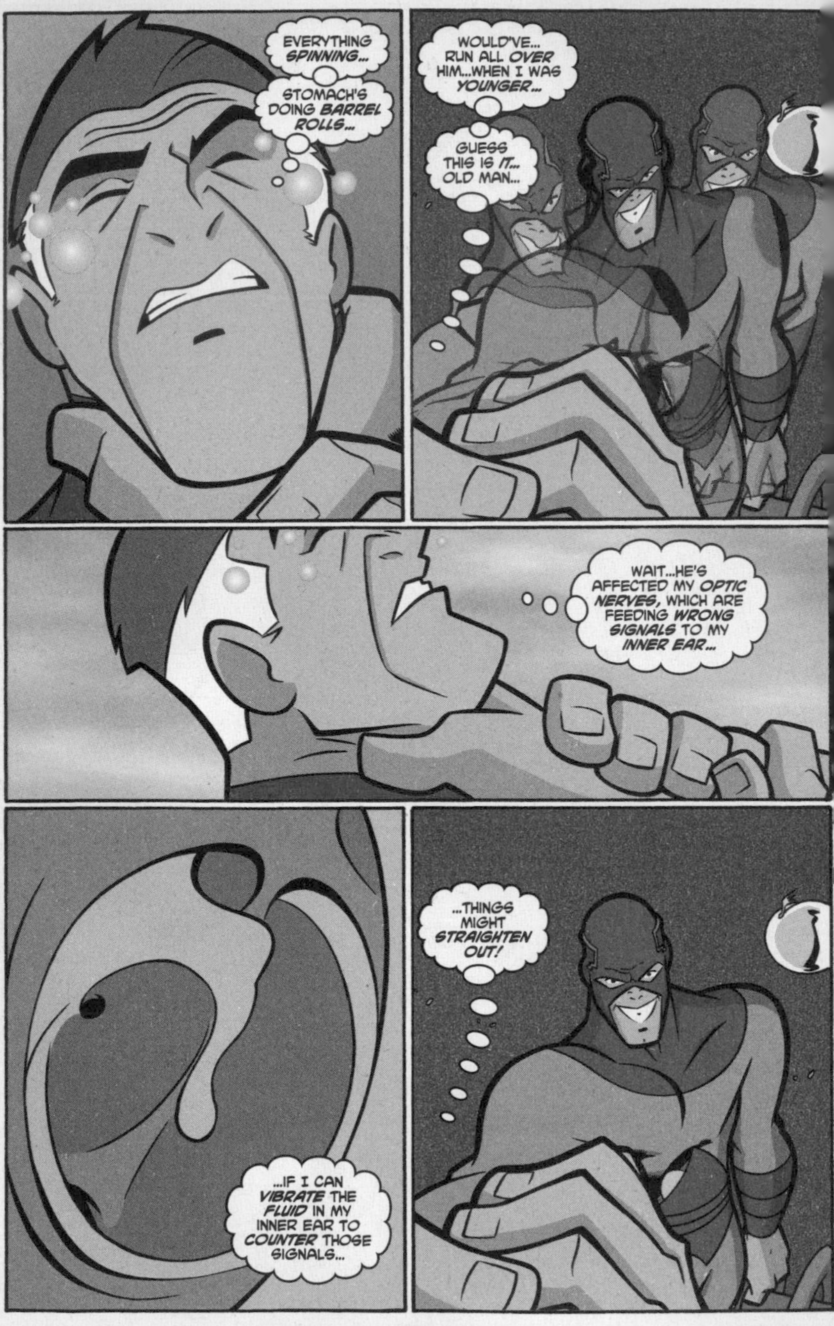
EVERYTHING SPINNING...
STOMACH'S DOING BARREL ROLLS...
WOULD'VE... RUN ALL OVER HIM...WHEN I WAS YOUNGER...
GUESS THIS IS IT... OLD MAN...
WAIT...HE'S AFFECTED MY OPTIC NERVES, WHICH ARE FEEDING WRONG SIGNALS TO MY INNER EAR...
...IF I CAN VIBRATE THE FLUID IN MY INNER EAR TO COUNTER THOSE SIGNALS...
...THINGS MIGHT STRAIGHTEN OUT!

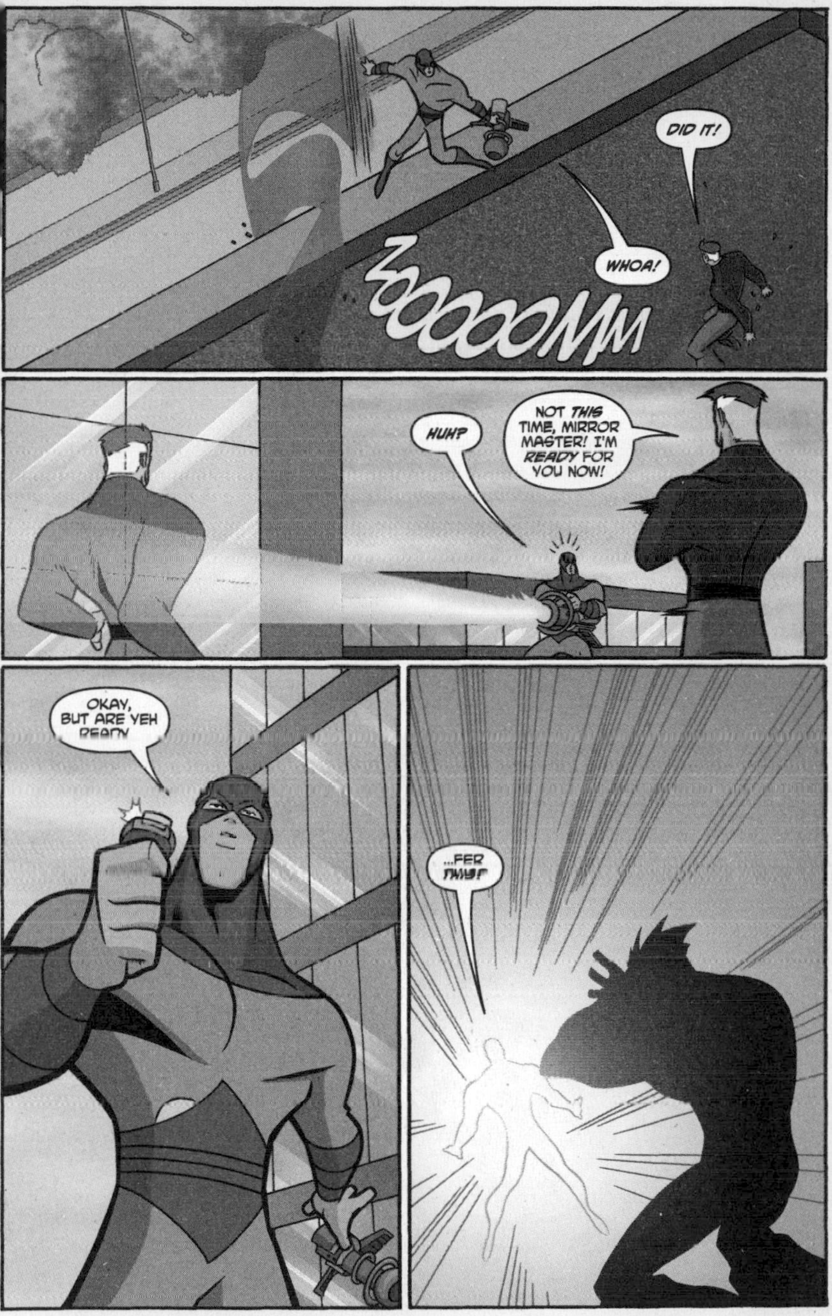
DID IT!
WHOA!
ZOOOOOMM
NOT THIS TIME, MIRROR MASTER! I'M READY FOR YOU NOW!
HUH?
OKAY, BUT ARE YEH READY
...FER THIS!

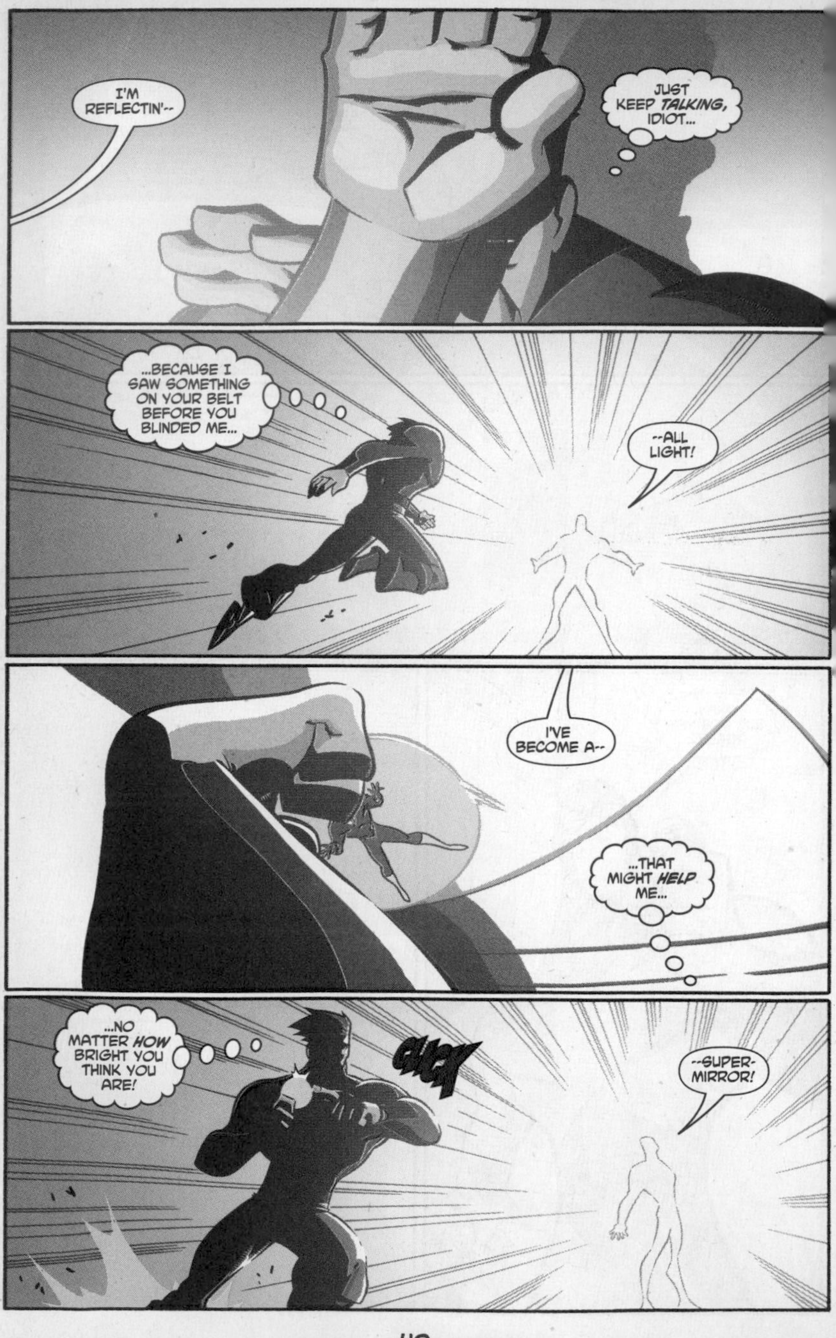
I'M REFLECTIN'--
JUST KEEP *TALKING*, IDIOT...
...BECAUSE I SAW SOMETHING ON YOUR BELT BEFORE YOU BLINDED ME...
--ALL LIGHT!
I'VE BECOME A--
...THAT MIGHT *HELP* ME...
...NO MATTER *HOW* BRIGHT YOU THINK YOU ARE!
--SUPER-MIRROR!

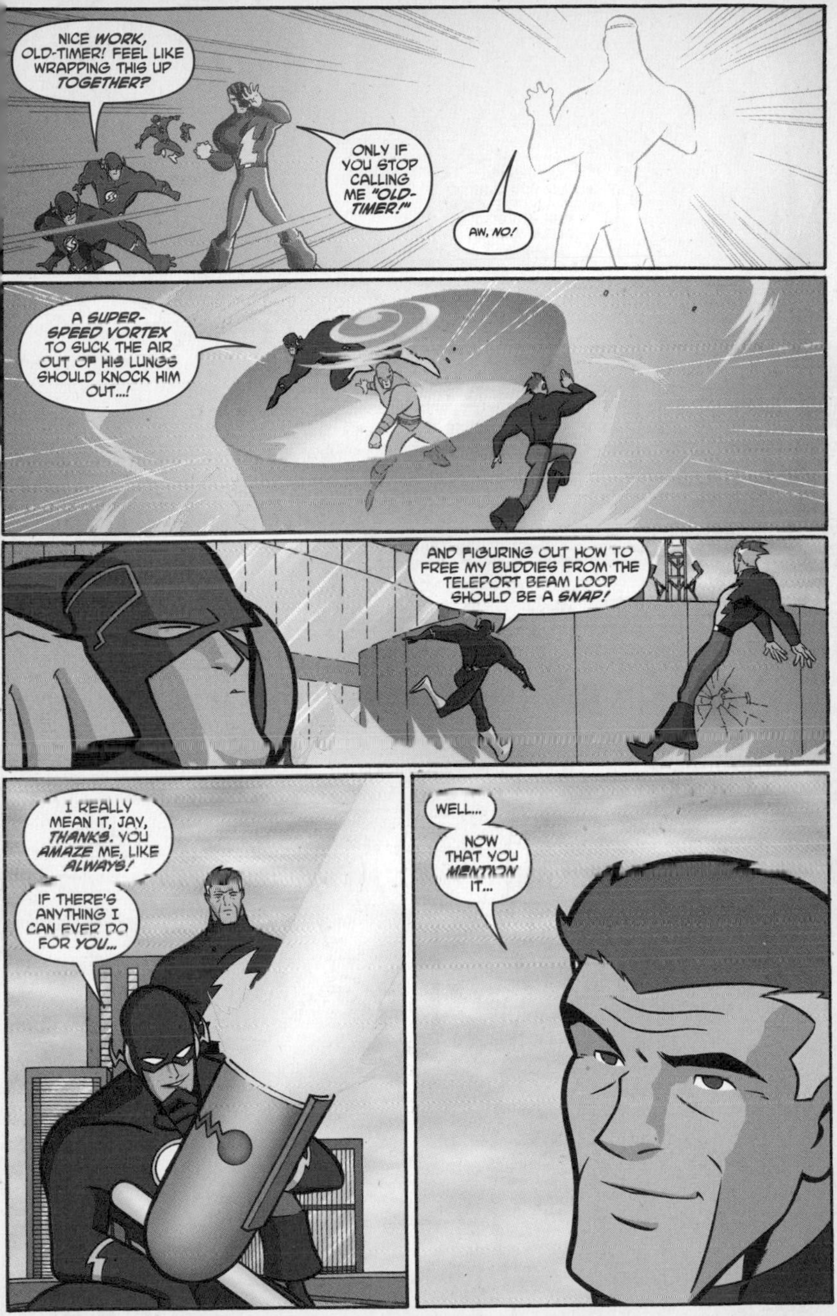
NICE WORK, OLD-TIMER! FEEL LIKE WRAPPING THIS UP TOGETHER?
ONLY IF YOU STOP CALLING ME "OLD-TIMER!"
AW, NO!
A SUPER-SPEED VORTEX TO SUCK THE AIR OUT OF HIS LUNGS SHOULD KNOCK HIM OUT...!
AND FIGURING OUT HOW TO FREE MY BUDDIES FROM THE TELEPORT BEAM LOOP SHOULD BE A SNAP!
I REALLY MEAN IT, JAY, THANKS. YOU AMAZE ME, LIKE ALWAYS!
IF THERE'S ANYTHING I CAN EVER DO FOR YOU...
WELL...
NOW THAT YOU MENTION IT...

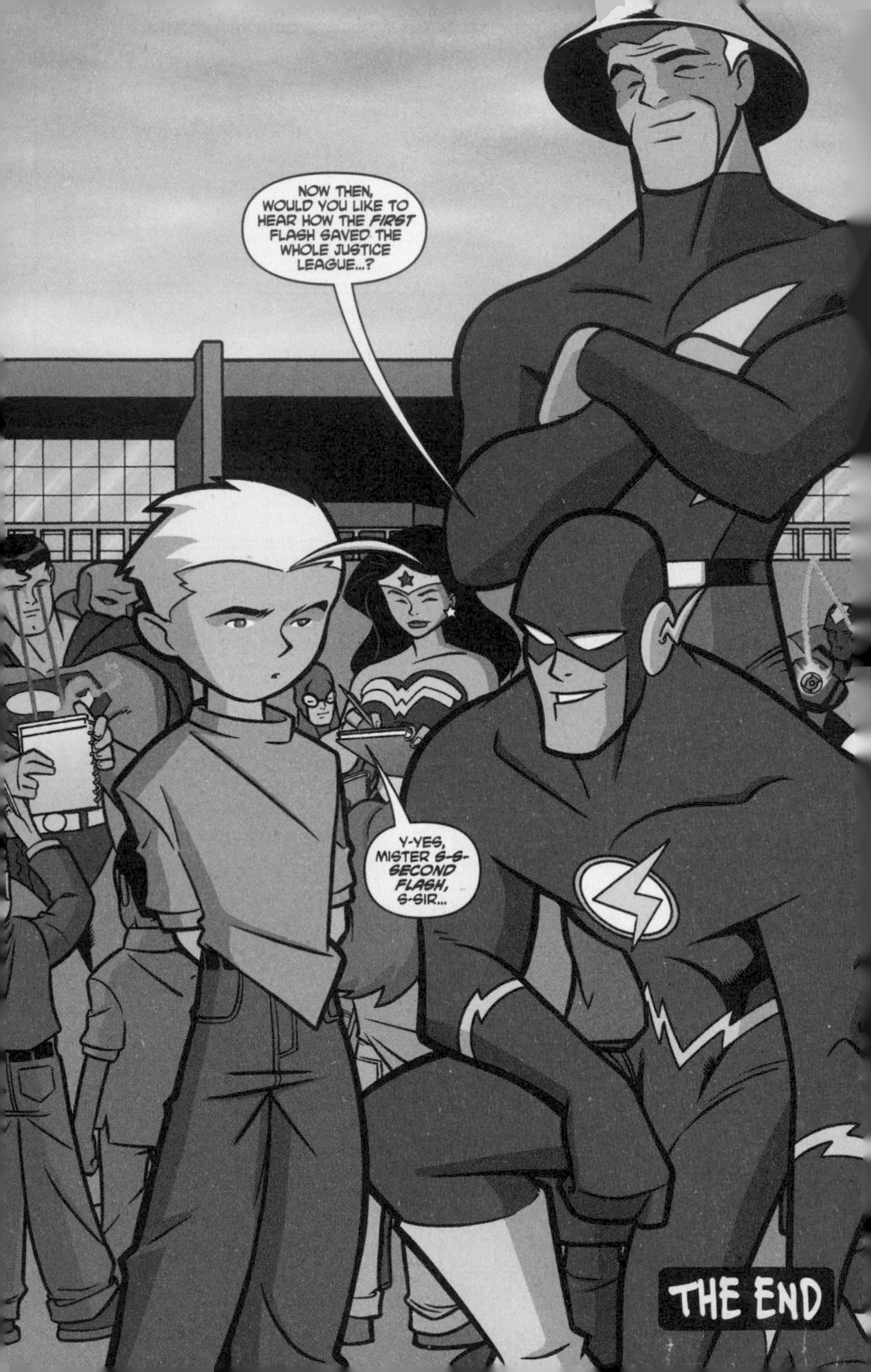
NOW THEN, WOULD YOU LIKE TO HEAR HOW THE *FIRST* FLASH SAVED THE WHOLE JUSTICE LEAGUE...?
Y-YES, MISTER *S-S-SECOND FLASH,* S-SIR...
THE END

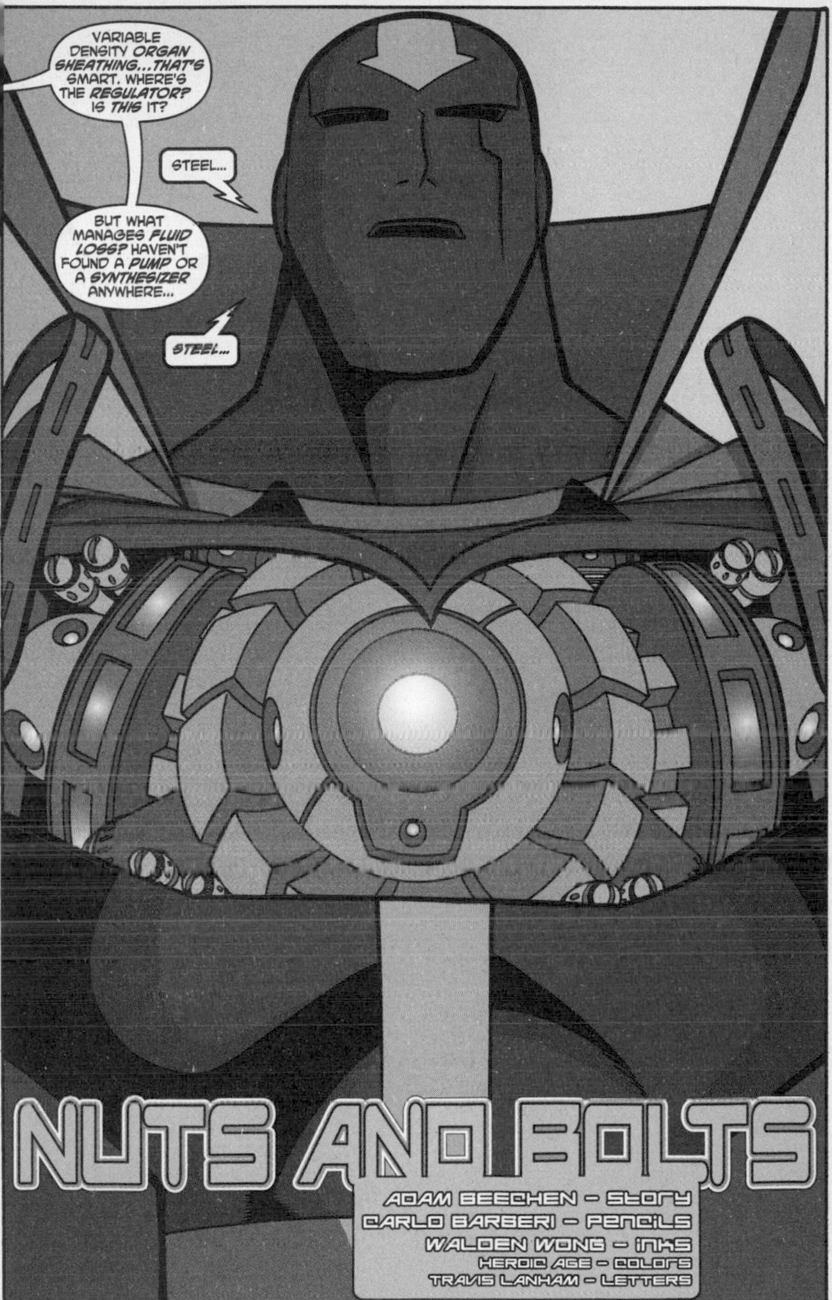
VARIABLE DENSITY ORGAN SHEATHING...THAT'S SMART. WHERE'S THE REGULATOR? IS THIS IT?
STEEL...
BUT WHAT MANAGES FLUID LOSS? HAVEN'T FOUND A PUMP OR A SYNTHESIZER ANYWHERE...
STEEL...
NUTS AND BOLTS
ADAM BEECHEN - STORY
CARLO BARBERI - PENCILS
WALDEN WONG - INKS
HEROIC AGE - COLORS
TRAVIS LANHAM - LETTERS

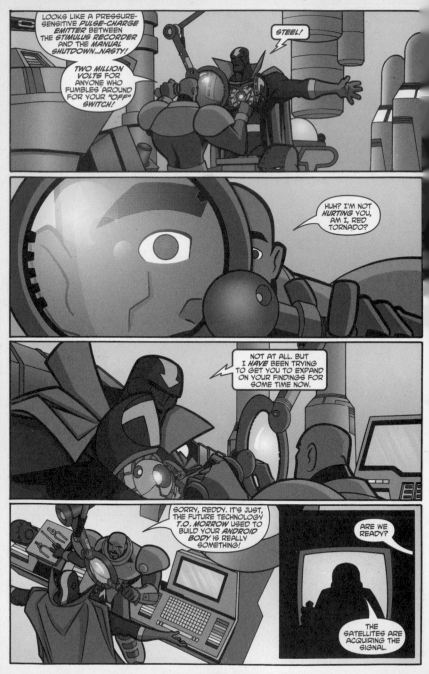

LOOKS LIKE A PRESSURE-SENSITIVE *PULSE-CHARGE EMITTER* BETWEEN THE *STIMULUS RECORDER* AND THE *MANUAL SHUTDOWN...NASTY!*

TWO MILLION VOLTS FOR ANYONE WHO FUMBLES AROUND FOR YOUR "OFF" SWITCH!

STEEL!

HUH? I'M NOT *HURTING* YOU, AM I, RED TORNADO?

NOT AT ALL. BUT I *HAVE* BEEN TRYING TO GET YOU TO EXPAND ON YOUR FINDINGS FOR SOME TIME NOW.

SORRY, REDDY. IT'S JUST, THE FUTURE TECHNOLOGY *T.O. MORROW* USED TO BUILD YOUR *ANDROID BODY* IS REALLY SOMETHING!

ARE WE READY?

THE SATELLITES ARE ACQUIRING THE SIGNAL.

44

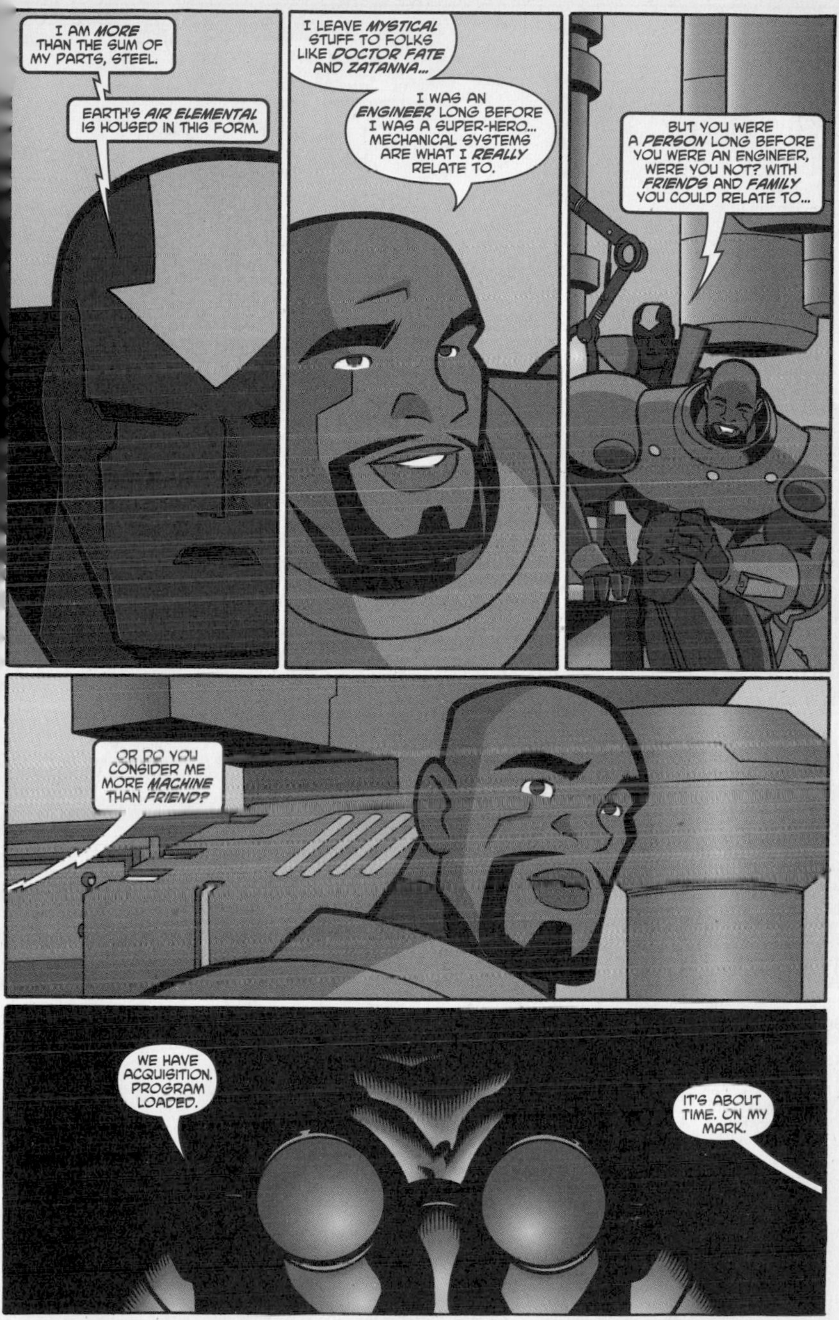
I AM MORE THAN THE SUM OF MY PARTS, STEEL.
EARTH'S AIR ELEMENTAL IS HOUSED IN THIS FORM.
I LEAVE MYSTICAL STUFF TO FOLKS LIKE DOCTOR FATE AND ZATANNA...
I WAS AN ENGINEER LONG BEFORE I WAS A SUPER-HERO... MECHANICAL SYSTEMS ARE WHAT I REALLY RELATE TO.
BUT YOU WERE A PERSON LONG BEFORE YOU WERE AN ENGINEER, WERE YOU NOT? WITH FRIENDS AND FAMILY YOU COULD RELATE TO...
OR DO YOU CONSIDER ME MORE MACHINE THAN FRIEND?
WE HAVE ACQUISITION. PROGRAM LOADED.
IT'S ABOUT TIME. ON MY MARK.

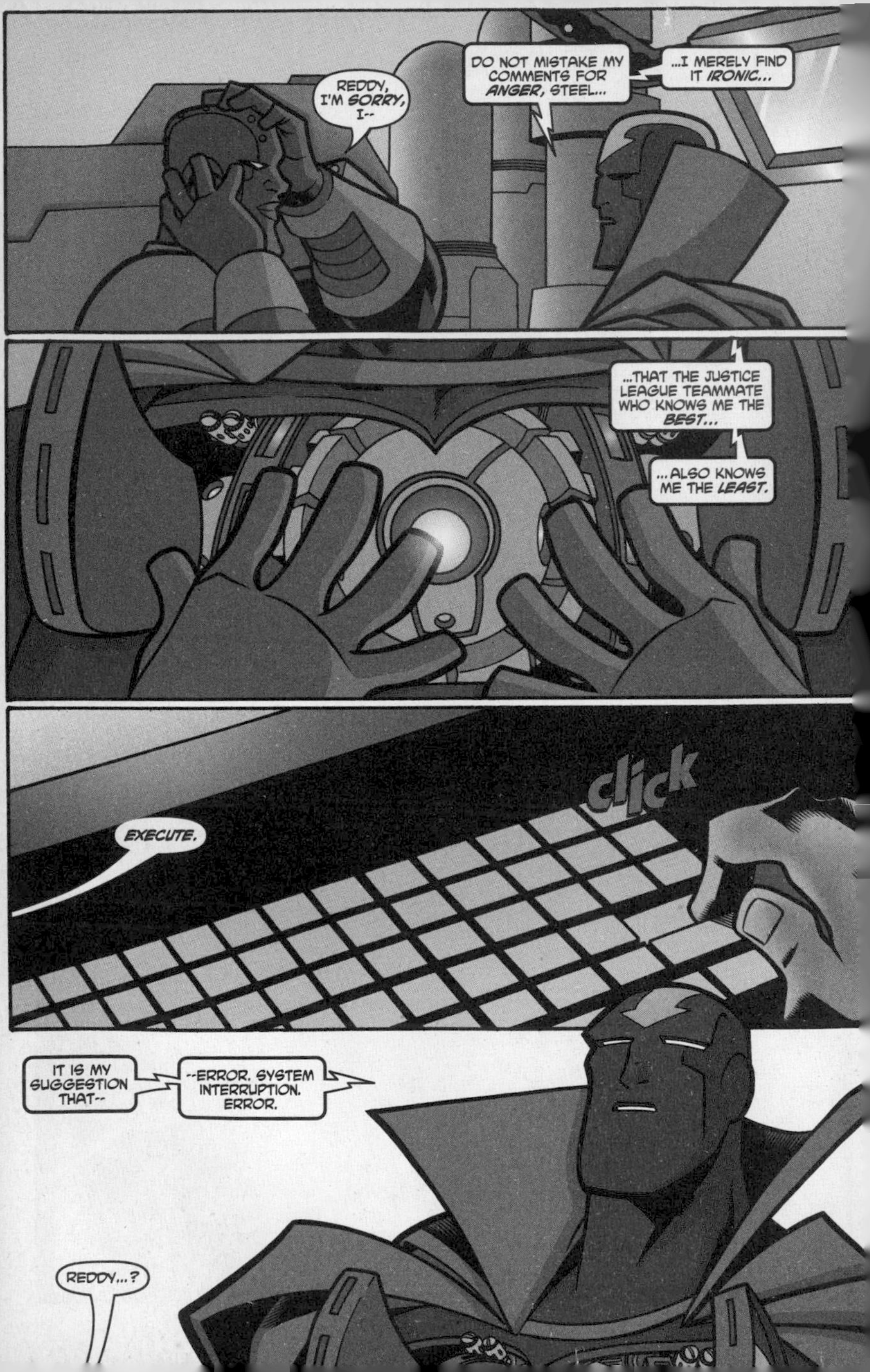
REDDY, I'M SORRY, I--
DO NOT MISTAKE MY COMMENTS FOR ANGER, STEEL...
...I MERELY FIND IT IRONIC...
...THAT THE JUSTICE LEAGUE TEAMMATE WHO KNOWS ME THE BEST...
...ALSO KNOWS ME THE LEAST.
EXECUTE.
click
IT IS MY SUGGESTION THAT--
--ERROR. SYSTEM INTERRUPTION. ERROR.
REDDY...?

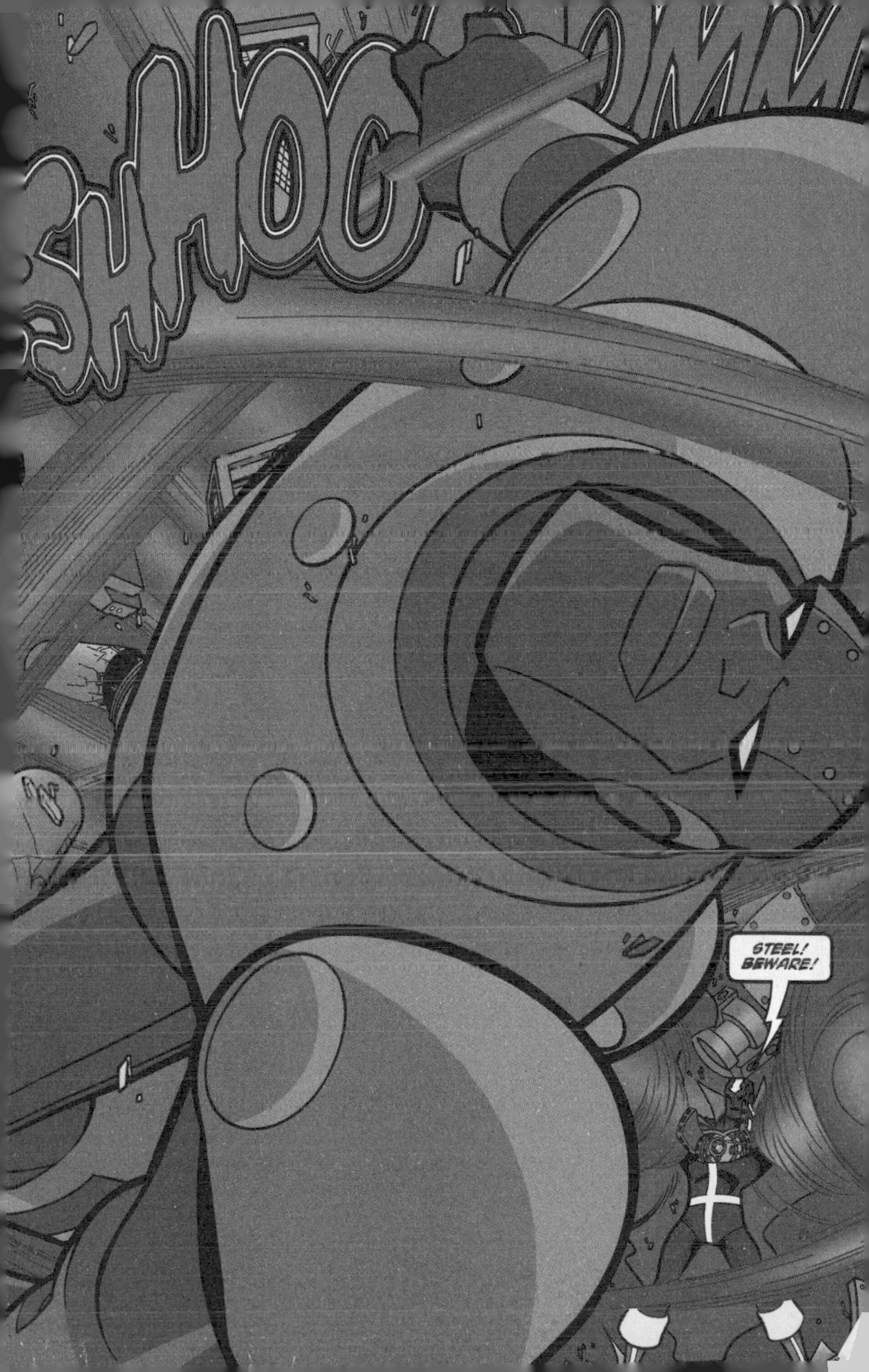
STEEL! BEWARE!

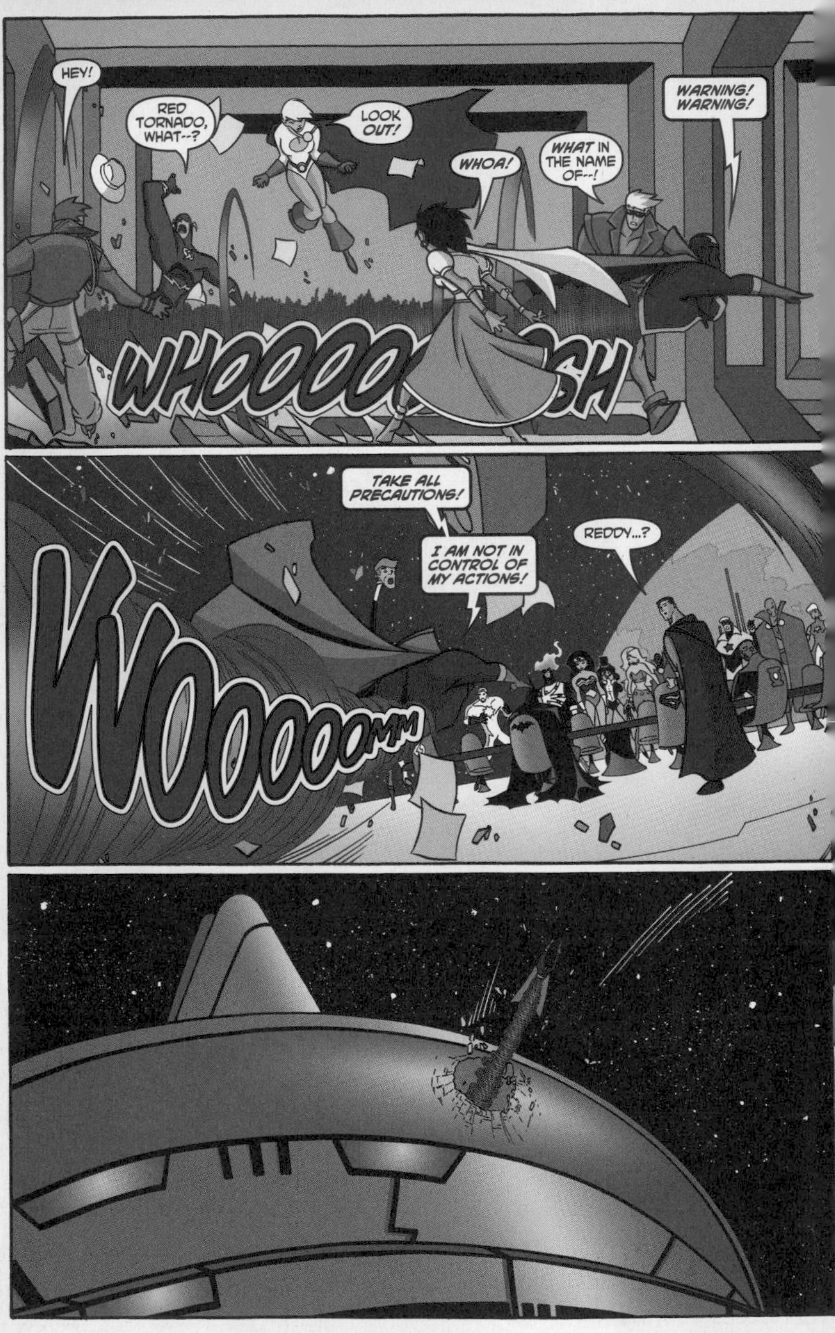
HEY!
RED TORNADO, WHAT--?
LOOK OUT!
WHOA!
WHAT IN THE NAME OF--!
WARNING! WARNING!
WHOOOOO
SH
TAKE ALL PRECAUTIONS!
I AM NOT IN CONTROL OF MY ACTIONS!
REDDY...?
VVOOOOOOMM

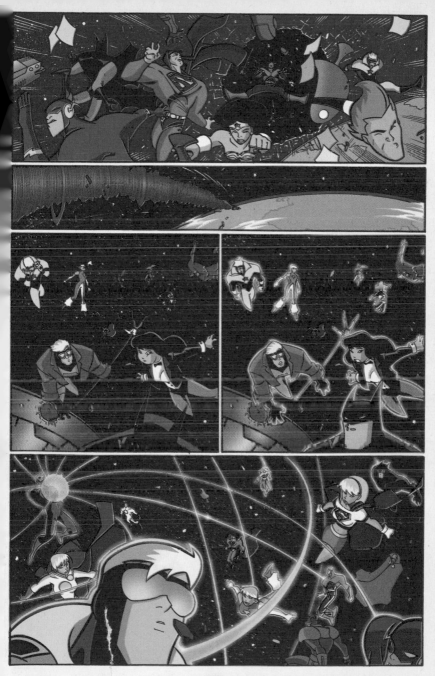

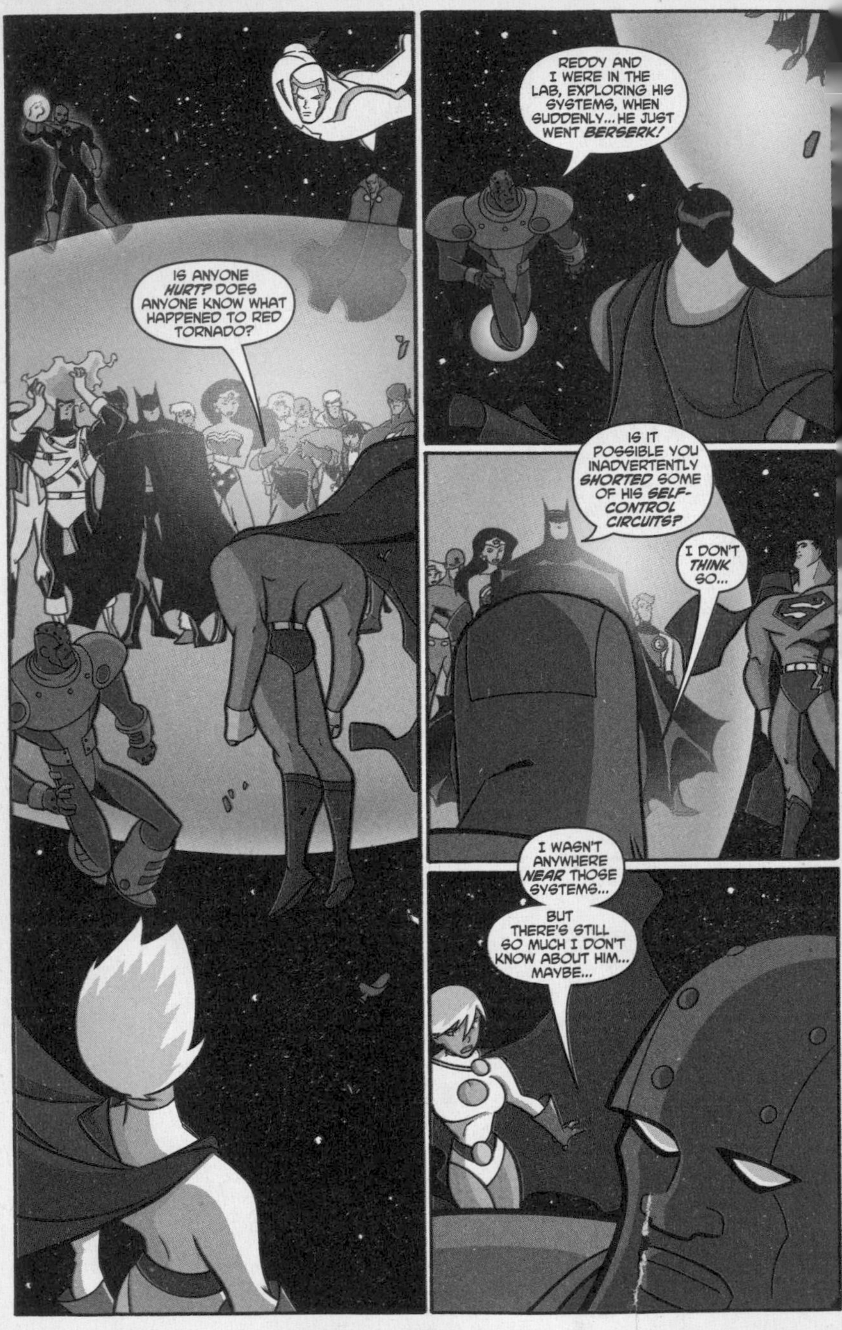
IS ANYONE HURT? DOES ANYONE KNOW WHAT HAPPENED TO RED TORNADO?
REDDY AND I WERE IN THE LAB, EXPLORING HIS SYSTEMS, WHEN SUDDENLY... HE JUST WENT BERSERK!
IS IT POSSIBLE YOU INADVERTENTLY SHORTED SOME OF HIS SELF-CONTROL CIRCUITS?
I DON'T THINK SO...
I WASN'T ANYWHERE NEAR THOSE SYSTEMS...
BUT THERE'S STILL SO MUCH I DON'T KNOW ABOUT HIM... MAYBE...

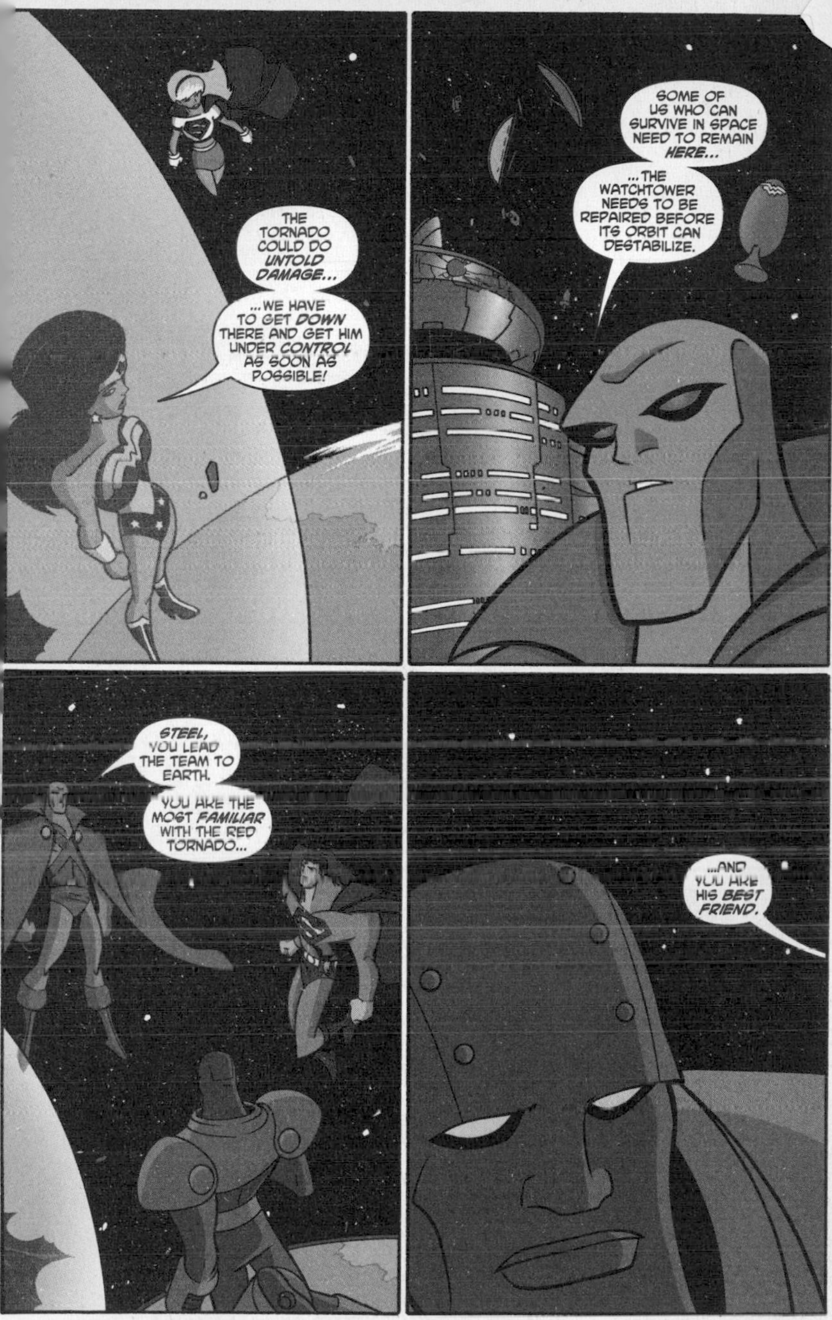
THE TORNADO COULD DO *UNTOLD DAMAGE*...
...WE HAVE TO GET *DOWN* THERE AND GET HIM UNDER *CONTROL* AS SOON AS POSSIBLE!
SOME OF US WHO CAN SURVIVE IN SPACE NEED TO REMAIN *HERE*...
...THE WATCHTOWER NEEDS TO BE REPAIRED BEFORE ITS ORBIT CAN DESTABILIZE.
STEEL, YOU LEAD THE TEAM TO EARTH.
YOU ARE THE MOST *FAMILIAR* WITH THE RED TORNADO...
...AND YOU ARE HIS *BEST FRIEND*.

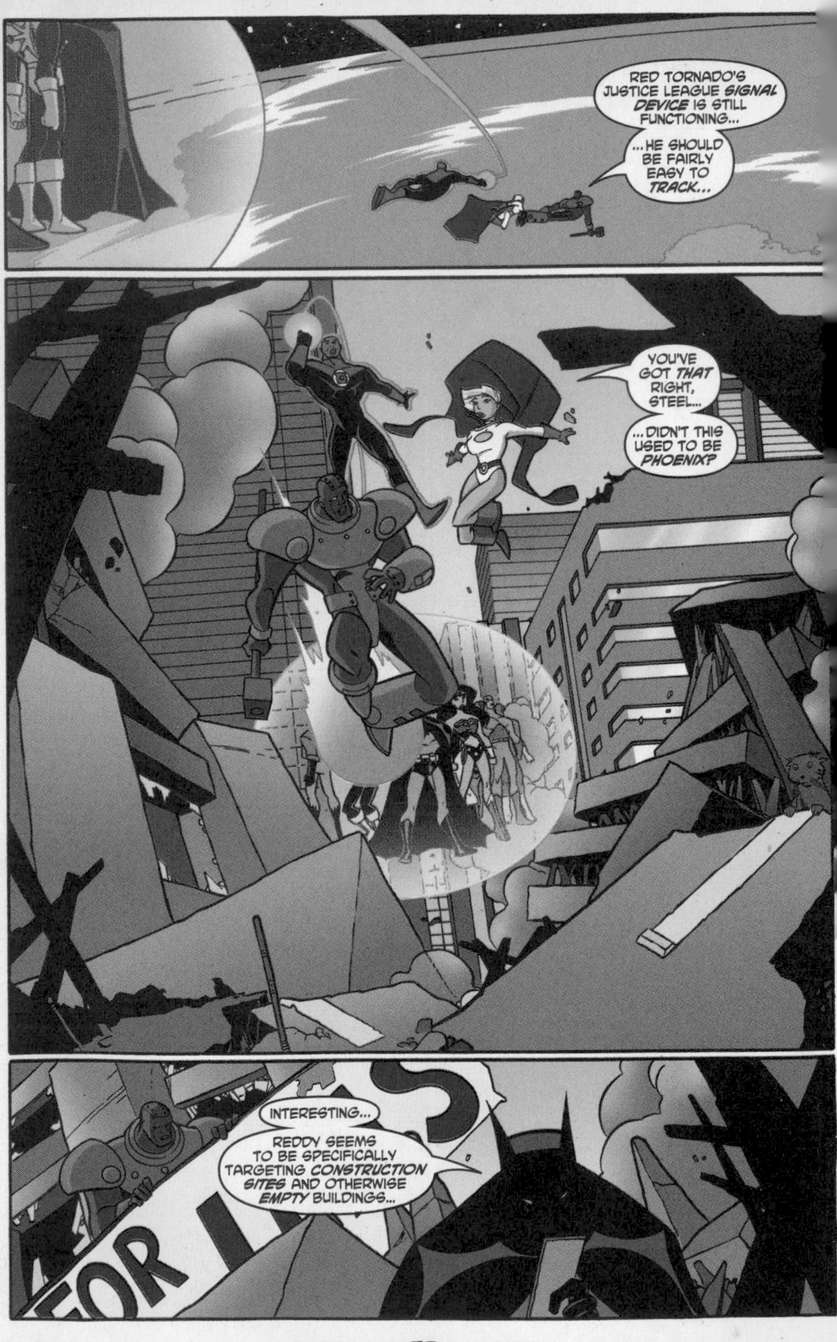
RED TORNADO'S JUSTICE LEAGUE SIGNAL DEVICE IS STILL FUNCTIONING...
...HE SHOULD BE FAIRLY EASY TO TRACK...
YOU'VE GOT THAT RIGHT, STEEL...
...DIDN'T THIS USED TO BE PHOENIX?
INTERESTING...
REDDY SEEMS TO BE SPECIFICALLY TARGETING CONSTRUCTION SITES AND OTHERWISE EMPTY BUILDINGS...
FOR

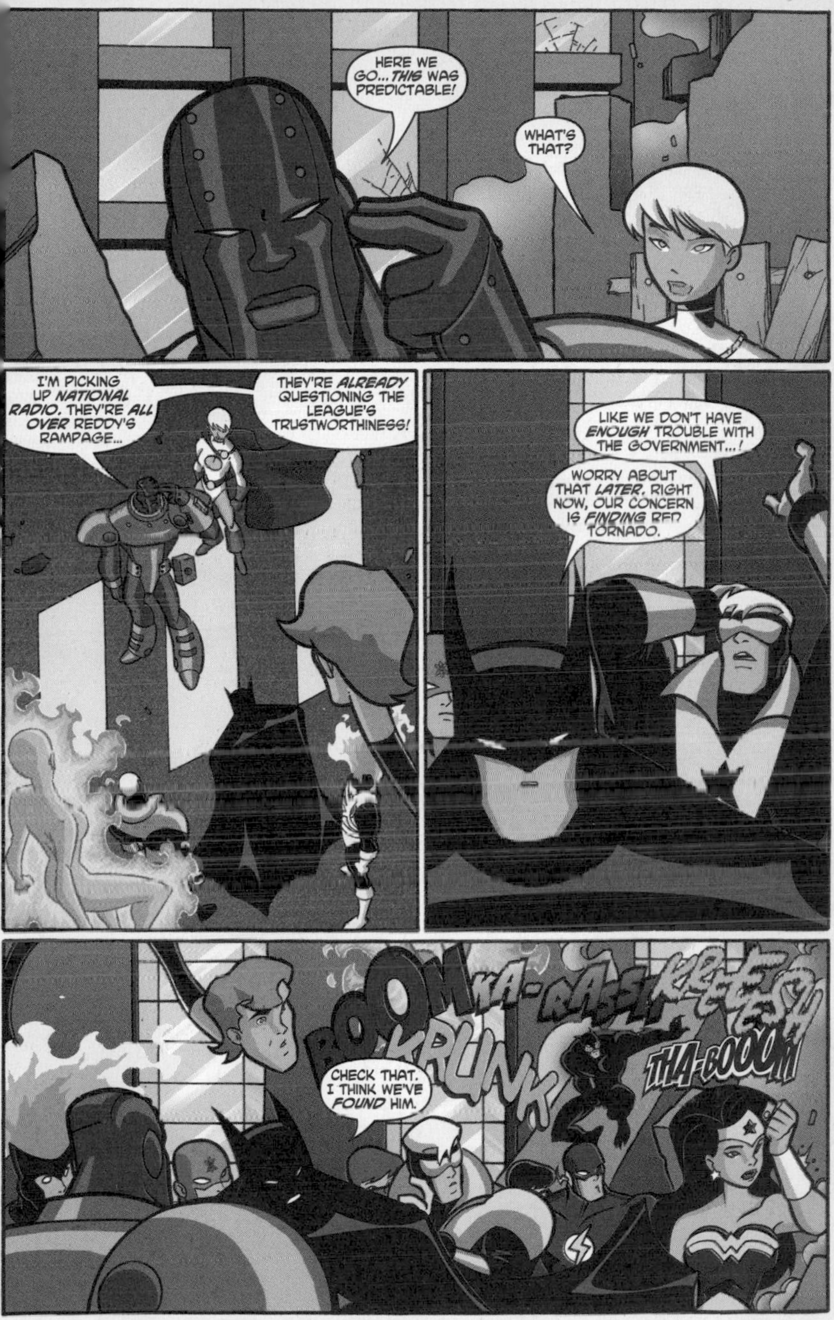
HERE WE GO...THIS WAS PREDICTABLE!
WHAT'S THAT?
I'M PICKING UP NATIONAL RADIO. THEY'RE ALL OVER REDDY'S RAMPAGE...
THEY'RE ALREADY QUESTIONING THE LEAGUE'S TRUSTWORTHINESS!
LIKE WE DON'T HAVE ENOUGH TROUBLE WITH THE GOVERNMENT...!
WORRY ABOUT THAT LATER. RIGHT NOW, OUR CONCERN IS FINDING RED TORNADO.
BOOOM
KA-RASSH
KREESH
KRUNK
THA-BOOOM
CHECK THAT. I THINK WE'VE FOUND HIM.

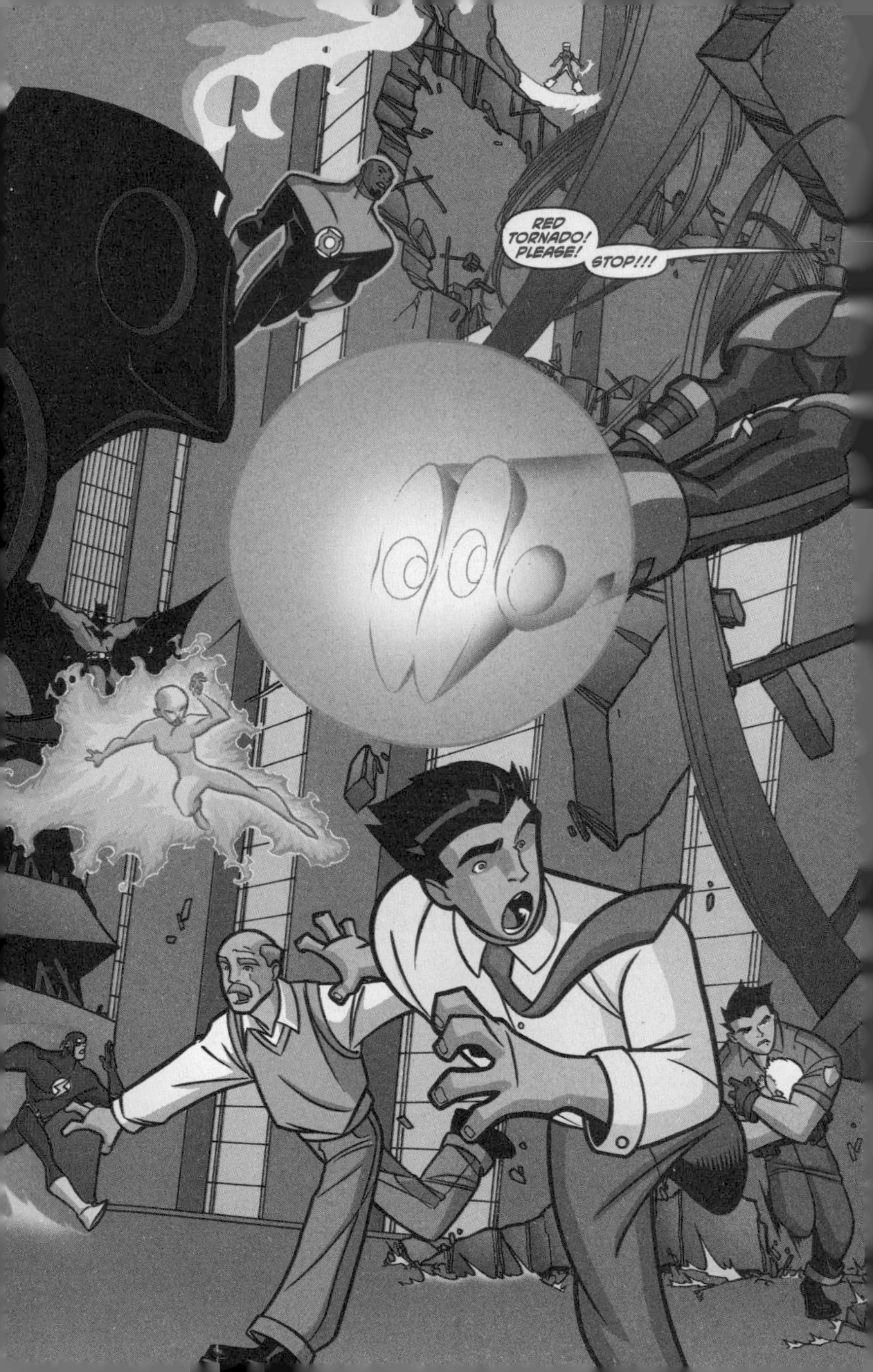
RED TORNADO! PLEASE!
STOP!!!

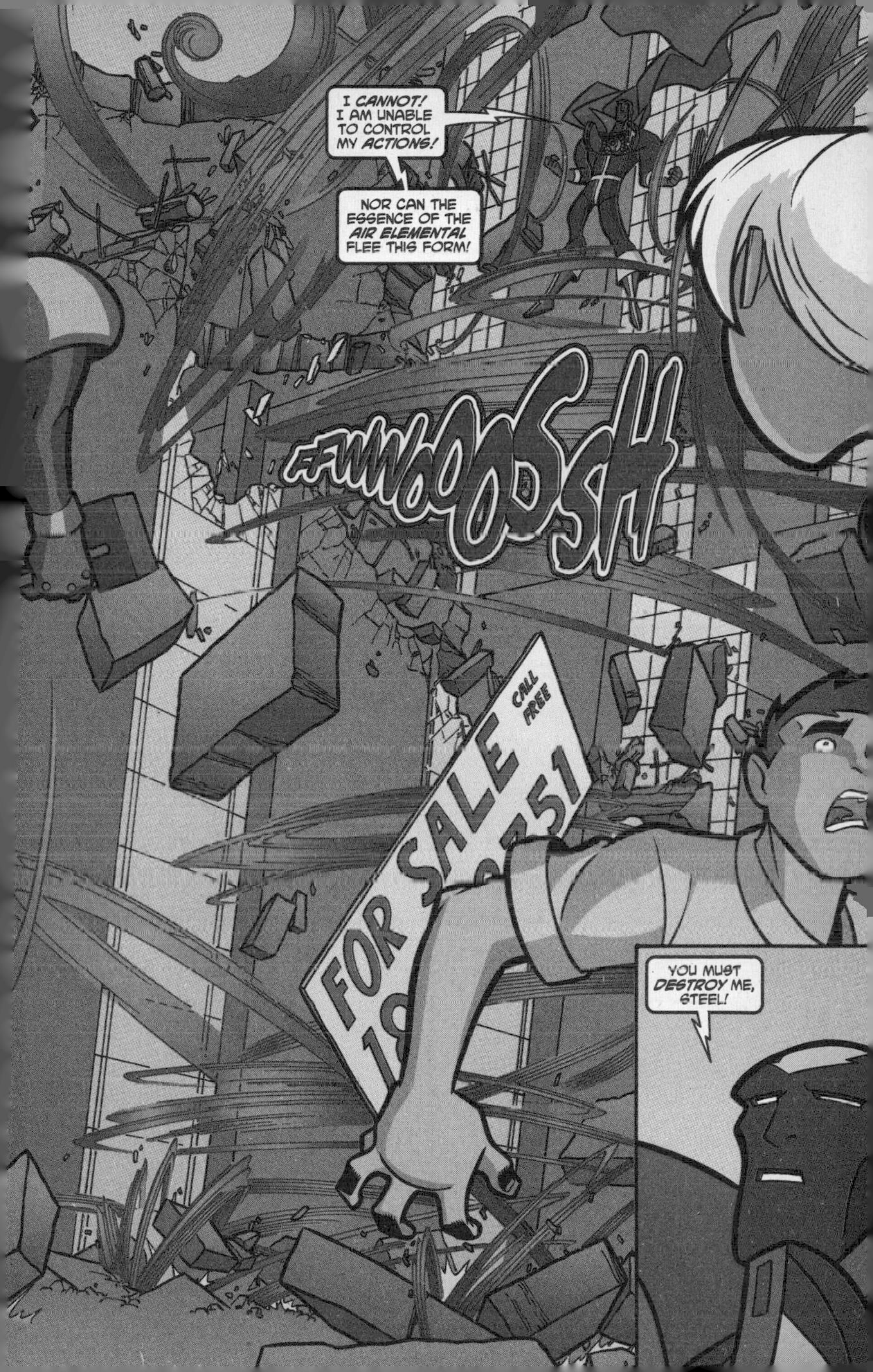

I CANNOT! I AM UNABLE TO CONTROL MY ACTIONS!
NOR CAN THE ESSENCE OF THE AIR ELEMENTAL FLEE THIS FORM!
FWWOOOSH
FOR SALE
CALL FREE
YOU MUST DESTROY ME, STEEL!

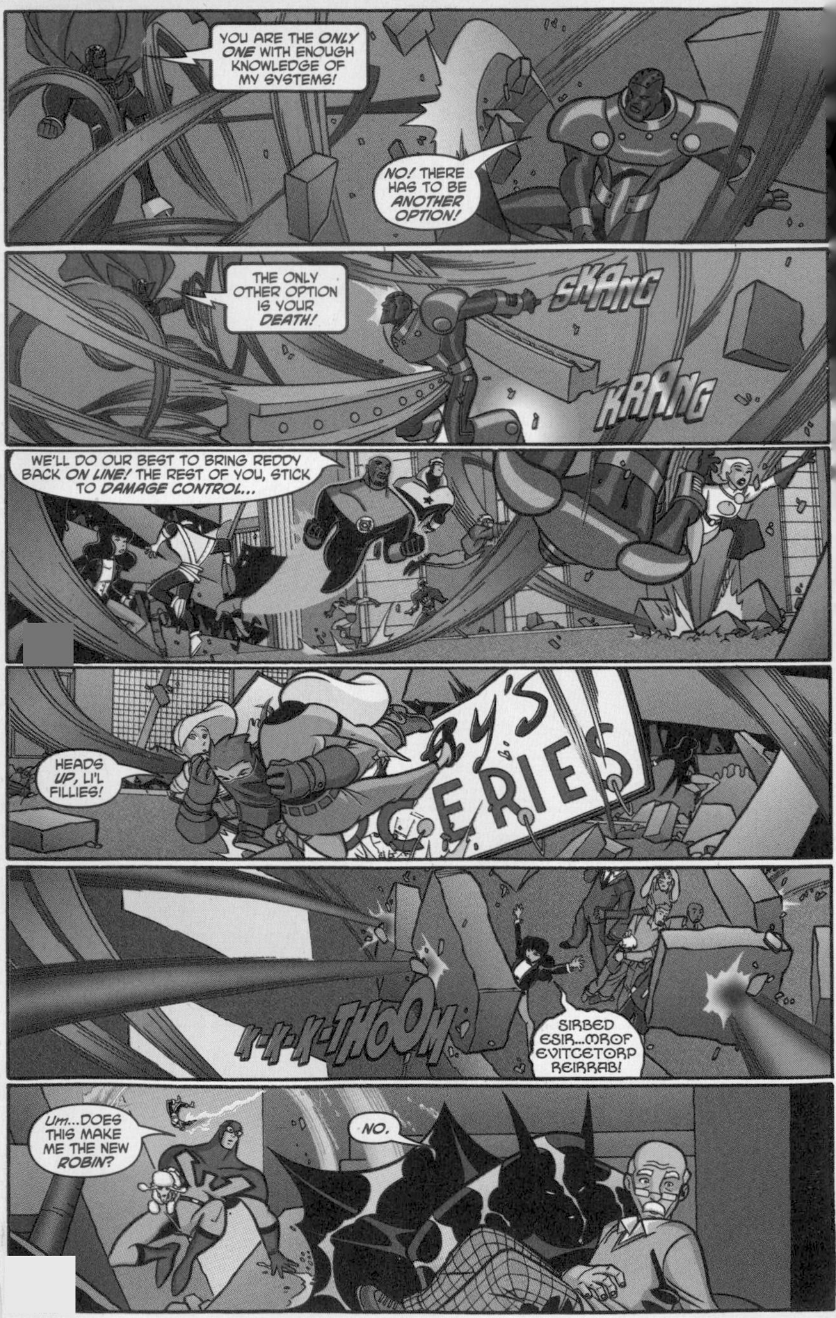

YOU ARE THE ONLY ONE WITH ENOUGH KNOWLEDGE OF MY SYSTEMS!
NO! THERE HAS TO BE ANOTHER OPTION!
THE ONLY OTHER OPTION IS YOUR DEATH!
SKANG
KRANG
WE'LL DO OUR BEST TO BRING REDDY BACK ON LINE! THE REST OF YOU, STICK TO DAMAGE CONTROL...
HEADS UP, LI'L FILLIES!
ERIES
K-K-K-THOOM
SIRBED ESIR...MROF EVITCETORP REIRRAB!
Um...DOES THIS MAKE ME THE NEW ROBIN?
NO.

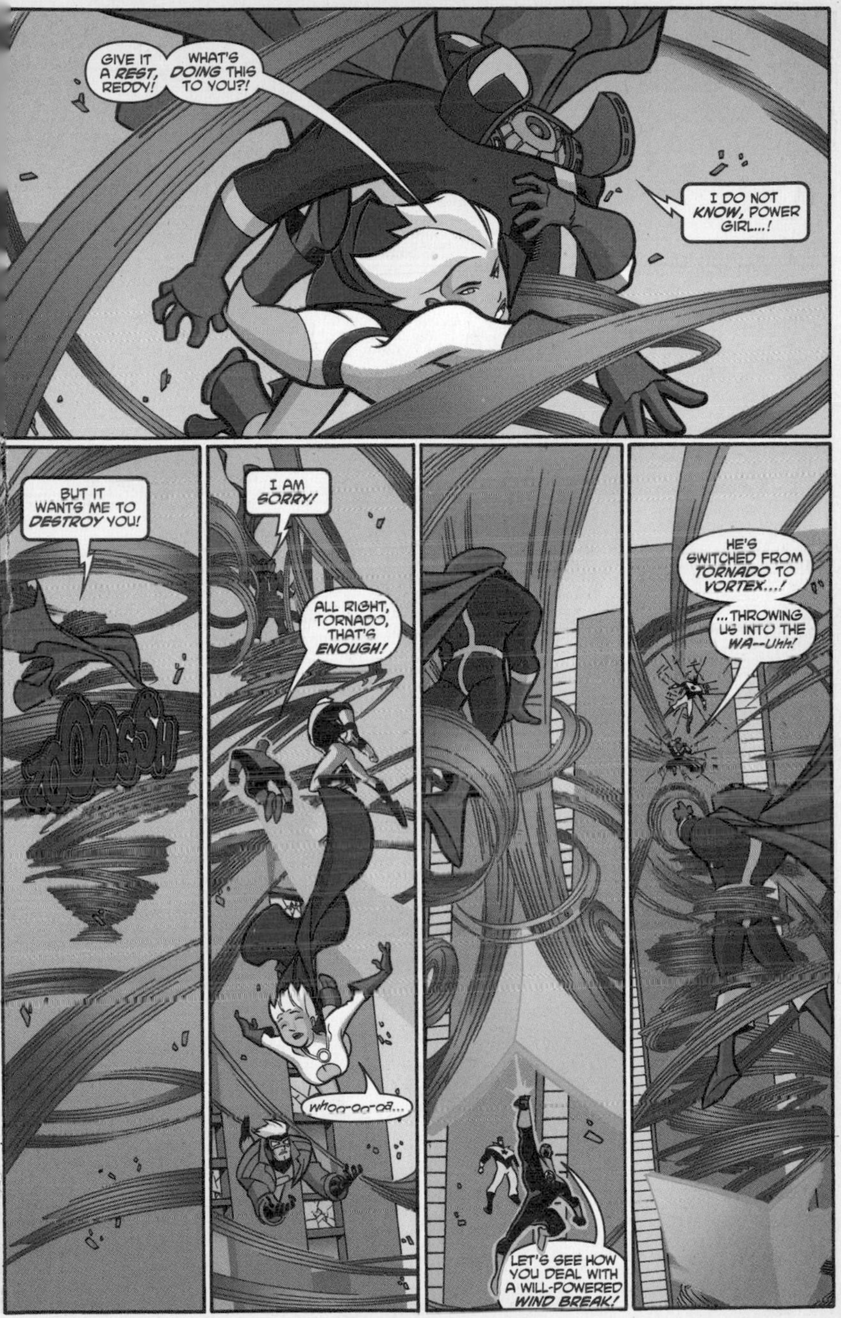
GIVE IT A REST, REDDY!
WHAT'S DOING THIS TO YOU?!
I DO NOT KNOW, POWER GIRL...!
BUT IT WANTS ME TO DESTROY YOU!
ZOOOOSSSH
I AM SORRY!
ALL RIGHT, TORNADO, THAT'S ENOUGH!
WHOA-OA-OA...
LET'S SEE HOW YOU DEAL WITH A WILL-POWERED WIND BREAK!
HE'S SWITCHED FROM TORNADO TO VORTEX...!
...THROWING US INTO THE WA--Uhh!

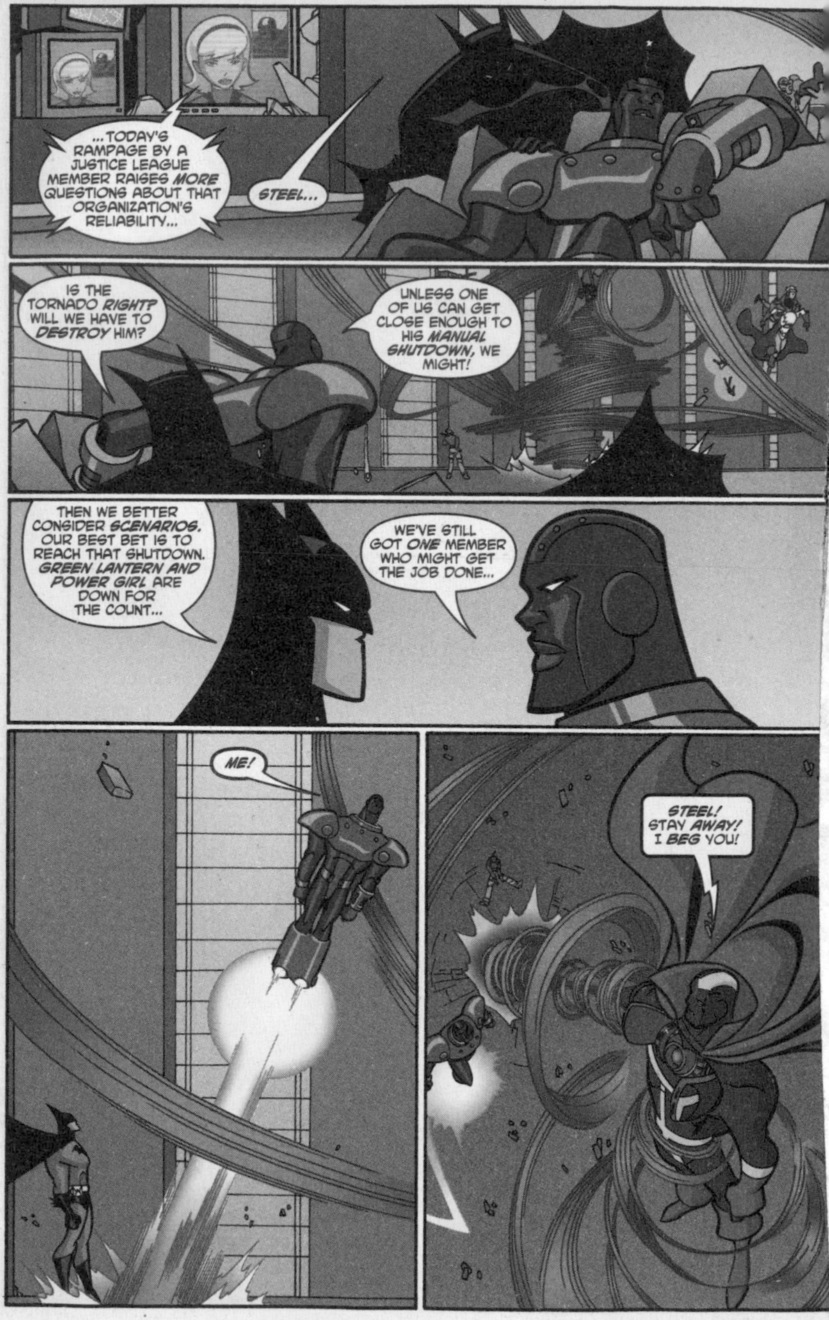
...TODAY'S RAMPAGE BY A JUSTICE LEAGUE MEMBER RAISES MORE QUESTIONS ABOUT THAT ORGANIZATION'S RELIABILITY...
STEEL...
IS THE TORNADO RIGHT? WILL WE HAVE TO DESTROY HIM?
UNLESS ONE OF US CAN GET CLOSE ENOUGH TO HIS MANUAL SHUTDOWN, WE MIGHT!
THEN WE BETTER CONSIDER SCENARIOS. OUR BEST BET IS TO REACH THAT SHUTDOWN. GREEN LANTERN AND POWER GIRL ARE DOWN FOR THE COUNT...
WE'VE STILL GOT ONE MEMBER WHO MIGHT GET THE JOB DONE...
ME!
STEEL! STAY AWAY! I BEG YOU!

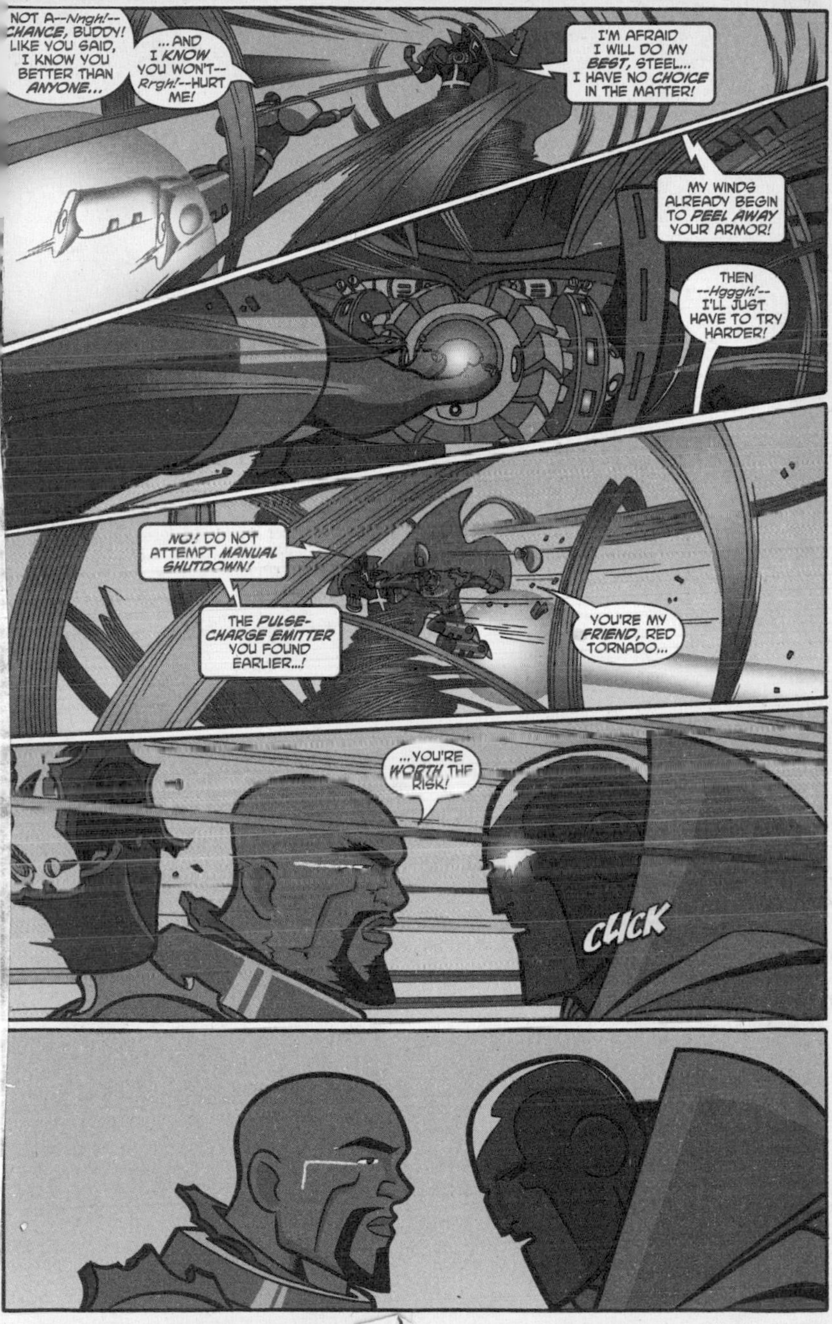
NOT A--*Nngh!*--*CHANCE*, BUDDY! LIKE YOU SAID, I KNOW YOU BETTER THAN *ANYONE*...
...AND I *KNOW* YOU WON'T--*Rrgh!*--HURT ME!
I'M AFRAID I WILL DO MY *BEST*, STEEL... I HAVE NO *CHOICE* IN THE MATTER!
MY WINDS ALREADY BEGIN TO *PEEL AWAY* YOUR ARMOR!
THEN --*Hgggh!*-- I'LL JUST HAVE TO TRY HARDER!
NO! DO NOT ATTEMPT *MANUAL SHUTDOWN!*
THE *PULSE-CHARGE EMITTER* YOU FOUND EARLIER...!
YOU'RE MY *FRIEND*, RED TORNADO...
...YOU'RE *WORTH* THE RISK!
CLICK

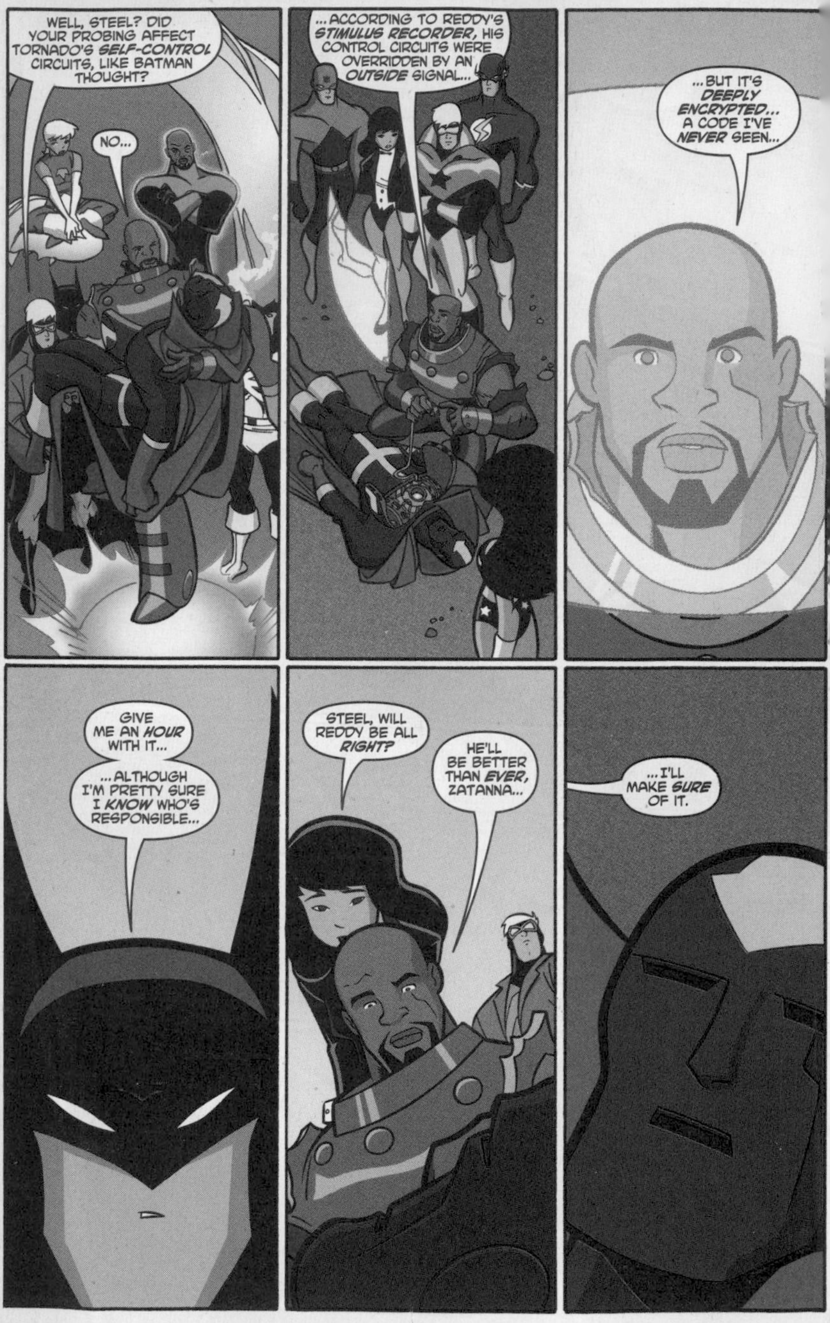
WELL, STEEL? DID YOUR PROBING AFFECT TORNADO'S SELF-CONTROL CIRCUITS, LIKE BATMAN THOUGHT?
NO...
...ACCORDING TO REDDY'S STIMULUS RECORDER, HIS CONTROL CIRCUITS WERE OVERRIDDEN BY AN OUTSIDE SIGNAL...
...BUT IT'S DEEPLY ENCRYPTED... A CODE I'VE NEVER SEEN...
GIVE ME AN HOUR WITH IT...
...ALTHOUGH I'M PRETTY SURE I KNOW WHO'S RESPONSIBLE...
STEEL, WILL REDDY BE ALL RIGHT?
HE'LL BE BETTER THAN EVER, ZATANNA...
...I'LL MAKE SURE OF IT.

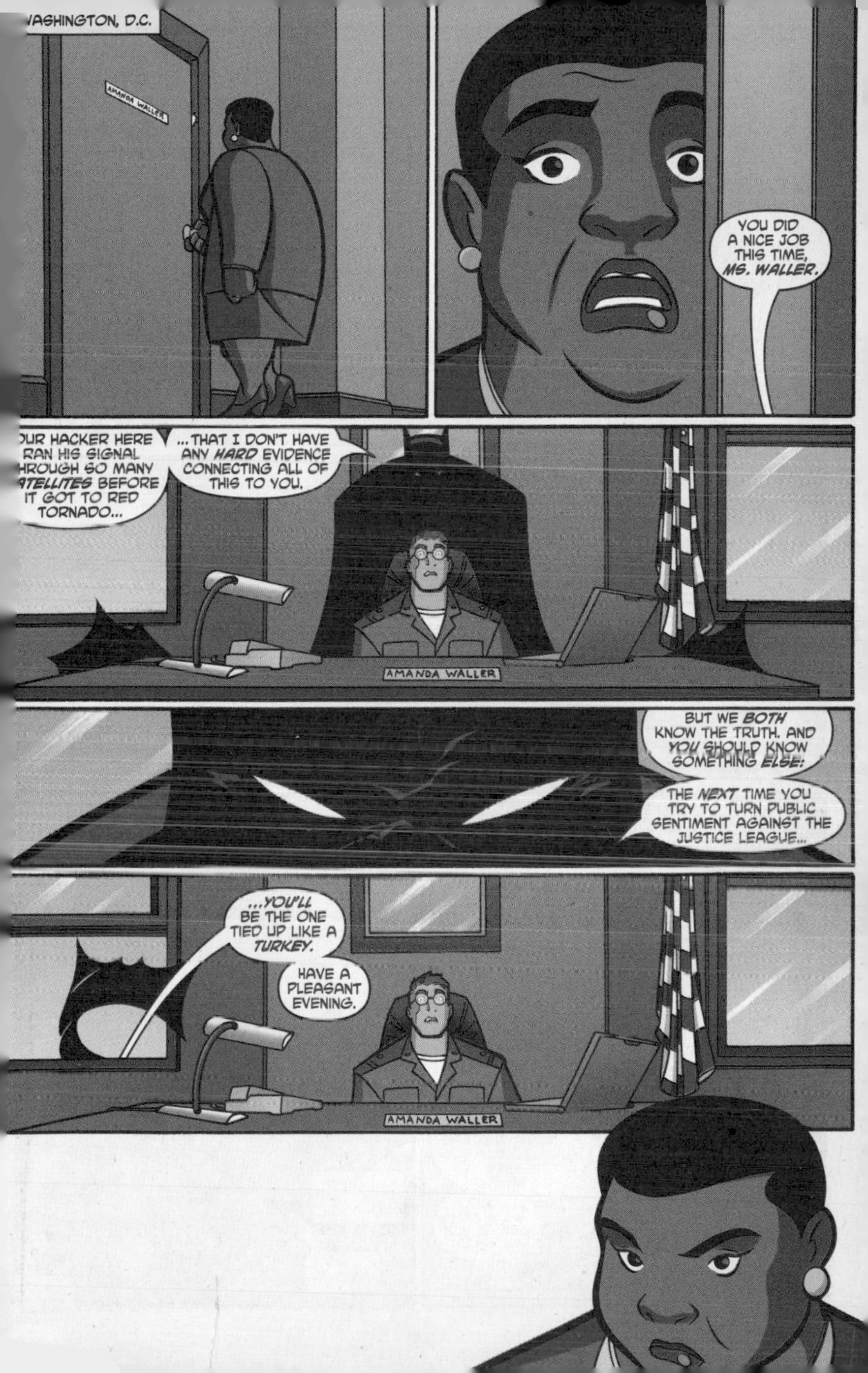
WASHINGTON, D.C.
AMANDA WALLER
YOU DID A NICE JOB THIS TIME, MS. WALLER.
OUR HACKER HERE RAN HIS SIGNAL THROUGH SO MANY SATELLITES BEFORE IT GOT TO RED TORNADO...
...THAT I DON'T HAVE ANY HARD EVIDENCE CONNECTING ALL OF THIS TO YOU.
AMANDA WALLER
BUT WE BOTH KNOW THE TRUTH. AND YOU SHOULD KNOW SOMETHING ELSE:
THE NEXT TIME YOU TRY TO TURN PUBLIC SENTIMENT AGAINST THE JUSTICE LEAGUE...
...YOU'LL BE THE ONE TIED UP LIKE A TURKEY.
HAVE A PLEASANT EVENING.
AMANDA WALLER

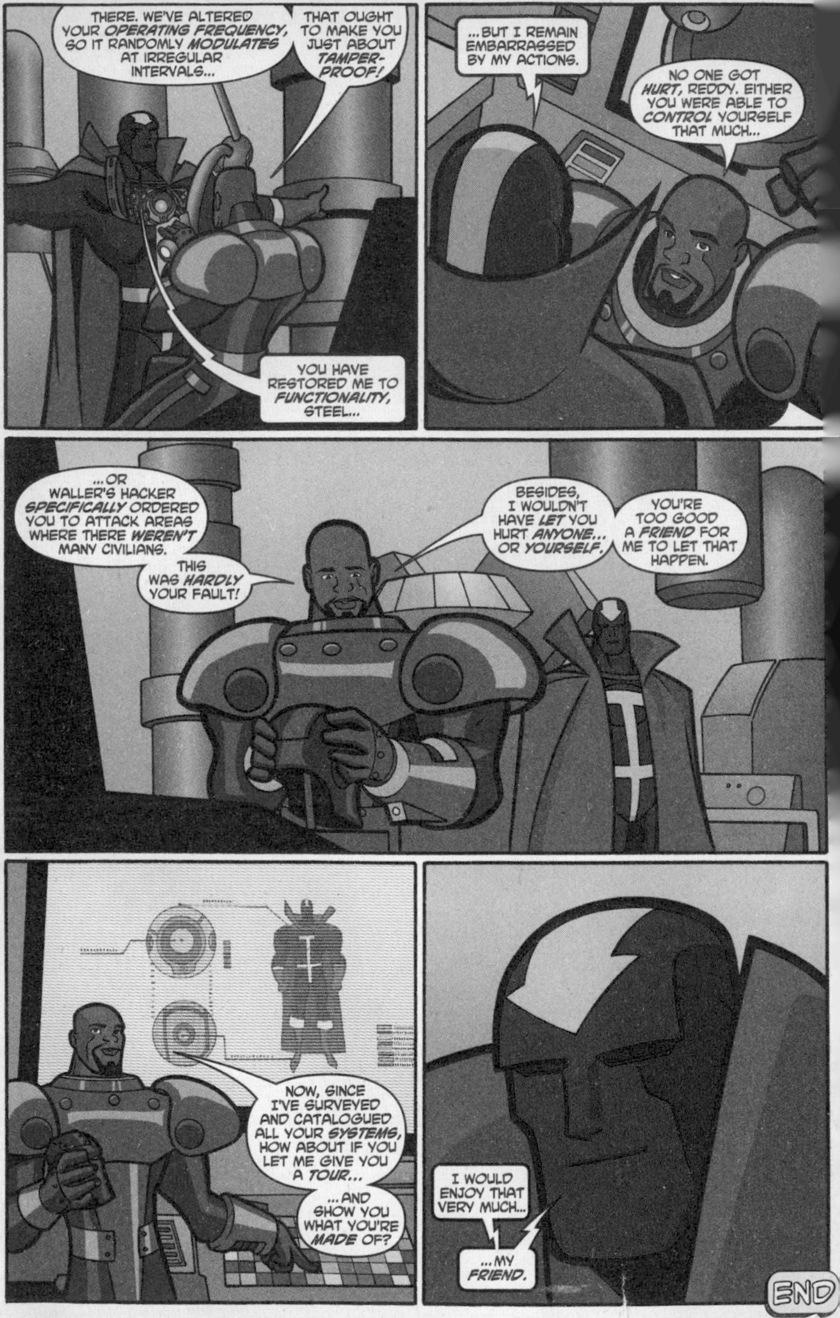
THERE. WE'VE ALTERED YOUR OPERATING FREQUENCY, SO IT RANDOMLY MODULATES AT IRREGULAR INTERVALS...
THAT OUGHT TO MAKE YOU JUST ABOUT TAMPER-PROOF!
YOU HAVE RESTORED ME TO FUNCTIONALITY, STEEL...
...BUT I REMAIN EMBARRASSED BY MY ACTIONS.
NO ONE GOT HURT, REDDY. EITHER YOU WERE ABLE TO CONTROL YOURSELF THAT MUCH...
...OR WALLER'S HACKER SPECIFICALLY ORDERED YOU TO ATTACK AREAS WHERE THERE WEREN'T MANY CIVILIANS.
THIS WAS HARDLY YOUR FAULT!
BESIDES, I WOULDN'T HAVE LET YOU HURT ANYONE... OR YOURSELF.
YOU'RE TOO GOOD A FRIEND FOR ME TO LET THAT HAPPEN.
NOW, SINCE I'VE SURVEYED AND CATALOGUED ALL YOUR SYSTEMS, HOW ABOUT IF YOU LET ME GIVE YOU A TOUR...
...AND SHOW YOU WHAT YOU'RE MADE OF?
I WOULD ENJOY THAT VERY MUCH...
...MY FRIEND.
END

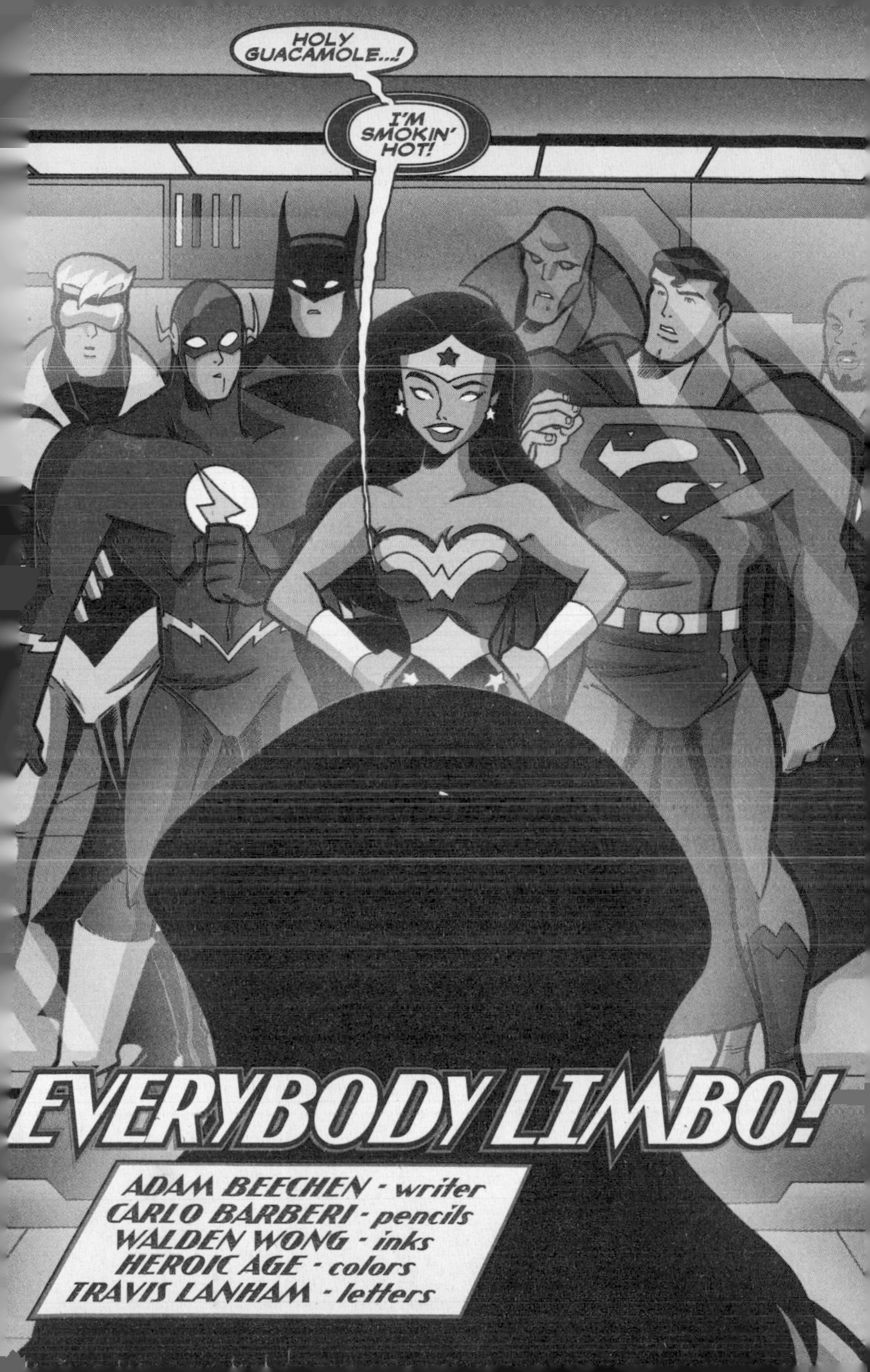
HOLY GUACAMOLE...!
I'M SMOKIN' HOT!
EVERYBODY LIMBO!
ADAM BEECHEN - writer
CARLO BARBERI - pencils
WALDEN WONG - inks
HEROIC AGE - colors
TRAVIS LANHAM - letters

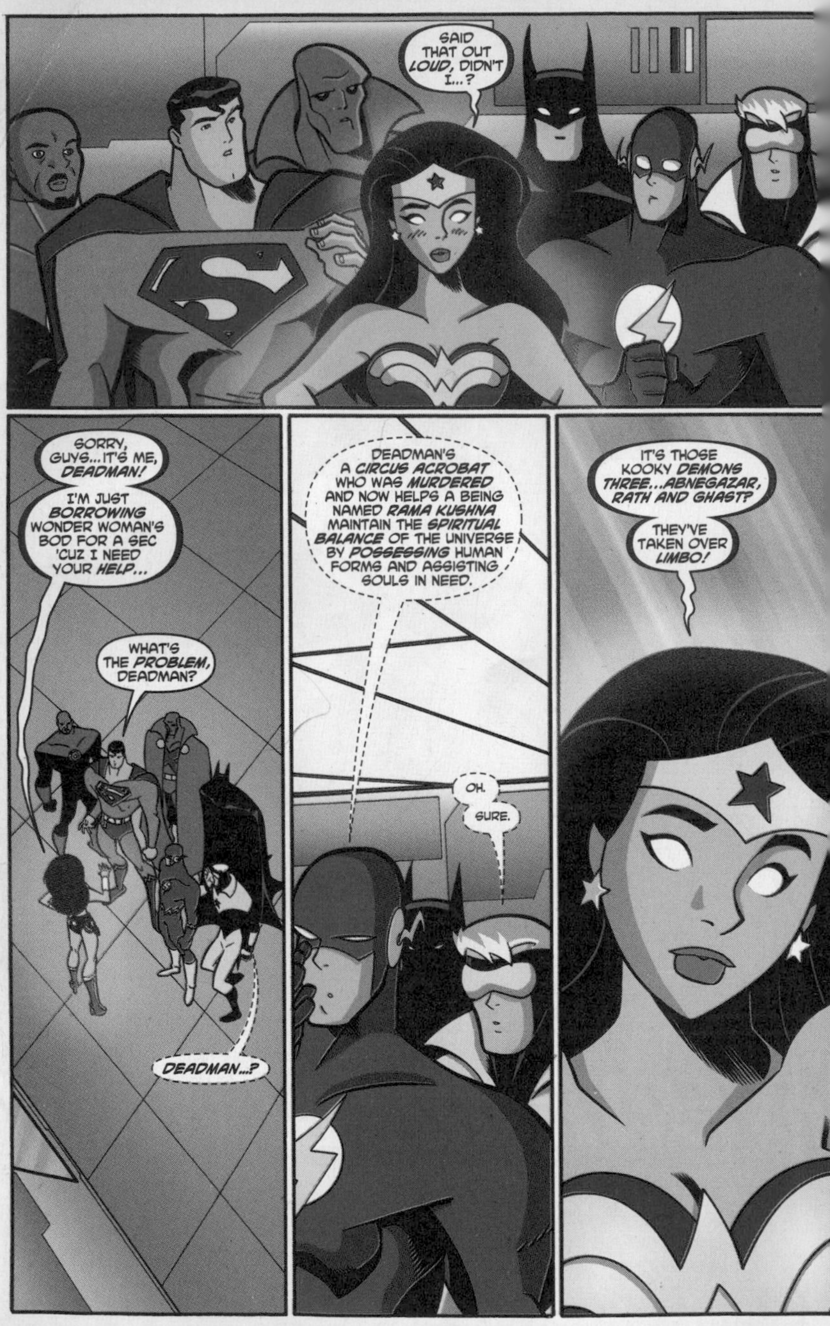
SAID THAT OUT LOUD, DIDN'T I...?
SORRY, GUYS...IT'S ME, DEADMAN!
I'M JUST BORROWING WONDER WOMAN'S BOD FOR A SEC 'CUZ I NEED YOUR HELP...
WHAT'S THE PROBLEM, DEADMAN?
DEADMAN...?
DEADMAN'S A CIRCUS ACROBAT WHO WAS MURDERED AND NOW HELPS A BEING NAMED RAMA KUSHNA MAINTAIN THE SPIRITUAL BALANCE OF THE UNIVERSE BY POSSESSING HUMAN FORMS AND ASSISTING SOULS IN NEED.
OH.
SURE.
IT'S THOSE KOOKY DEMONS THREE...ABNEGAZAR, RATH AND GHAST?
THEY'VE TAKEN OVER LIMBO!

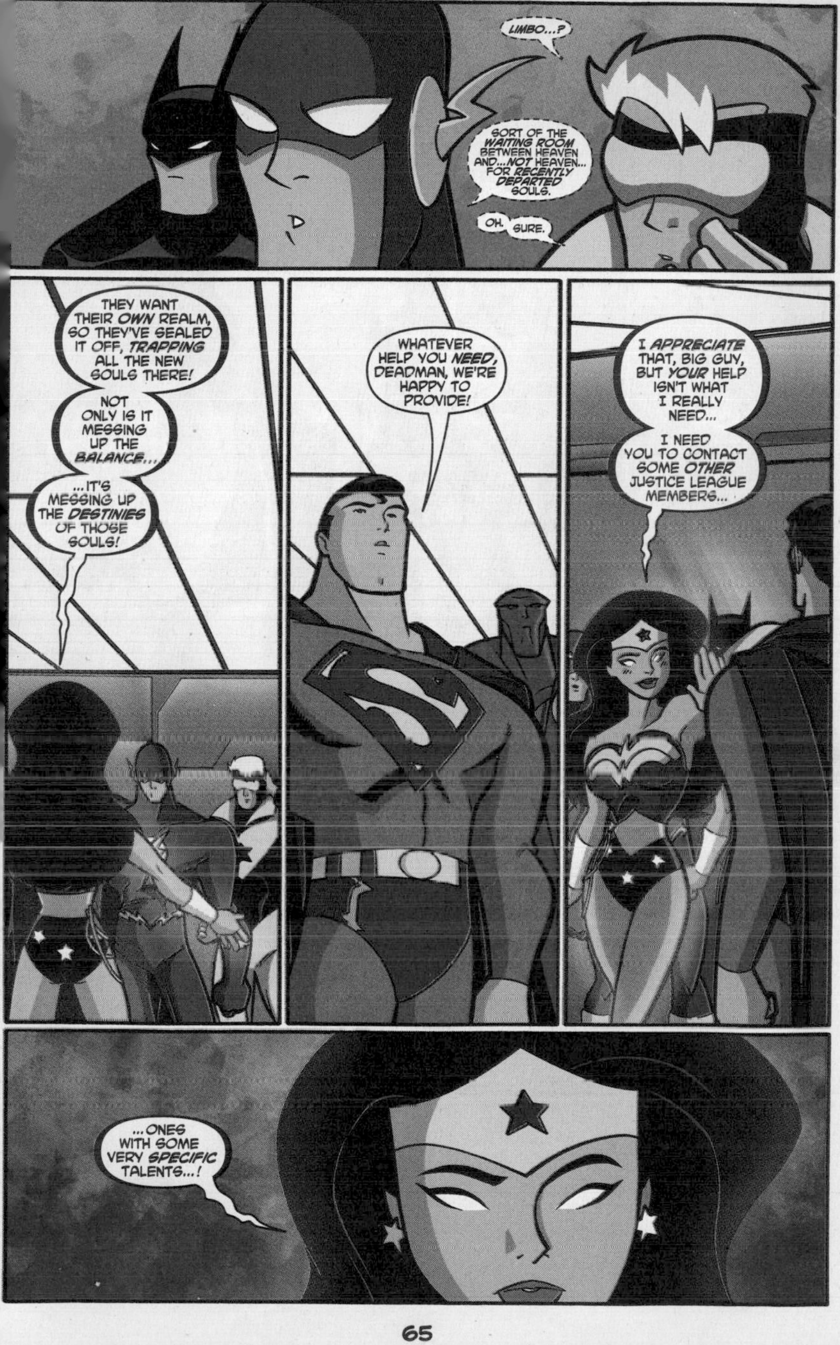
LIMBO...?
SORT OF THE WAITING ROOM BETWEEN HEAVEN AND...NOT HEAVEN... FOR RECENTLY DEPARTED SOULS.
OH. SURE.
THEY WANT THEIR OWN REALM, SO THEY'VE SEALED IT OFF, TRAPPING ALL THE NEW SOULS THERE!
NOT ONLY IS IT MESSING UP THE BALANCE...
...IT'S MESSING UP THE DESTINIES OF THOSE SOULS!
WHATEVER HELP YOU NEED, DEADMAN, WE'RE HAPPY TO PROVIDE!
I APPRECIATE THAT, BIG GUY, BUT YOUR HELP ISN'T WHAT I REALLY NEED...
I NEED YOU TO CONTACT SOME OTHER JUSTICE LEAGUE MEMBERS...
...ONES WITH SOME VERY SPECIFIC TALENTS...!

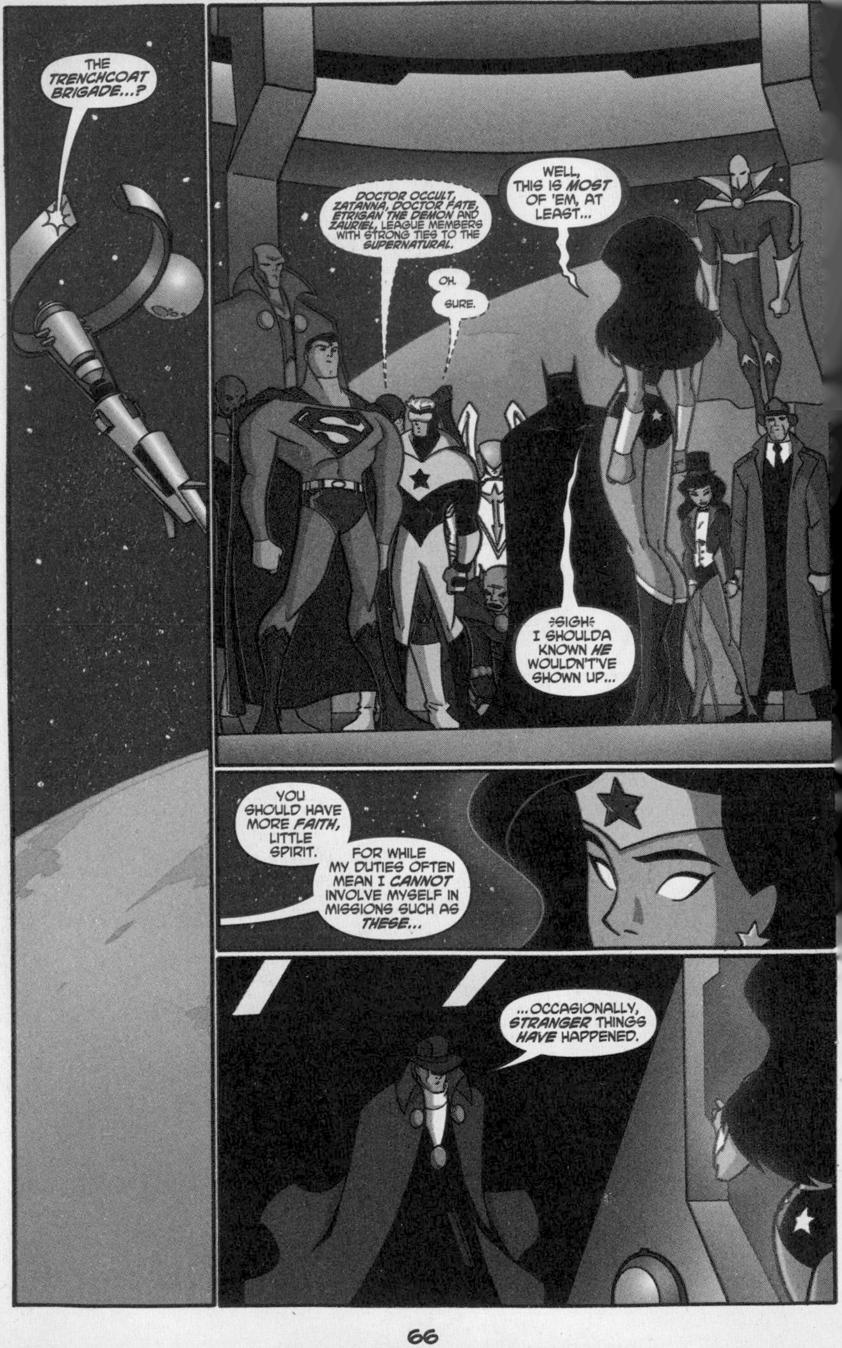
THE TRENCHCOAT BRIGADE...?
DOCTOR OCCULT, ZATANNA, DOCTOR FATE, ETRIGAN THE DEMON AND ZAURIEL, LEAGUE MEMBERS WITH STRONG TIES TO THE SUPERNATURAL.
WELL, THIS IS MOST OF 'EM, AT LEAST...
OH.
SURE.
SIGH I SHOULDA KNOWN HE WOULDN'T'VE SHOWN UP...
YOU SHOULD HAVE MORE FAITH, LITTLE SPIRIT.
FOR WHILE MY DUTIES OFTEN MEAN I CANNOT INVOLVE MYSELF IN MISSIONS SUCH AS THESE...
...OCCASIONALLY, STRANGER THINGS HAVE HAPPENED.

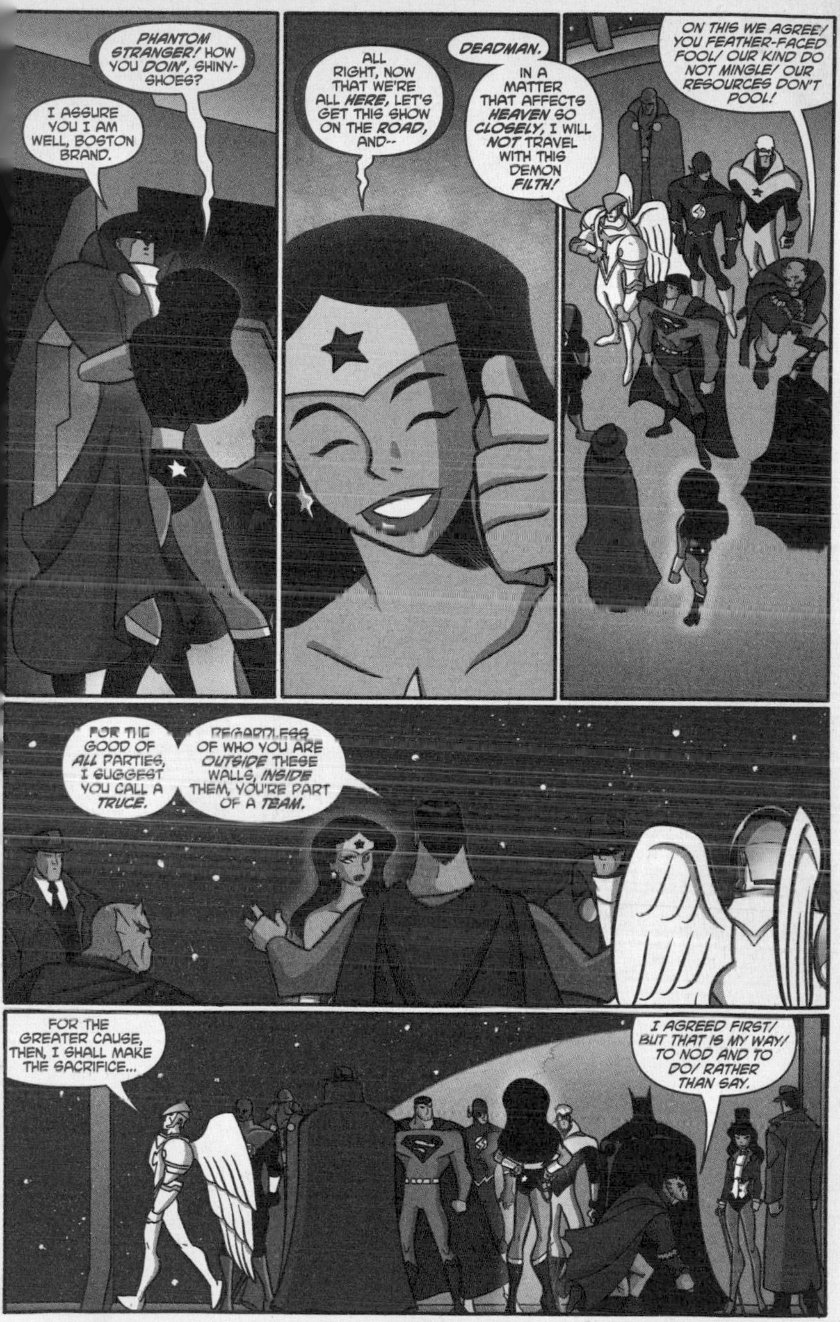
PHANTOM STRANGER! HOW YOU DOIN', SHINY-SHOES?
I ASSURE YOU I AM WELL, BOSTON BRAND.
ALL RIGHT, NOW THAT WE'RE ALL HERE, LET'S GET THIS SHOW ON THE ROAD, AND--
DEADMAN.
IN A MATTER THAT AFFECTS HEAVEN SO CLOSELY, I WILL NOT TRAVEL WITH THIS DEMON FILTH!
ON THIS WE AGREE/ YOU FEATHER-FACED FOOL/ OUR KIND DO NOT MINGLE/ OUR RESOURCES DON'T POOL!
FOR THE GOOD OF ALL PARTIES, I SUGGEST YOU CALL A TRUCE.
REGARDLESS OF WHO YOU ARE OUTSIDE THESE WALLS, INSIDE THEM, YOU'RE PART OF A TEAM.
FOR THE GREATER CAUSE, THEN, I SHALL MAKE THE SACRIFICE...
I AGREED FIRST/ BUT THAT IS MY WAY/ TO NOD AND TO DO/ RATHER THAN SAY.

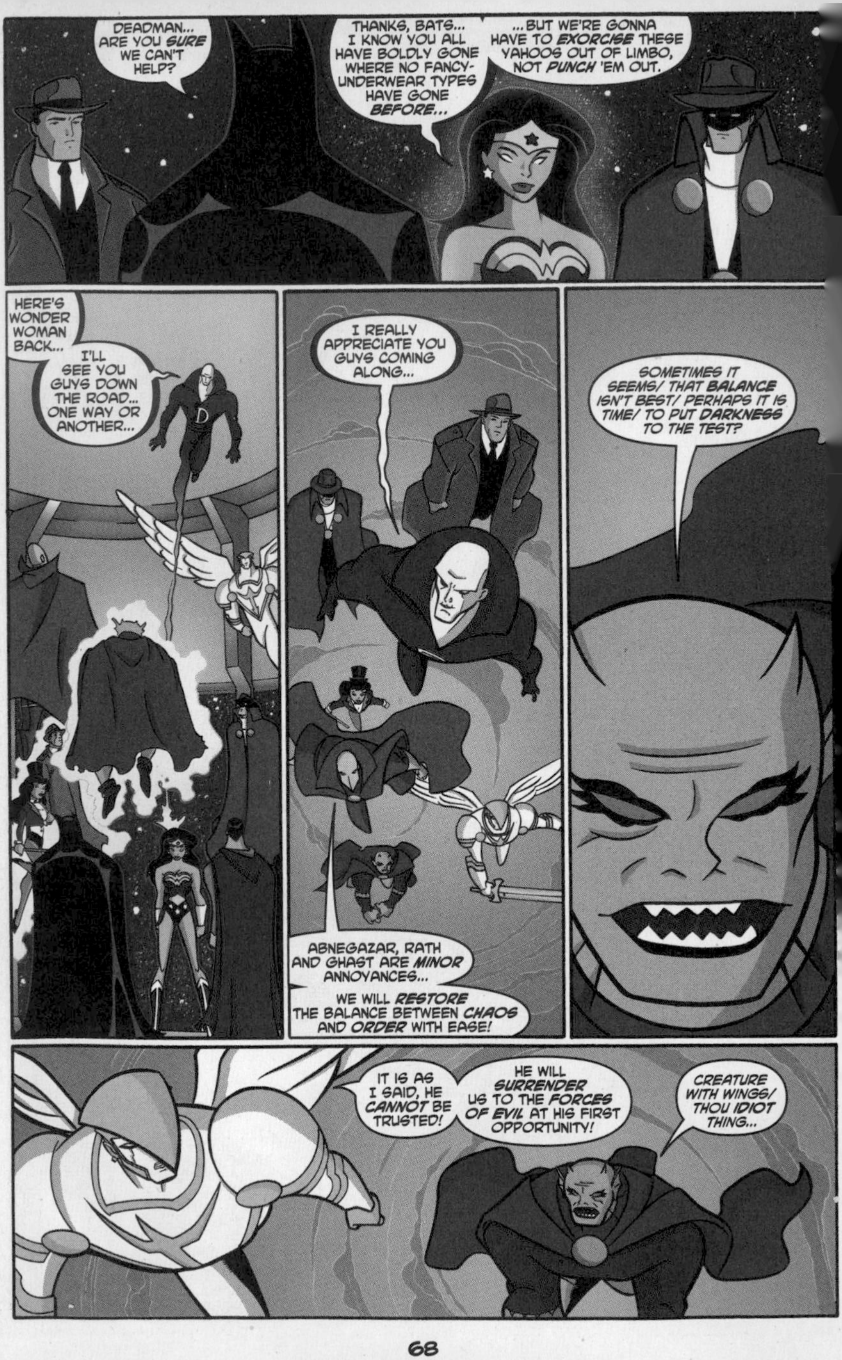
DEADMAN... ARE YOU SURE WE CAN'T HELP?
THANKS, BATS... I KNOW YOU ALL HAVE BOLDLY GONE WHERE NO FANCY-UNDERWEAR TYPES HAVE GONE BEFORE...
...BUT WE'RE GONNA HAVE TO EXORCISE THESE YAHOOS OUT OF LIMBO, NOT PUNCH 'EM OUT.
HERE'S WONDER WOMAN BACK...
I'LL SEE YOU GUYS DOWN THE ROAD... ONE WAY OR ANOTHER...
I REALLY APPRECIATE YOU GUYS COMING ALONG...
ABNEGAZAR, RATH AND GHAST ARE MINOR ANNOYANCES...
WE WILL RESTORE THE BALANCE BETWEEN CHAOS AND ORDER WITH EASE!
SOMETIMES IT SEEMS/ THAT BALANCE ISN'T BEST/ PERHAPS IT IS TIME/ TO PUT DARKNESS TO THE TEST?
IT IS AS I SAID, HE CANNOT BE TRUSTED!
HE WILL SURRENDER US TO THE FORCES OF EVIL AT HIS FIRST OPPORTUNITY!
CREATURE WITH WINGS/ THOU IDIOT THING...

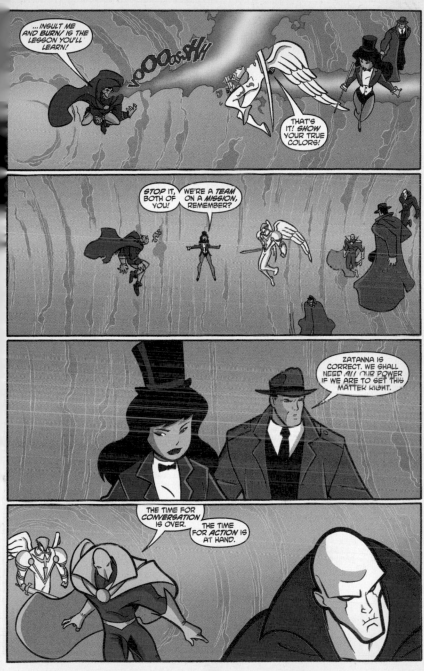

...INSULT ME AND BURN! IS THE LESSON YOU'LL LEARN!

vOOOooSHH

THAT'S IT! *SHOW* YOUR TRUE COLORS!

STOP IT, BOTH OF YOU! WE'RE A *TEAM* ON A *MISSION*, REMEMBER?

ZATANNA IS CORRECT. WE SHALL NEED *ALL* OUR POWER IF WE ARE TO SET THIS MATTER RIGHT.

THE TIME FOR *CONVERSATION* IS OVER. THE TIME FOR *ACTION* IS AT HAND.

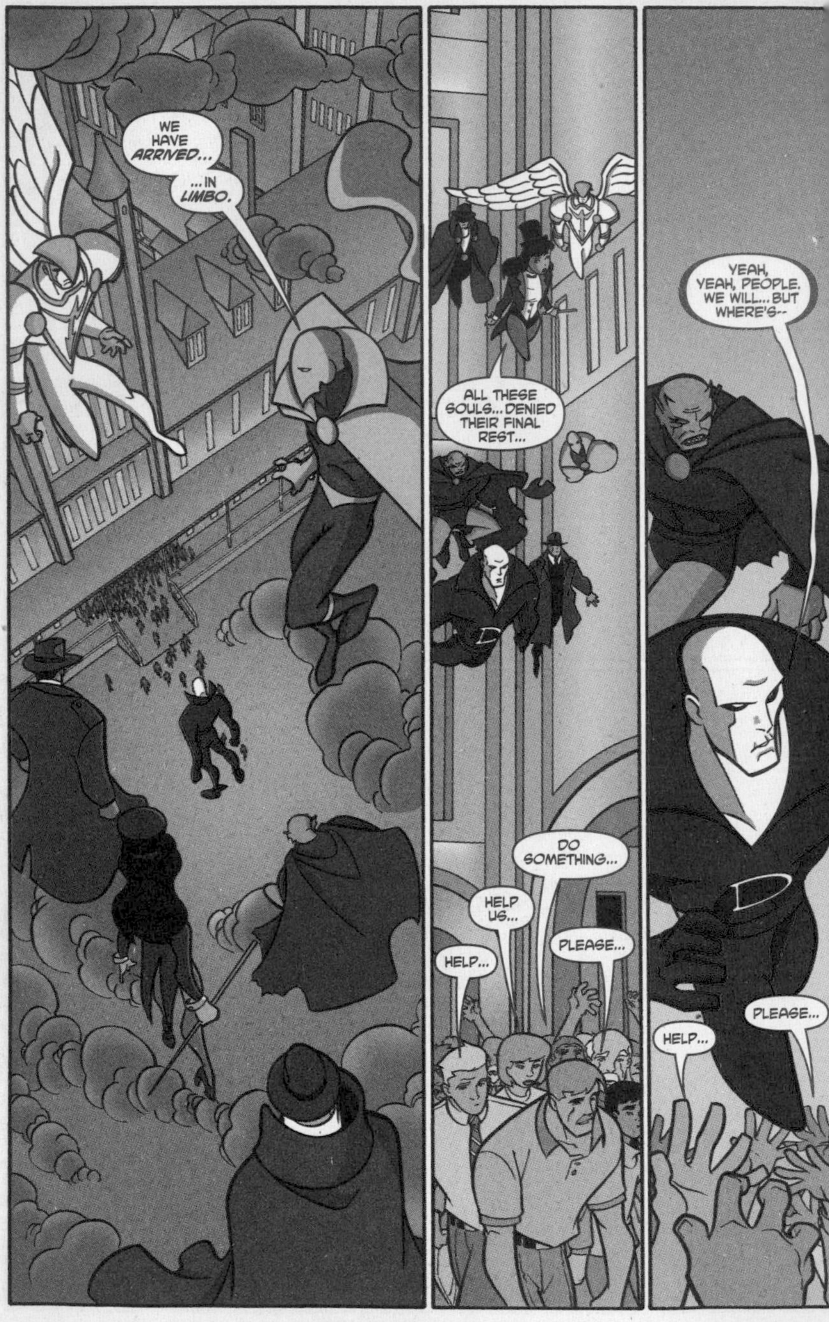
WE HAVE ARRIVED...
...IN LIMBO.
ALL THESE SOULS...DENIED THEIR FINAL REST...
DO SOMETHING...
HELP US...
PLEASE...
HELP...
YEAH, YEAH, PEOPLE. WE WILL...BUT WHERE'S--
PLEASE...
HELP...

IT WOULD APPEAR THE PROBLEM BEGINS AND ENDS HERE...

THE DEMONS THREE HAVE USED *COMPLICATED* MAGIC TO FORM THESE BARRIERS...

...REMOVING THEM WILL TAKE *TIME*...

FINE, BUT WHAT ABOUT--

DOESN'T LOOK SO TOUGH TO *ME,* DOCTOR OCCULT...

ONE *SPELL,* SPOKEN *BACKWARDS,* OUGHT TO TAKE CARE OF IT...

BRICRAAD--

ZATANNA, LOOK OUT--!

GLMMF!

TRESPASSERS! TRESPASSERS IN *OUR REALM!*

GHAST! I *KNEW* YOU GUYS HAD TO BE AROUND HERE *SOMEPLACE!*

WATCH *OUT,* EVERYBODY!

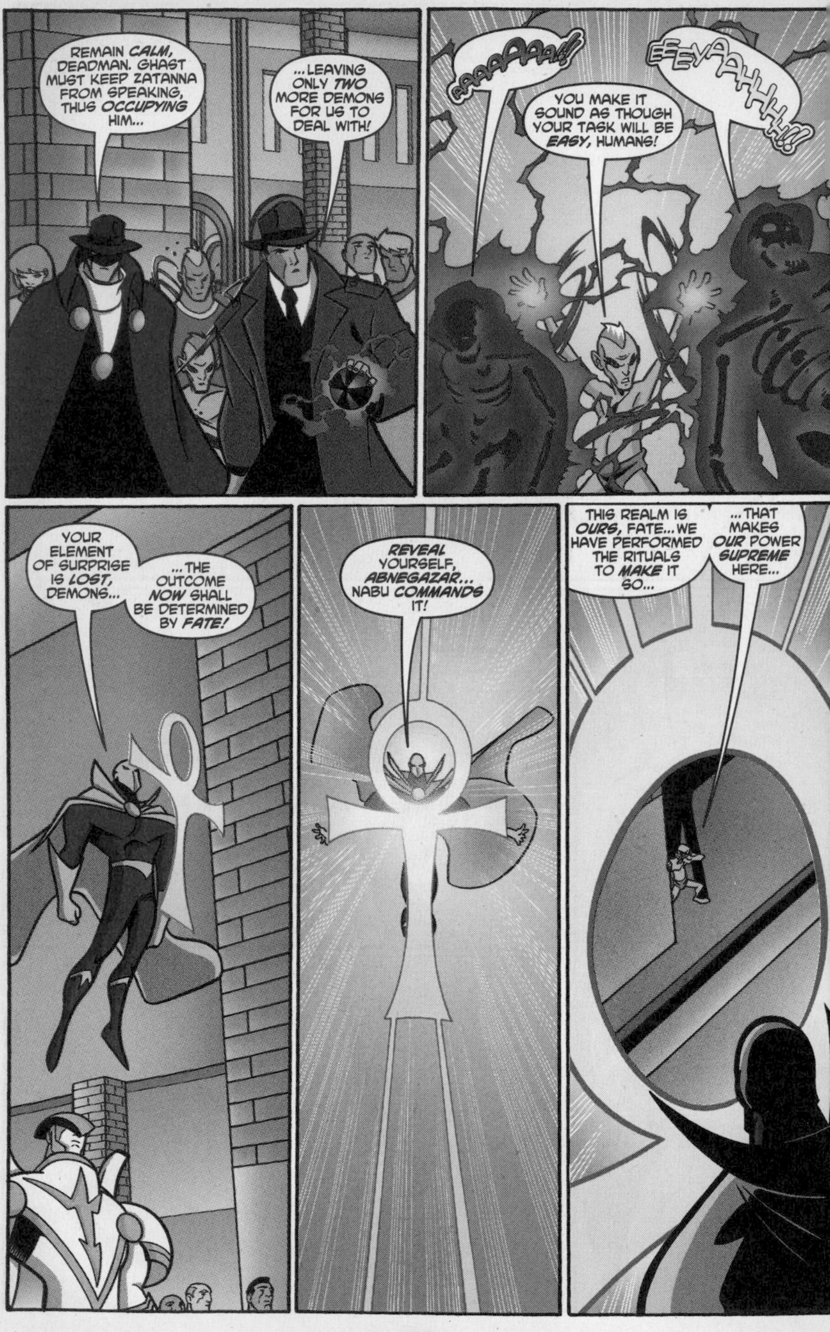
REMAIN CALM, DEADMAN. GHAST MUST KEEP ZATANNA FROM SPEAKING, THUS OCCUPYING HIM...
...LEAVING ONLY TWO MORE DEMONS FOR US TO DEAL WITH!
AAAAAAAA!!
EEEYAAHHHH!!!
YOU MAKE IT SOUND AS THOUGH YOUR TASK WILL BE EASY, HUMANS!
YOUR ELEMENT OF SURPRISE IS LOST, DEMONS...
...THE OUTCOME NOW SHALL BE DETERMINED BY FATE!
REVEAL YOURSELF, ABNEGAZAR... NABU COMMANDS IT!
THIS REALM IS OURS, FATE... WE HAVE PERFORMED THE RITUALS TO MAKE IT SO...
...THAT MAKES OUR POWER SUPREME HERE...

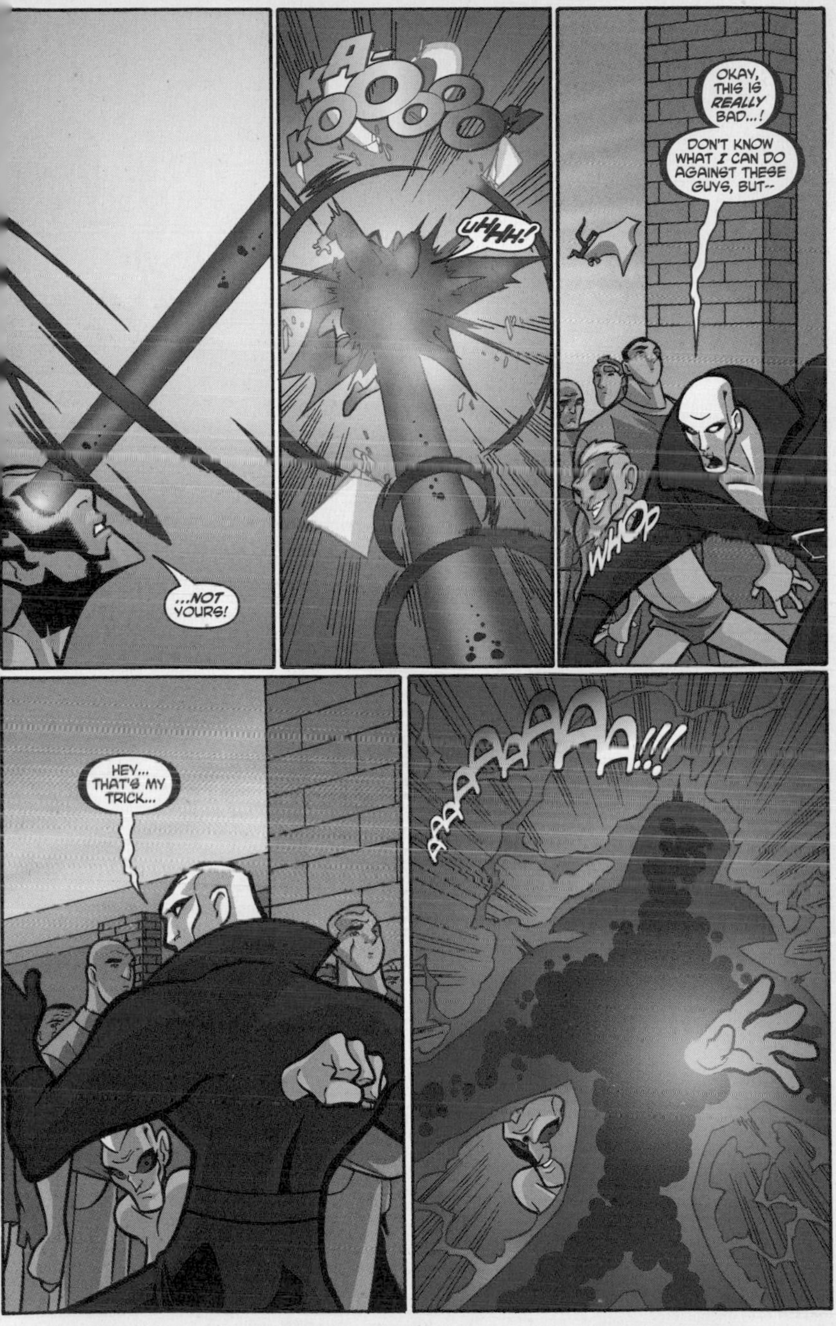
...NOT YOURS!
KA-KOOOOOOOM
UHHHH!
OKAY, THIS IS REALLY BAD...!
DON'T KNOW WHAT I CAN DO AGAINST THESE GUYS, BUT--
WHOP
HEY... THAT'S MY TRICK...
AAAAAAAAAAAAAA!!!

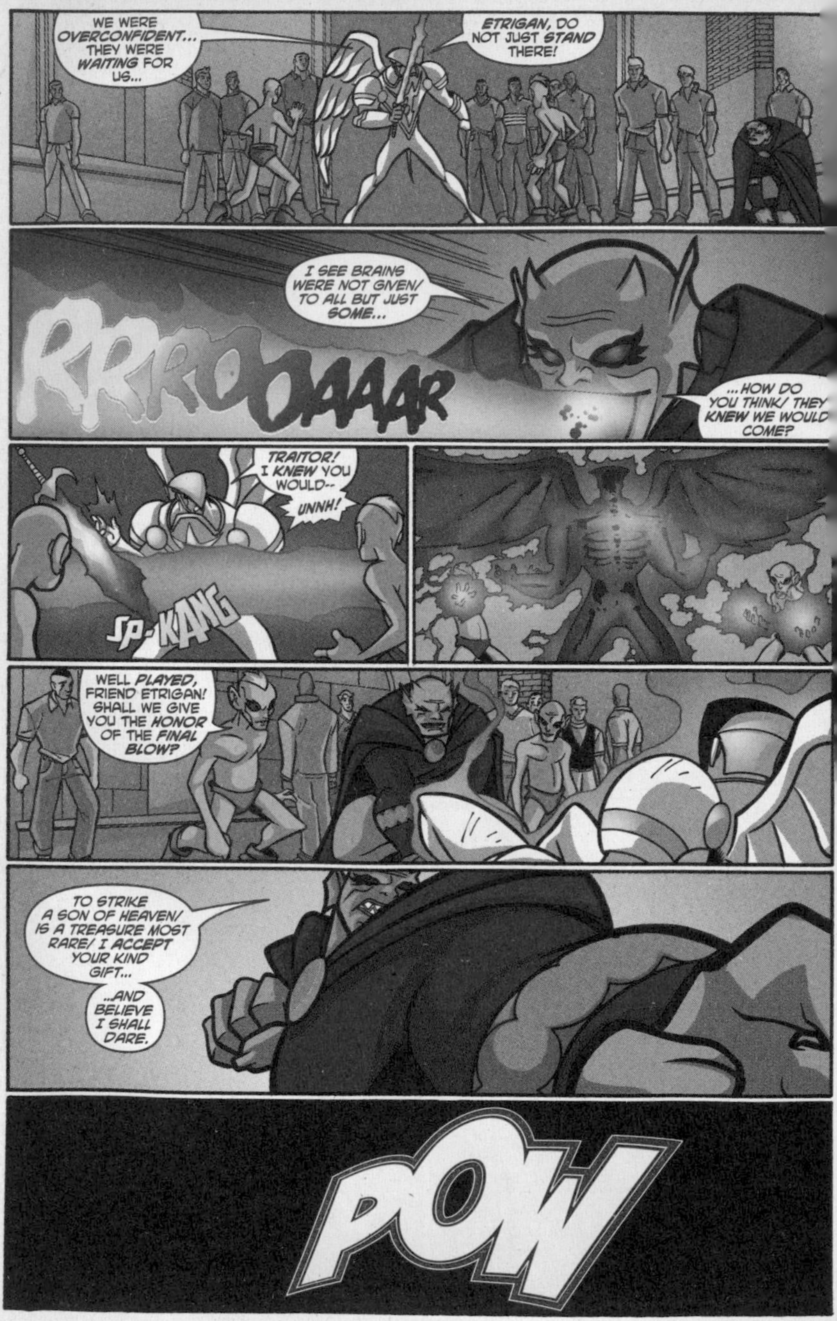
WE WERE OVERCONFIDENT... THEY WERE WAITING FOR US...
ETRIGAN, DO NOT JUST STAND THERE!
I SEE BRAINS WERE NOT GIVEN/ TO ALL BUT JUST SOME...
RRROOAAAR
...HOW DO YOU THINK/ THEY KNEW WE WOULD COME?
TRAITOR! I KNEW YOU WOULD--
UNNH!
SP-KANG
WELL PLAYED, FRIEND ETRIGAN! SHALL WE GIVE YOU THE HONOR OF THE FINAL BLOW?
TO STRIKE A SON OF HEAVEN/ IS A TREASURE MOST RARE/ I ACCEPT YOUR KIND GIFT...
...AND BELIEVE I SHALL DARE.
POW

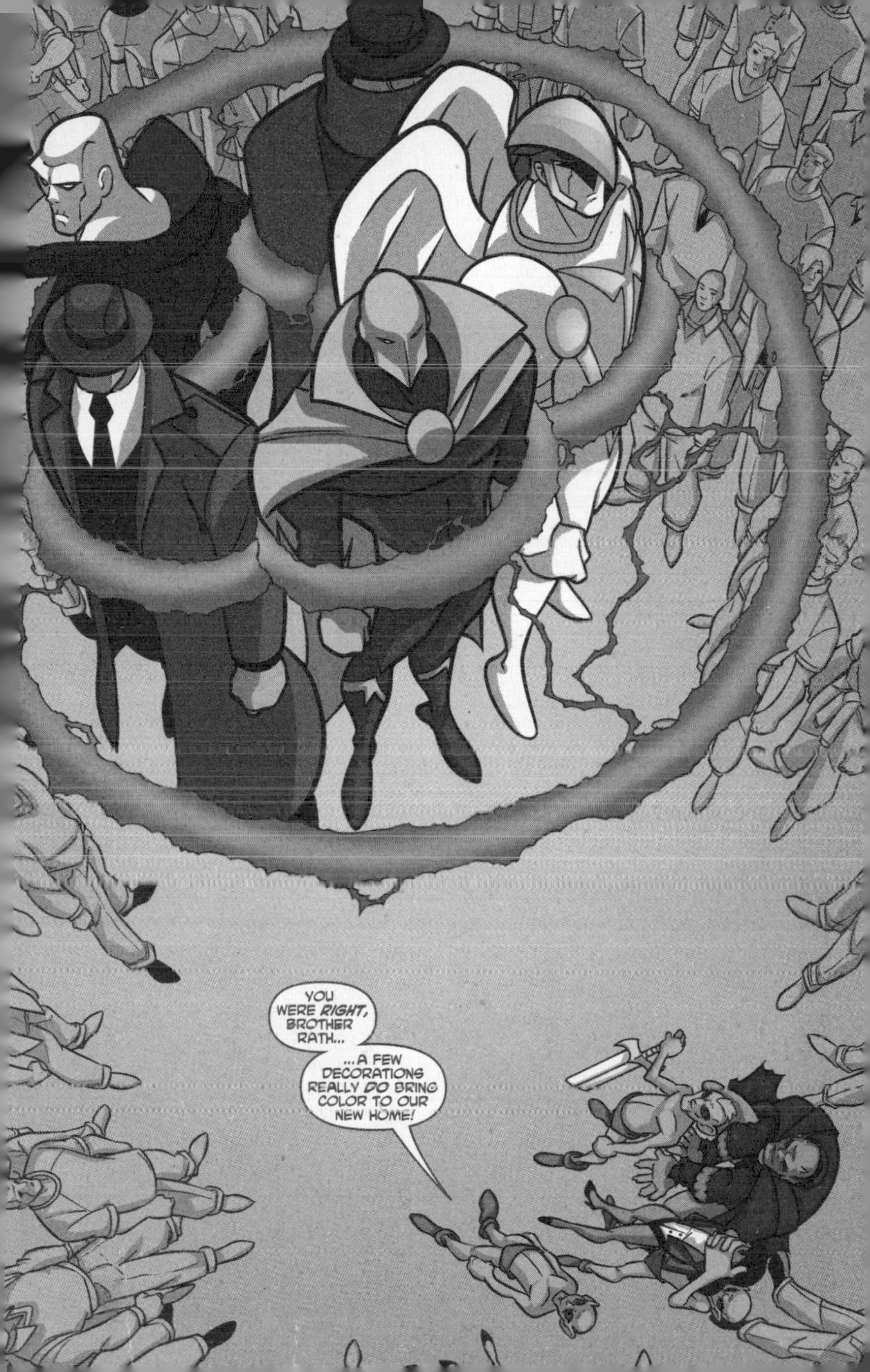
YOU WERE RIGHT, BROTHER RATH...
...A FEW DECORATIONS REALLY DO BRING COLOR TO OUR NEW HOME!

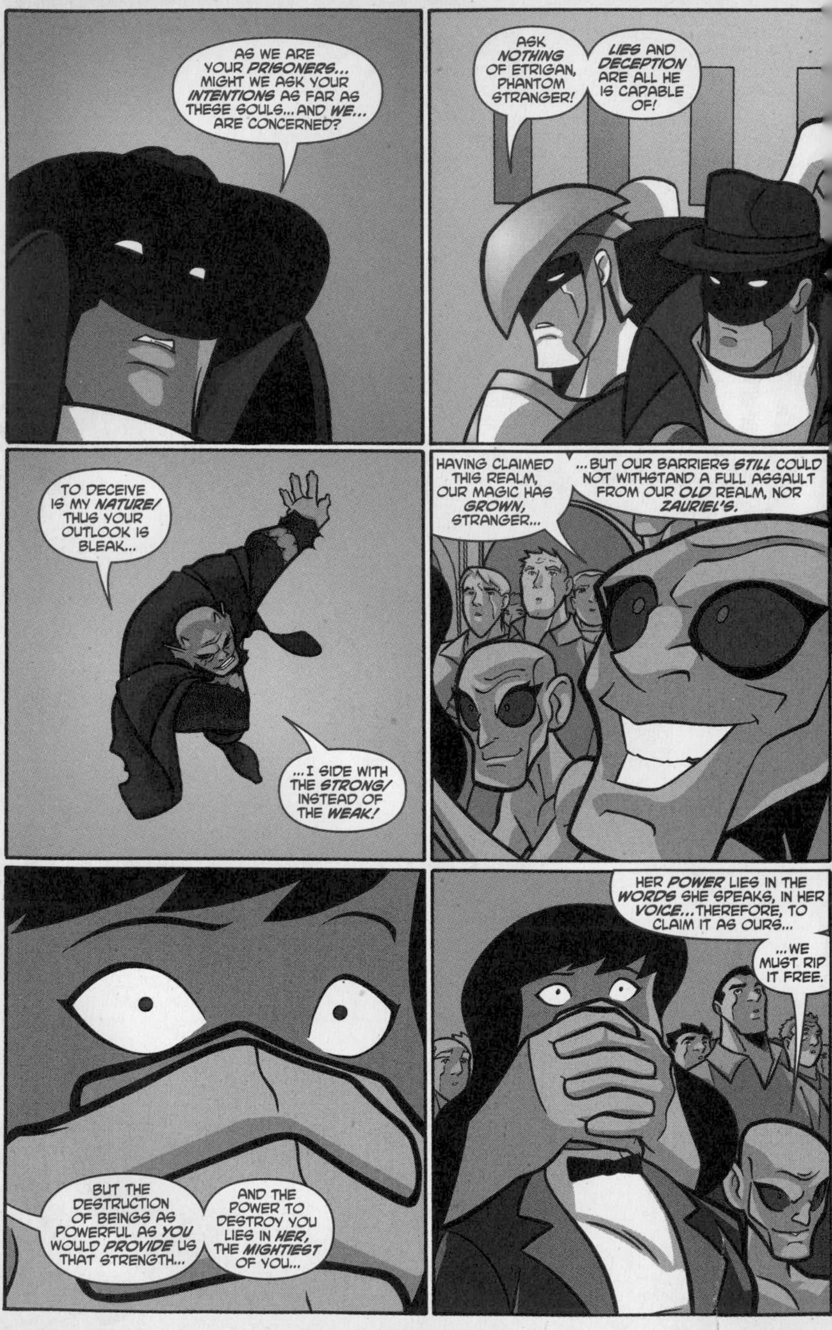
AS WE ARE YOUR PRISONERS... MIGHT WE ASK YOUR INTENTIONS AS FAR AS THESE SOULS...AND WE... ARE CONCERNED?
ASK NOTHING OF ETRIGAN, PHANTOM STRANGER!
LIES AND DECEPTION ARE ALL HE IS CAPABLE OF!
TO DECEIVE IS MY NATURE! THUS YOUR OUTLOOK IS BLEAK...
...I SIDE WITH THE STRONG! INSTEAD OF THE WEAK!
HAVING CLAIMED THIS REALM, OUR MAGIC HAS GROWN, STRANGER...
...BUT OUR BARRIERS STILL COULD NOT WITHSTAND A FULL ASSAULT FROM OUR OLD REALM, NOR ZAURIEL'S.
BUT THE DESTRUCTION OF BEINGS AS POWERFUL AS YOU WOULD PROVIDE US THAT STRENGTH...
AND THE POWER TO DESTROY YOU LIES IN HER, THE MIGHTIEST OF YOU...
HER POWER LIES IN THE WORDS SHE SPEAKS, IN HER VOICE...THEREFORE, TO CLAIM IT AS OURS...
...WE MUST RIP IT FREE.

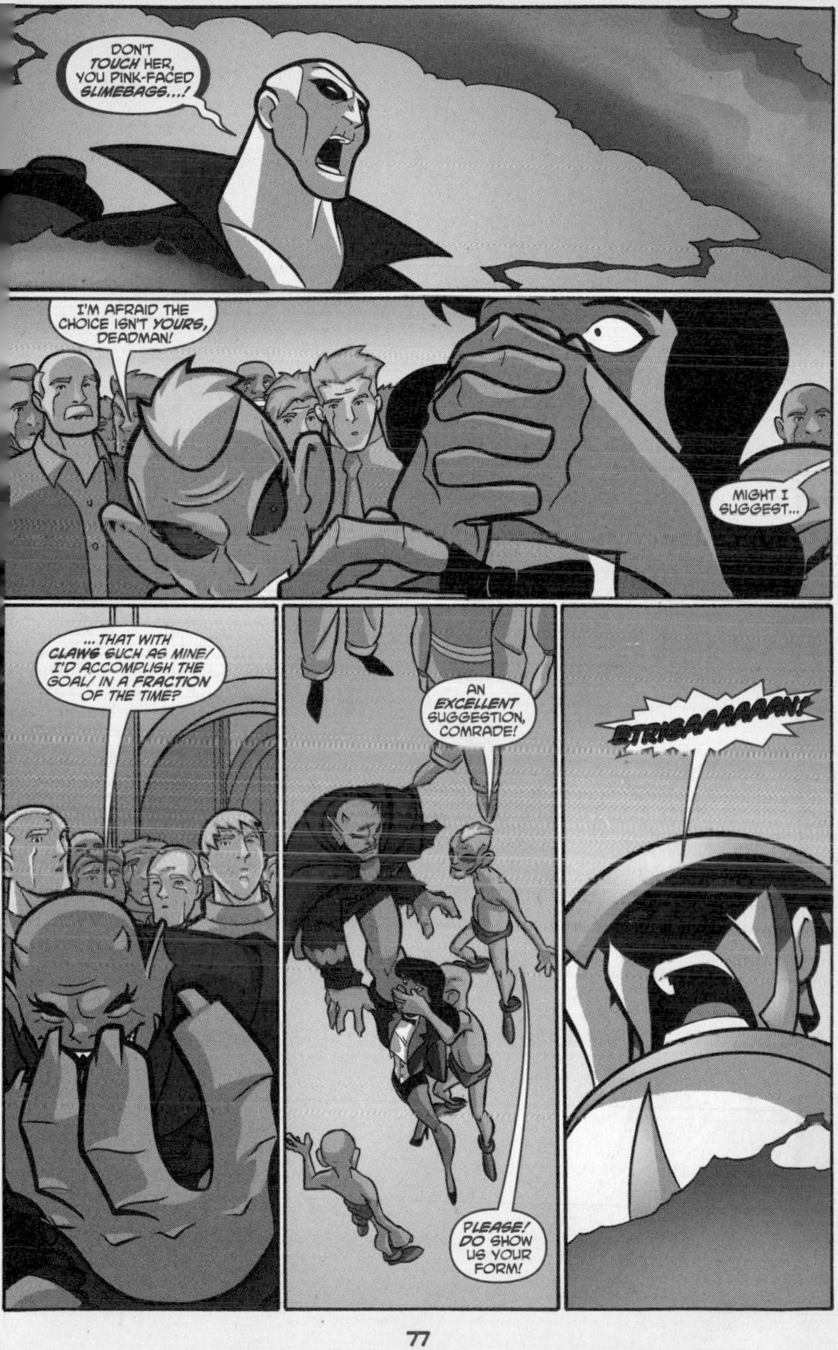
DON'T TOUCH HER, YOU PINK-FACED SLIMEBAGS...!
I'M AFRAID THE CHOICE ISN'T YOURS, DEADMAN!
MIGHT I SUGGEST...
...THAT WITH CLAWS SUCH AS MINE/ I'D ACCOMPLISH THE GOAL/ IN A FRACTION OF THE TIME?
AN EXCELLENT SUGGESTION, COMRADE!
PLEASE! DO SHOW US YOUR FORM!
ETRIGAAAAAAAN!

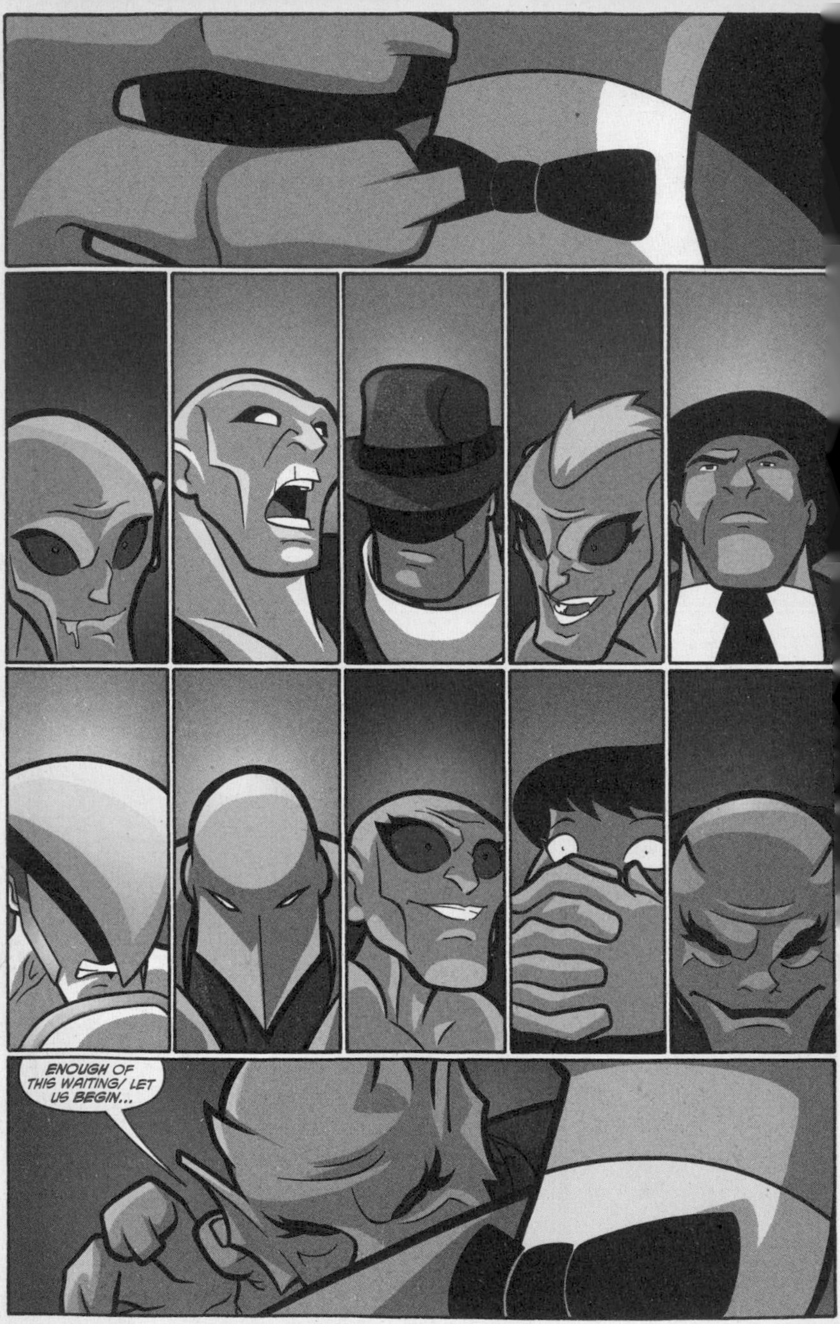
ENOUGH OF THIS WAITING/ LET US BEGIN...

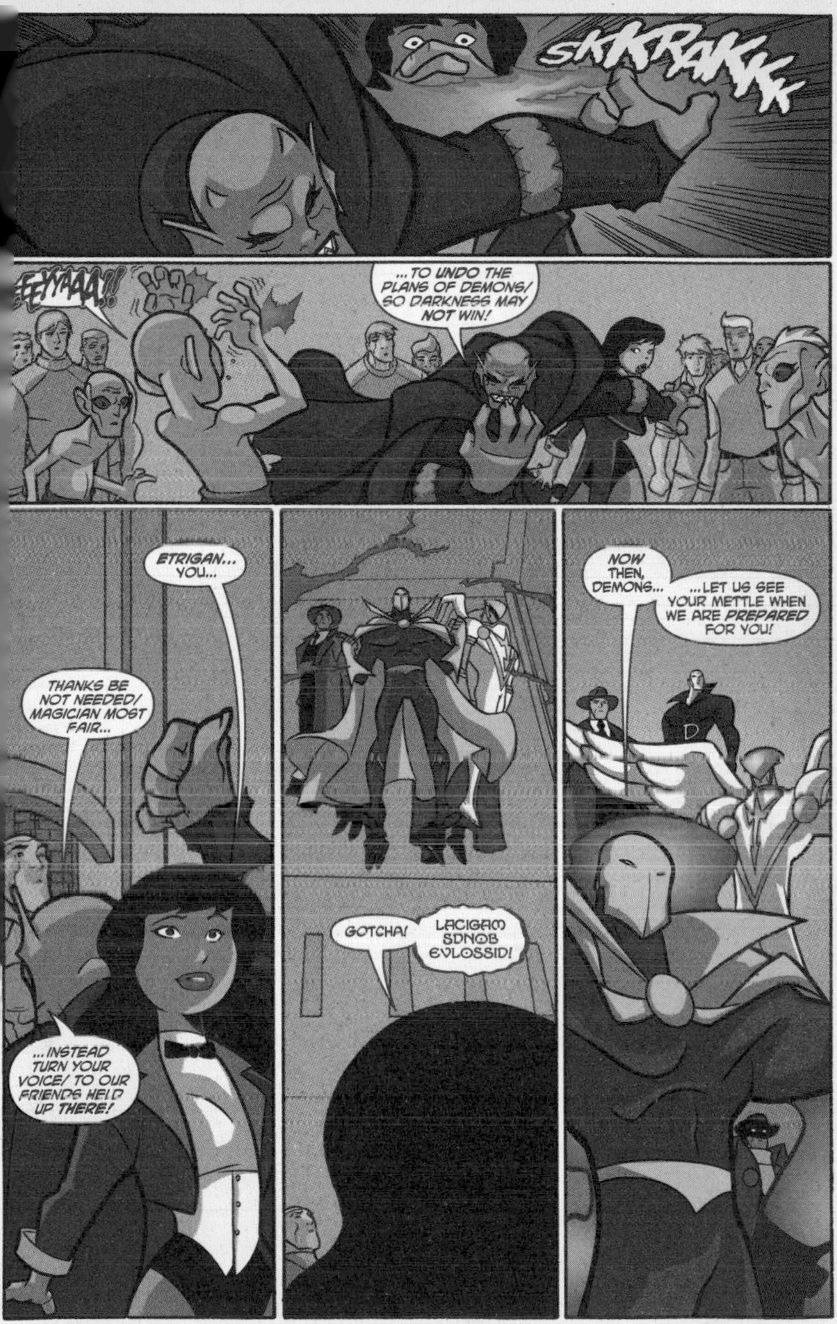
SKKRAKKK
EEEYAAA?!
...TO UNDO THE PLANS OF DEMONS/ SO DARKNESS MAY NOT WIN!
ETRIGAN... YOU...
THANKS BE NOT NEEDED/ MAGICIAN MOST FAIR...
...INSTEAD TURN YOUR VOICE/ TO OUR FRIENDS HELD UP THERE!
GOTCHA!
LACIGAM SDNOB EVLOSSID!
NOW THEN, DEMONS...
...LET US SEE YOUR METTLE WHEN WE ARE PREPARED FOR YOU!

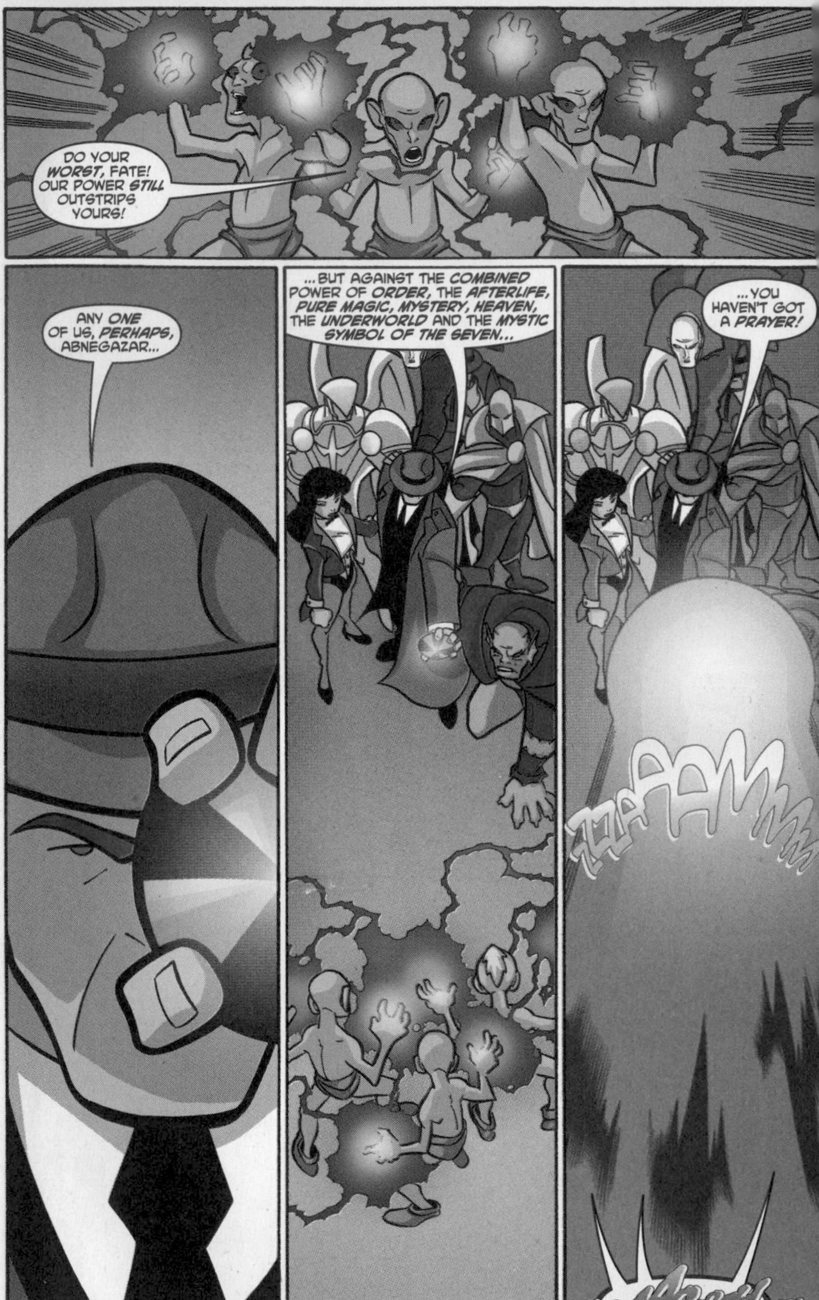
DO YOUR WORST, FATE! OUR POWER STILL OUTSTRIPS YOURS!
ANY ONE OF US, PERHAPS, ABNEGAZAR...
...BUT AGAINST THE COMBINED POWER OF ORDER, THE AFTERLIFE, PURE MAGIC, MYSTERY, HEAVEN, THE UNDERWORLD AND THE MYSTIC SYMBOL OF THE SEVEN...
...YOU HAVEN'T GOT A PRAYER!
ZZAAAMMM

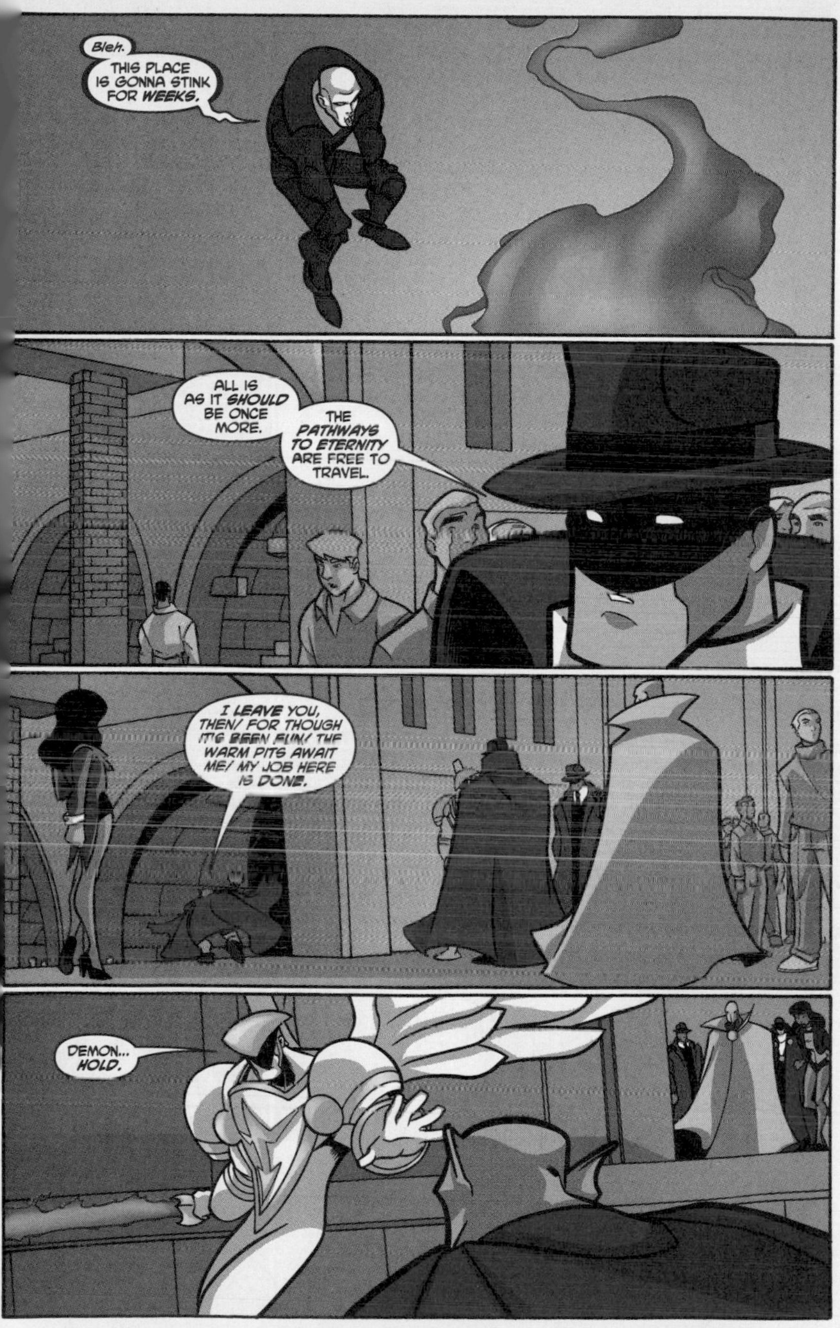
Bleh.
THIS PLACE IS GONNA STINK FOR WEEKS.
ALL IS AS IT SHOULD BE ONCE MORE.
THE PATHWAYS TO ETERNITY ARE FREE TO TRAVEL.
I LEAVE YOU, THEN! FOR THOUGH IT'S BEEN FUN! THE WARM PITS AWAIT ME! MY JOB HERE IS DONE.
DEMON... HOLD.

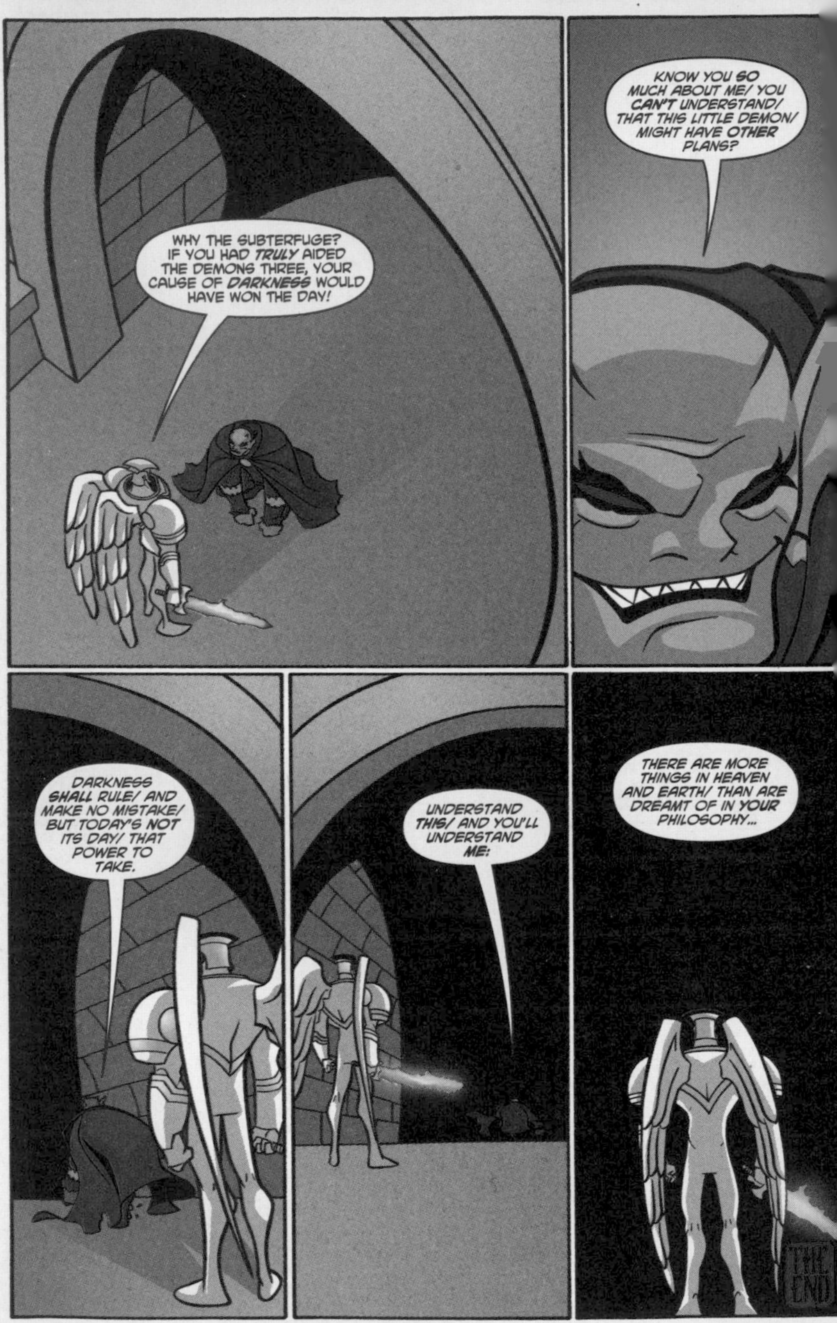
WHY THE SUBTERFUGE? IF YOU HAD TRULY AIDED THE DEMONS THREE, YOUR CAUSE OF DARKNESS WOULD HAVE WON THE DAY!
KNOW YOU SO MUCH ABOUT ME/ YOU CAN'T UNDERSTAND/ THAT THIS LITTLE DEMON/ MIGHT HAVE OTHER PLANS?
DARKNESS SHALL RULE/ AND MAKE NO MISTAKE/ BUT TODAY'S NOT ITS DAY/ THAT POWER TO TAKE.
UNDERSTAND THIS/ AND YOU'LL UNDERSTAND ME:
THERE ARE MORE THINGS IN HEAVEN AND EARTH/ THAN ARE DREAMT OF IN YOUR PHILOSOPHY...
THE END

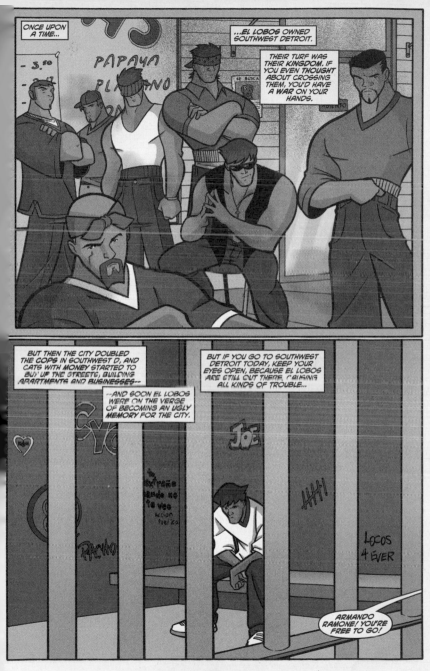

ONCE UPON A TIME...

...EL LOBOS OWNED SOUTHWEST DETROIT.

THEIR TURF WAS THEIR KINGDOM. IF YOU EVEN THOUGHT ABOUT CROSSING THEM, YOU'D HAVE A WAR ON YOUR HANDS.

BUT THEN THE CITY DOUBLED THE COPS IN SOUTHWEST D, AND CATS WITH MONEY STARTED TO BUY UP THE STREETS, BUILDING APARTMENTS AND BUSINESSES--

--AND SOON EL LOBOS WERE ON THE VERGE OF BECOMING AN UGLY MEMORY FOR THE CITY.

BUT IF YOU GO TO SOUTHWEST DETROIT TODAY, KEEP YOUR EYES OPEN, BECAUSE EL LOBOS ARE STILL OUT THERE, CAUSING ALL KINDS OF TROUBLE...

ARMANDO RAMONE! YOU'RE FREE TO GO!

83

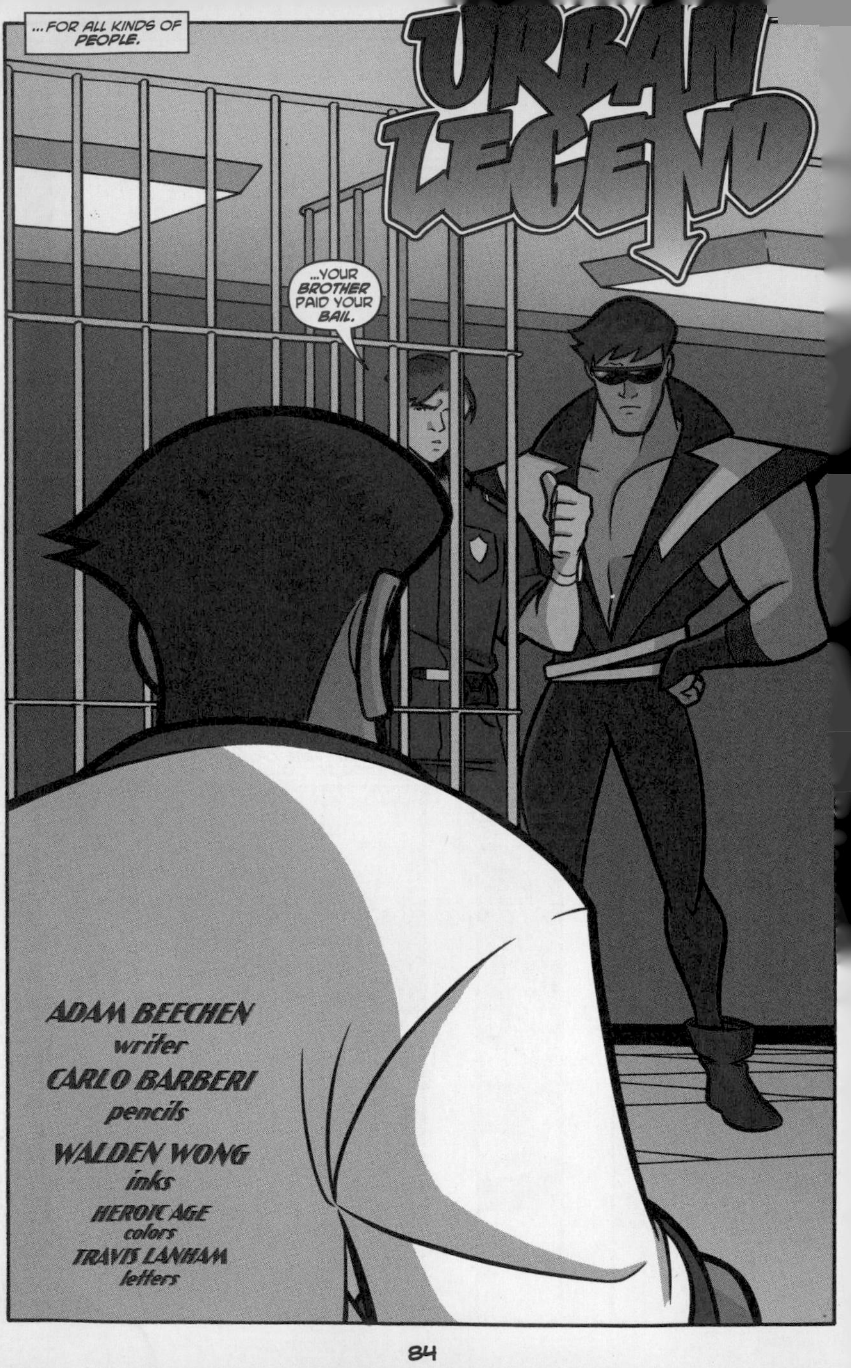

...FOR ALL KINDS OF PEOPLE.
URBAN LEGEND
...YOUR BROTHER PAID YOUR BAIL.
ADAM BEECHEN writer
CARLO BARBERI pencils
WALDEN WONG inks
HEROIC AGE colors
TRAVIS LANHAM letters

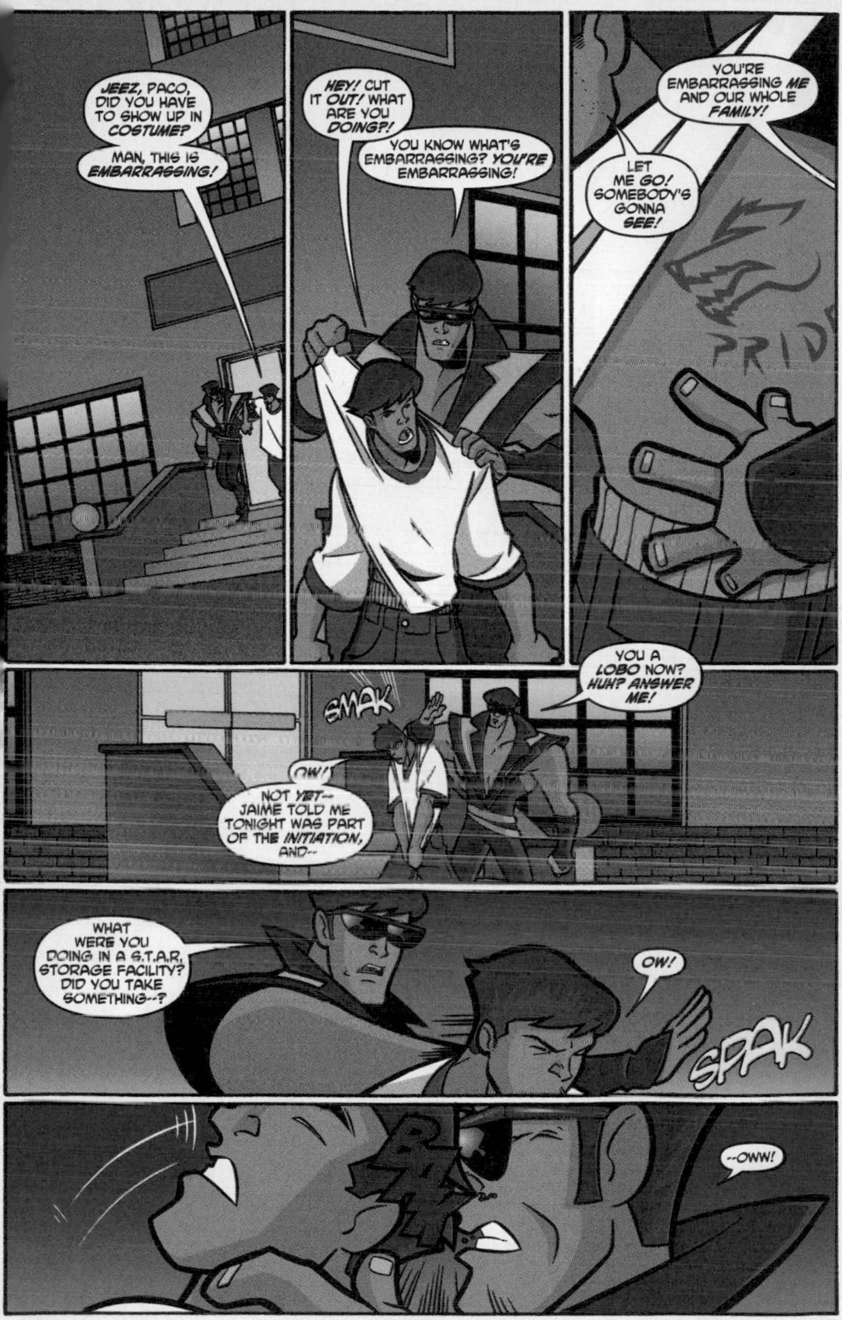

JEEZ, PACO, DID YOU HAVE TO SHOW UP IN COSTUME?
MAN, THIS IS EMBARRASSING!
HEY! CUT IT OUT! WHAT ARE YOU DOING?!
YOU KNOW WHAT'S EMBARRASSING? YOU'RE EMBARRASSING!
YOU'RE EMBARRASSING ME AND OUR WHOLE FAMILY!
LET ME GO! SOMEBODY'S GONNA SEE!
PRIDE
SMAK
YOU A LOBO NOW? HUH? ANSWER ME!
OW!
NOT YET-- JAIME TOLD ME TONIGHT WAS PART OF THE INITIATION, AND--
WHAT WERE YOU DOING IN A S.T.A.R. STORAGE FACILITY? DID YOU TAKE SOMETHING--?
OW!
SPAK
--OWW!

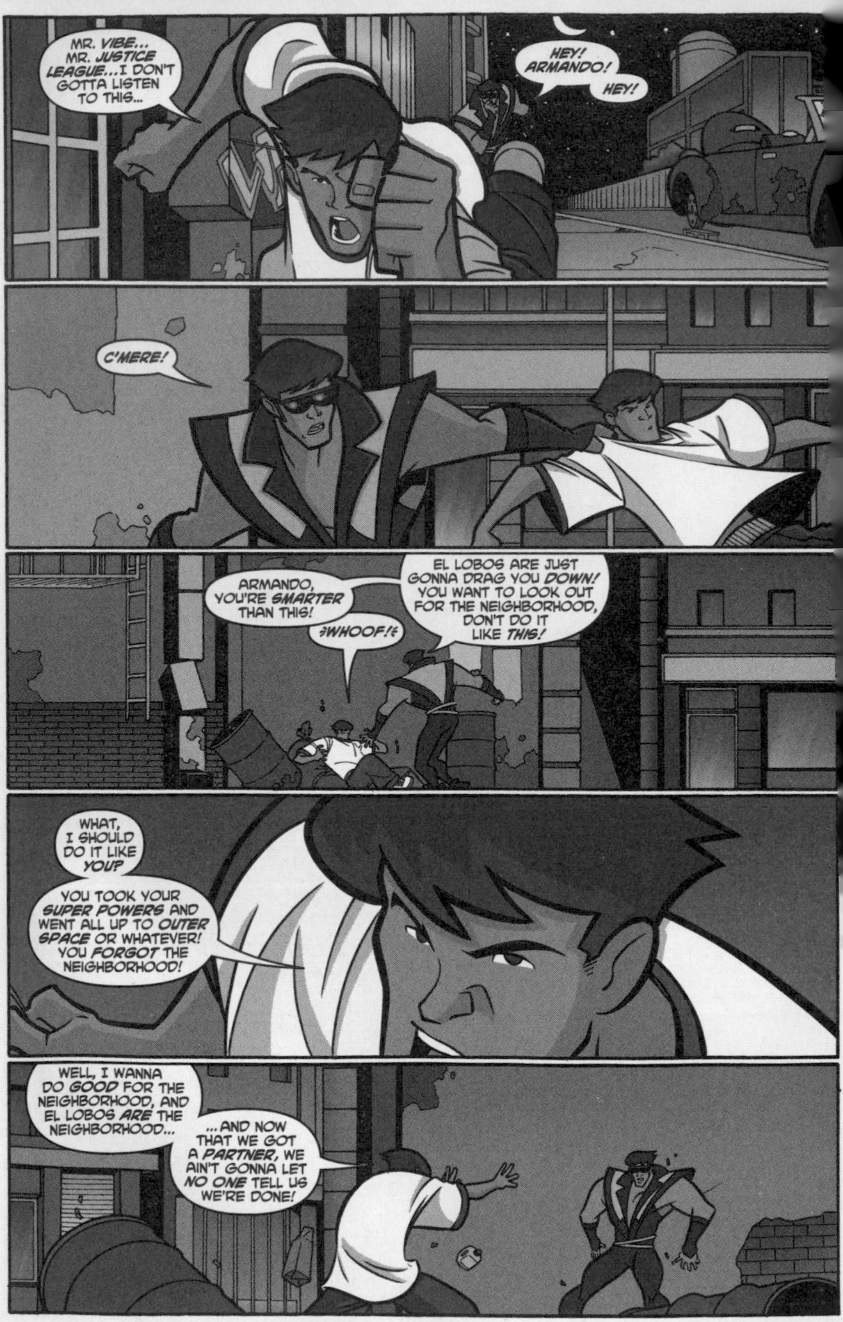
MR. VIBE... MR. JUSTICE LEAGUE...I DON'T GOTTA LISTEN TO THIS...
HEY! ARMANDO!
HEY!
C'MERE!
ARMANDO, YOU'RE SMARTER THAN THIS!
WHOOF!
EL LOBOS ARE JUST GONNA DRAG YOU DOWN! YOU WANT TO LOOK OUT FOR THE NEIGHBORHOOD, DON'T DO IT LIKE THIS!
WHAT, I SHOULD DO IT LIKE YOU?
YOU TOOK YOUR SUPER POWERS AND WENT ALL UP TO OUTER SPACE OR WHATEVER! YOU FORGOT THE NEIGHBORHOOD!
WELL, I WANNA DO GOOD FOR THE NEIGHBORHOOD, AND EL LOBOS ARE THE NEIGHBORHOOD...
...AND NOW THAT WE GOT A PARTNER, WE AIN'T GONNA LET NO ONE TELL US WE'RE DONE!

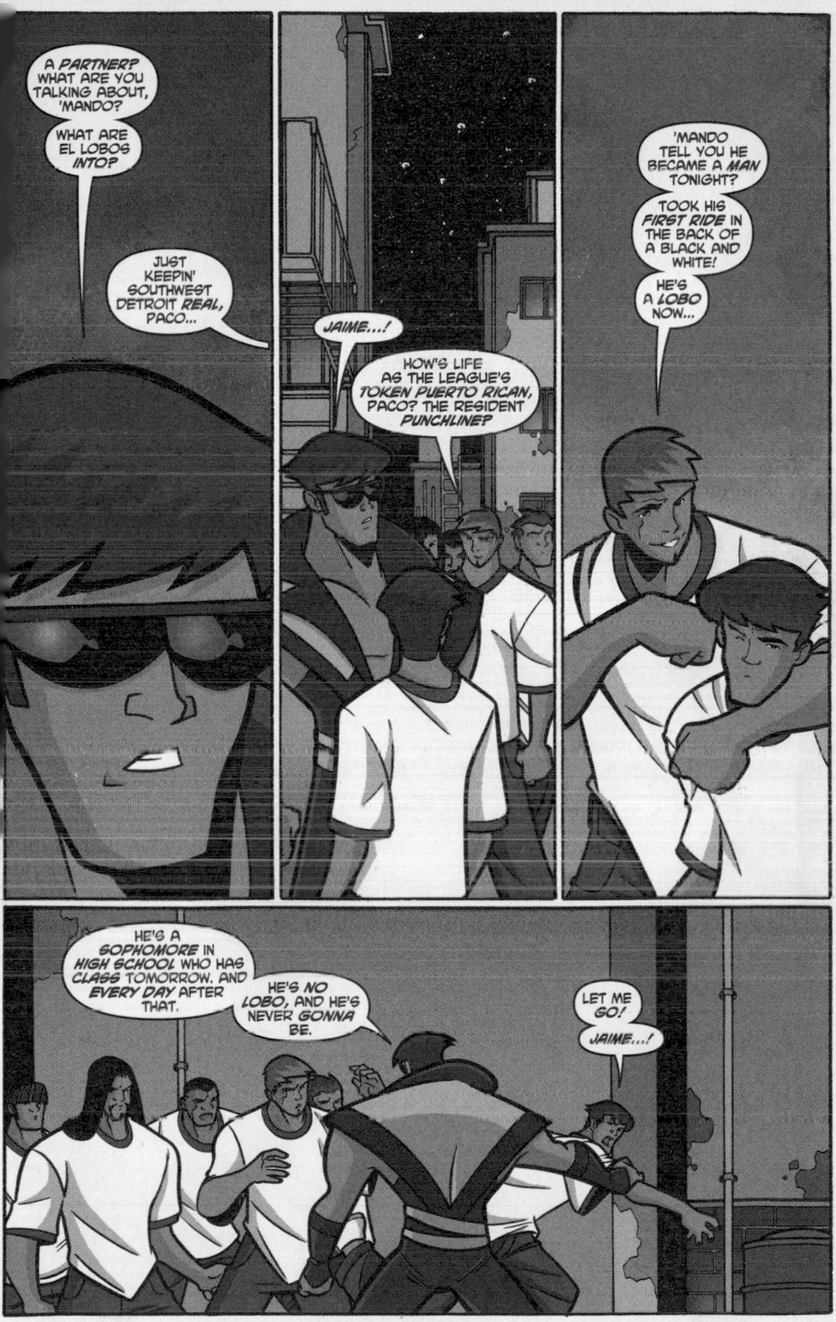
A PARTNER? WHAT ARE YOU TALKING ABOUT, 'MANDO?
WHAT ARE EL LOBOS INTO?
JUST KEEPIN' SOUTHWEST DETROIT REAL, PACO...
JAIME...!
HOW'S LIFE AS THE LEAGUE'S TOKEN PUERTO RICAN, PACO? THE RESIDENT PUNCHLINE?
'MANDO TELL YOU HE BECAME A MAN TONIGHT?
TOOK HIS FIRST RIDE IN THE BACK OF A BLACK AND WHITE!
HE'S A LOBO NOW...
HE'S A SOPHOMORE IN HIGH SCHOOL WHO HAS CLASS TOMORROW. AND EVERY DAY AFTER THAT.
HE'S NO LOBO, AND HE'S NEVER GONNA BE.
LET ME GO!
JAIME...!

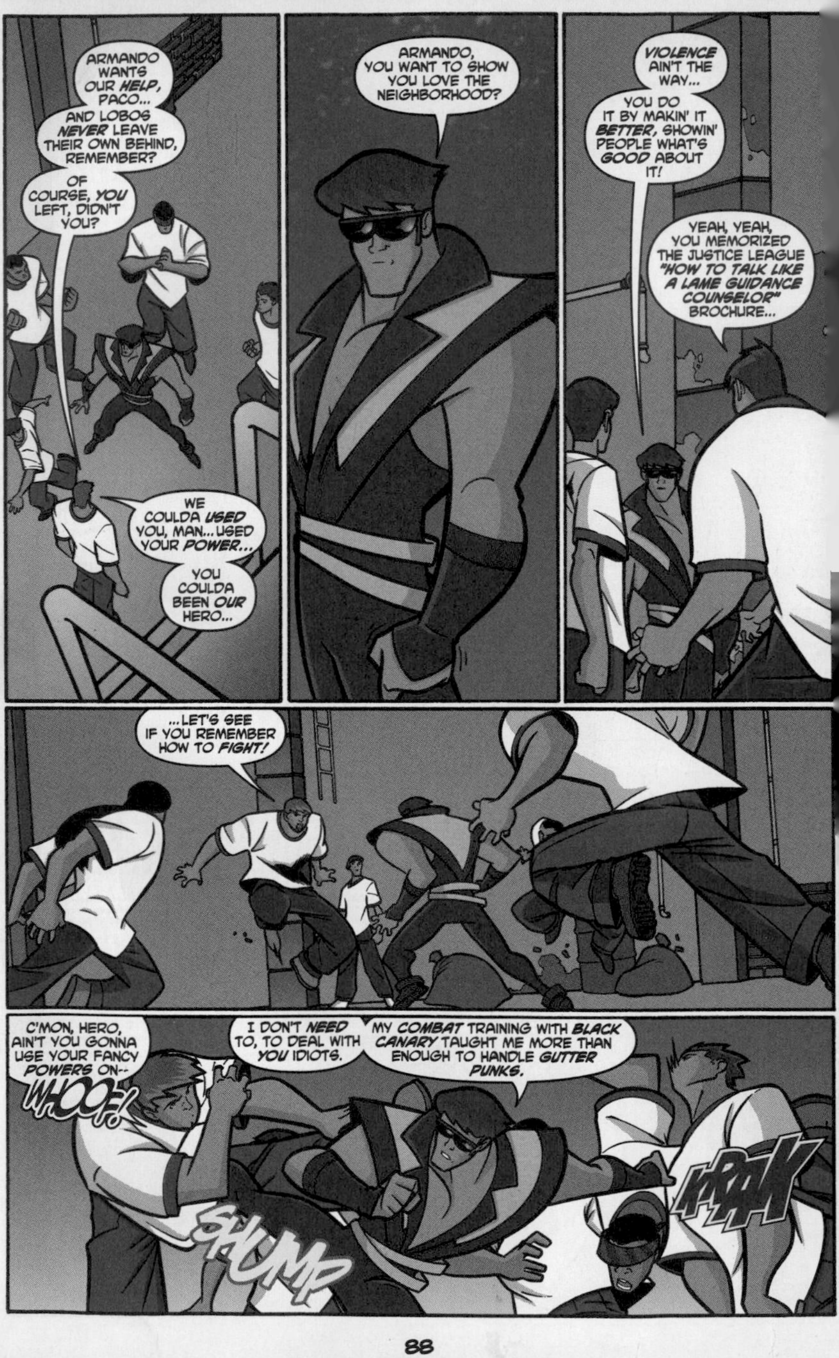
ARMANDO WANTS OUR HELP, PACO...
AND LOBOS NEVER LEAVE THEIR OWN BEHIND, REMEMBER?
OF COURSE, YOU LEFT, DIDN'T YOU?
WE COULDA USED YOU, MAN... USED YOUR POWER...
YOU COULDA BEEN OUR HERO...
ARMANDO, YOU WANT TO SHOW YOU LOVE THE NEIGHBORHOOD?
VIOLENCE AIN'T THE WAY...
YOU DO IT BY MAKIN' IT BETTER, SHOWIN' PEOPLE WHAT'S GOOD ABOUT IT!
YEAH, YEAH, YOU MEMORIZED THE JUSTICE LEAGUE "HOW TO TALK LIKE A LAME GUIDANCE COUNSELOR" BROCHURE...
...LET'S SEE IF YOU REMEMBER HOW TO FIGHT!
C'MON, HERO, AIN'T YOU GONNA USE YOUR FANCY POWERS ON--
WHOOF!
I DON'T NEED TO, TO DEAL WITH YOU IDIOTS.
MY COMBAT TRAINING WITH BLACK CANARY TAUGHT ME MORE THAN ENOUGH TO HANDLE GUTTER PUNKS.
KRAK
SHUMP

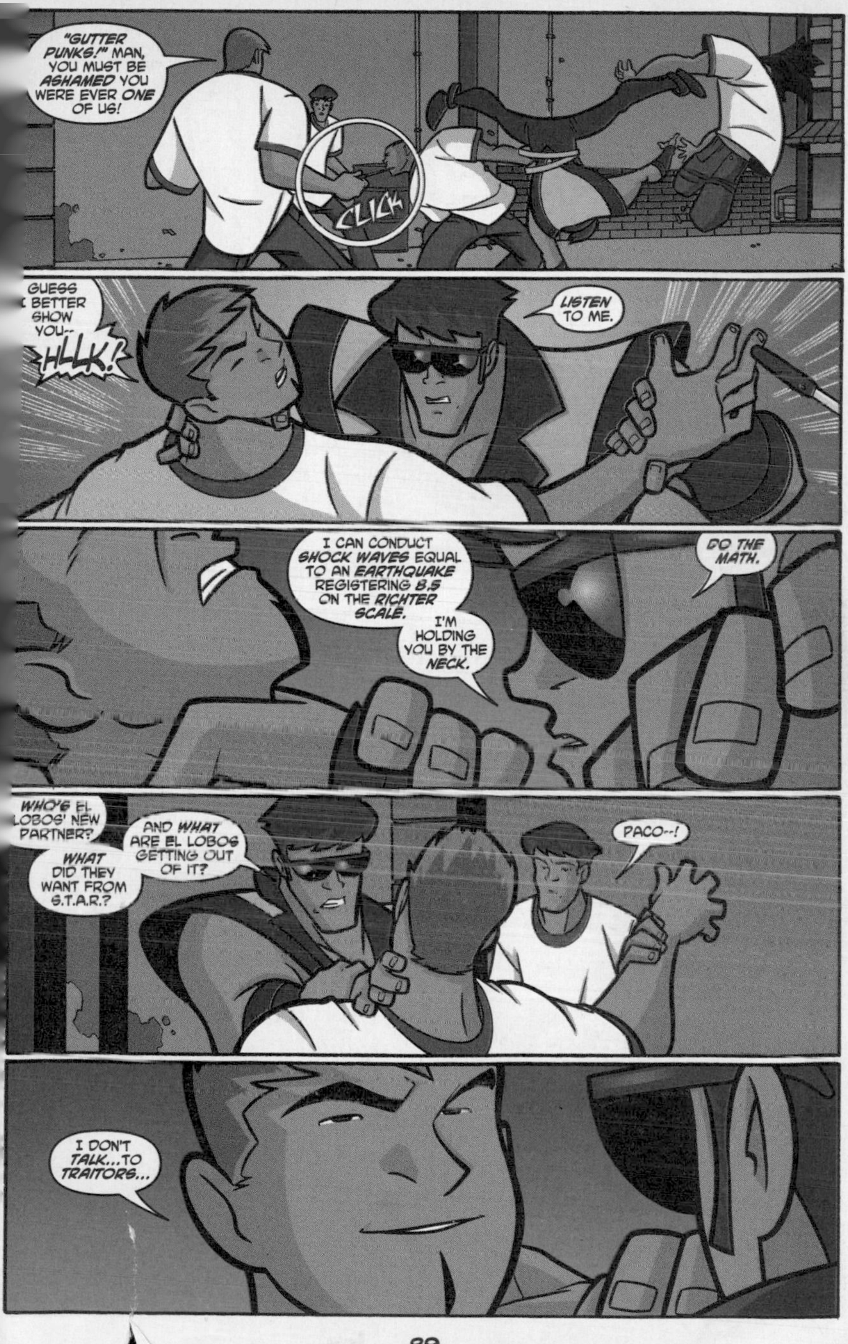
"GUTTER PUNKS!" MAN, YOU MUST BE ASHAMED YOU WERE EVER ONE OF US!
CLICK
GUESS I BETTER SHOW YOU--
HLLK!
LISTEN TO ME.
I CAN CONDUCT SHOCK WAVES EQUAL TO AN EARTHQUAKE REGISTERING 8.5 ON THE RICHTER SCALE.
I'M HOLDING YOU BY THE NECK.
DO THE MATH.
WHO'S EL LOBOS' NEW PARTNER?
WHAT DID THEY WANT FROM S.T.A.R.?
AND WHAT ARE EL LOBOS GETTING OUT OF IT?
PACO--!
I DON'T TALK...TO TRAITORS...

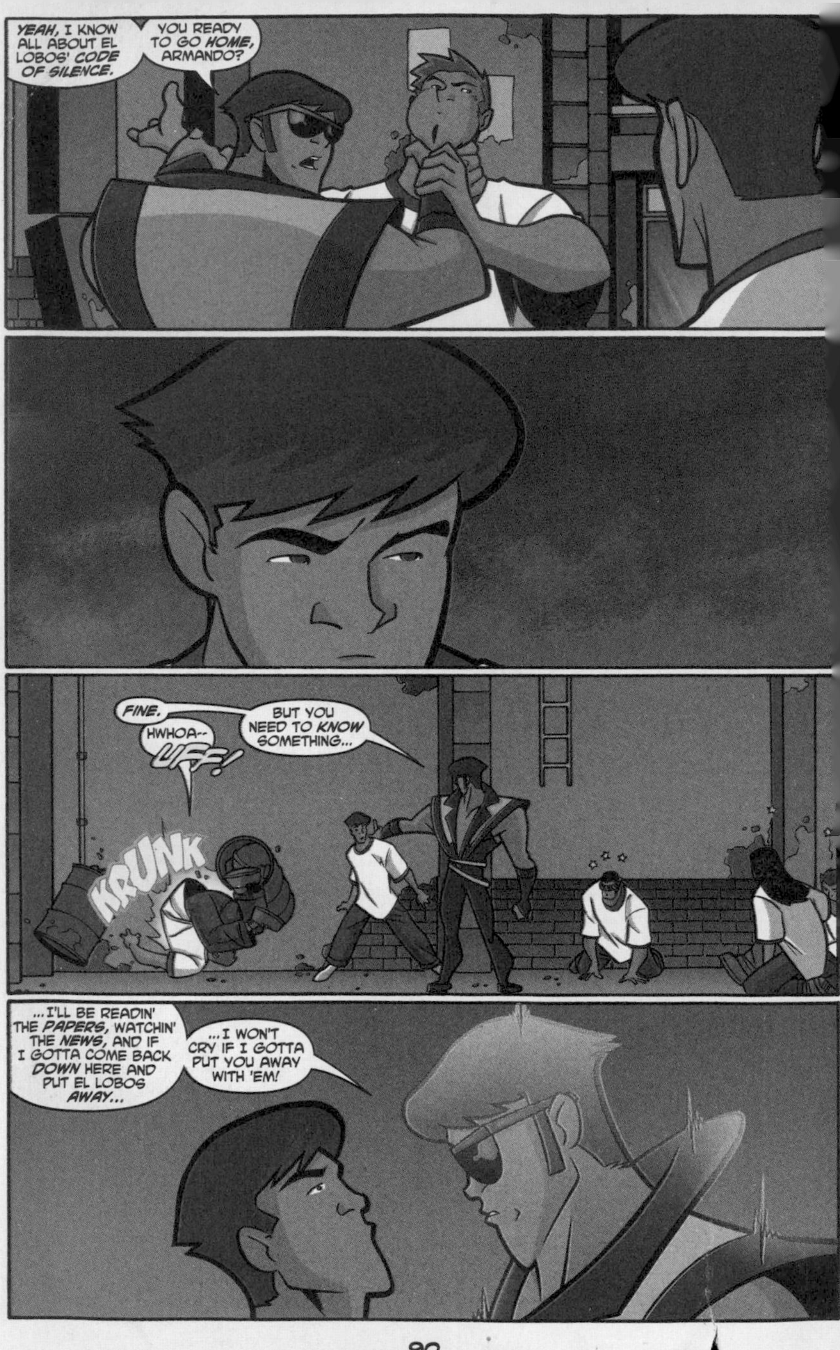
YEAH, I KNOW ALL ABOUT EL LOBOS' CODE OF SILENCE.
YOU READY TO GO HOME, ARMANDO?
FINE.
HWHOA-- UFF!
BUT YOU NEED TO KNOW SOMETHING...
KRUNK
...I'LL BE READIN' THE PAPERS, WATCHIN' THE NEWS, AND IF I GOTTA COME BACK DOWN HERE AND PUT EL LOBOS AWAY...
...I WON'T CRY IF I GOTTA PUT YOU AWAY WITH 'EM!

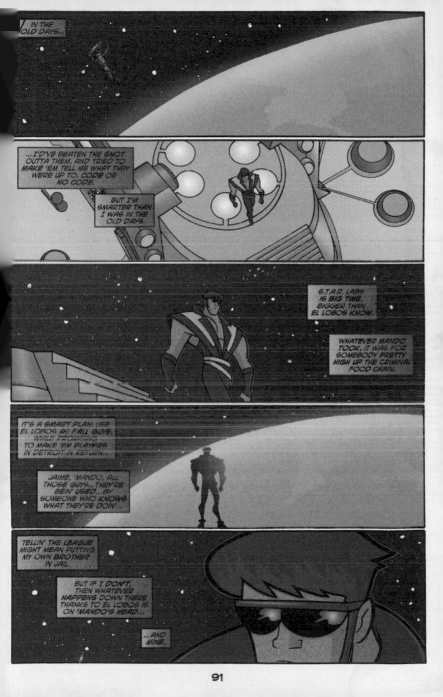

IN THE OLD DAYS...

...I'D'VE BEATEN THE SHOT OUTTA THEM, AND TRIED TO MAKE 'EM TELL ME WHAT THEY WERE UP TO, CODE OR NO CODE.

BUT I'M SMARTER THAN I WAS IN THE OLD DAYS.

S.T.A.R. LABS IS BIG TIME, BIGGER THAN EL LOBOS KNOW.

WHATEVER MANDO TOOK, IT WAS FOR SOMEBODY PRETTY HIGH UP THE CRIMINAL FOOD CHAIN.

IT'S A SMART PLAN: USE EL LOBOS AS FALL GUYS, WHILE PROMISING TO MAKE 'EM PLAYERS IN DETROIT IN RETURN...

JAIME, 'MANDO, ALL THOSE GUYS... THEY'RE BEIN' USED...BY SOMEONE WHO KNOWS WHAT THEY'RE DOIN'...

TELLIN' THE LEAGUE MIGHT MEAN PUTTING MY OWN BROTHER IN JAIL.

BUT IF I DON'T, THEN WHATEVER HAPPENS DOWN THERE THANKS TO EL LOBOS IS ON 'MANDO'S HEAD...

...AND MINE.

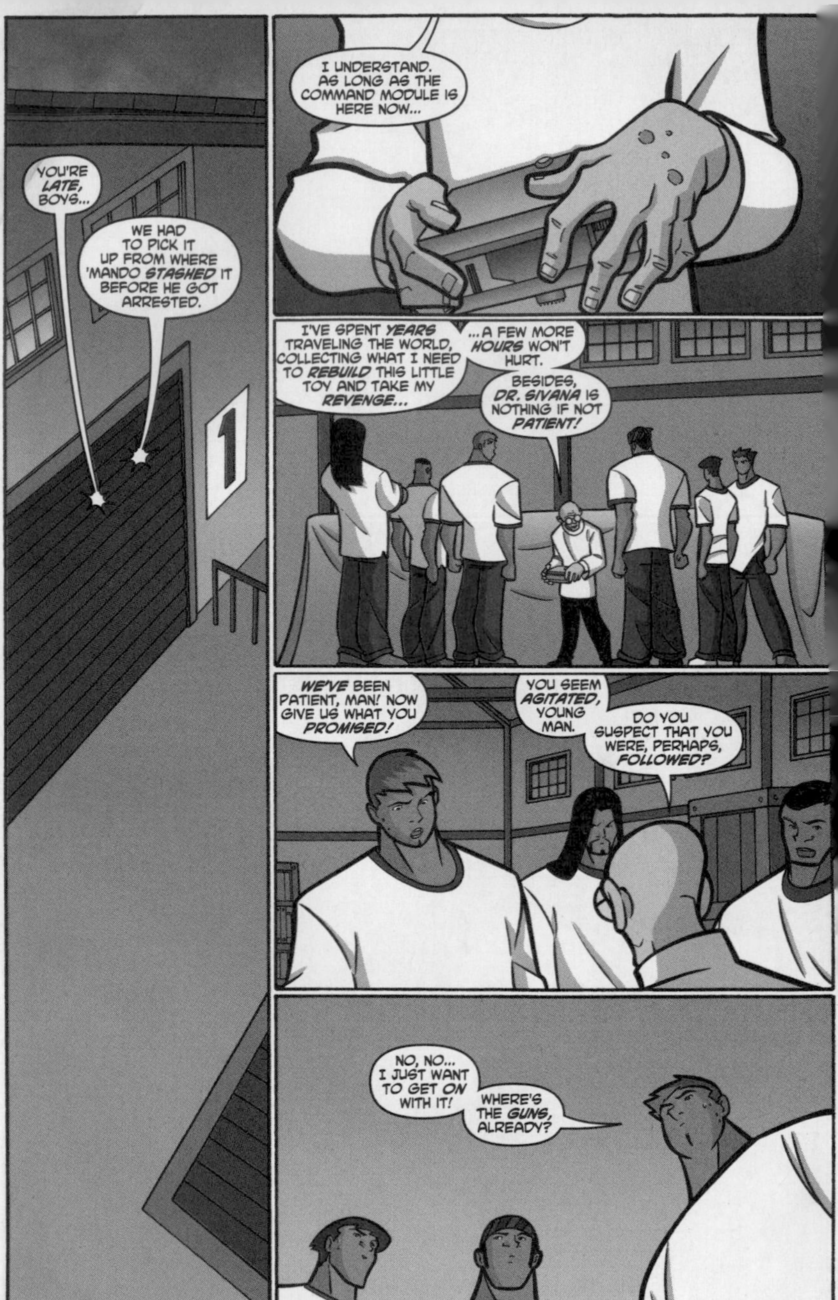
YOU'RE LATE, BOYS...
WE HAD TO PICK IT UP FROM WHERE 'MANDO STASHED IT BEFORE HE GOT ARRESTED.
I UNDERSTAND. AS LONG AS THE COMMAND MODULE IS HERE NOW...
I'VE SPENT YEARS TRAVELING THE WORLD, COLLECTING WHAT I NEED TO REBUILD THIS LITTLE TOY AND TAKE MY REVENGE...
...A FEW MORE HOURS WON'T HURT.
BESIDES, DR. SIVANA IS NOTHING IF NOT PATIENT!
1
WE'VE BEEN PATIENT, MAN! NOW GIVE US WHAT YOU PROMISED!
YOU SEEM AGITATED, YOUNG MAN.
DO YOU SUSPECT THAT YOU WERE, PERHAPS, FOLLOWED?
NO, NO... I JUST WANT TO GET ON WITH IT!
WHERE'S THE GUNS, ALREADY?

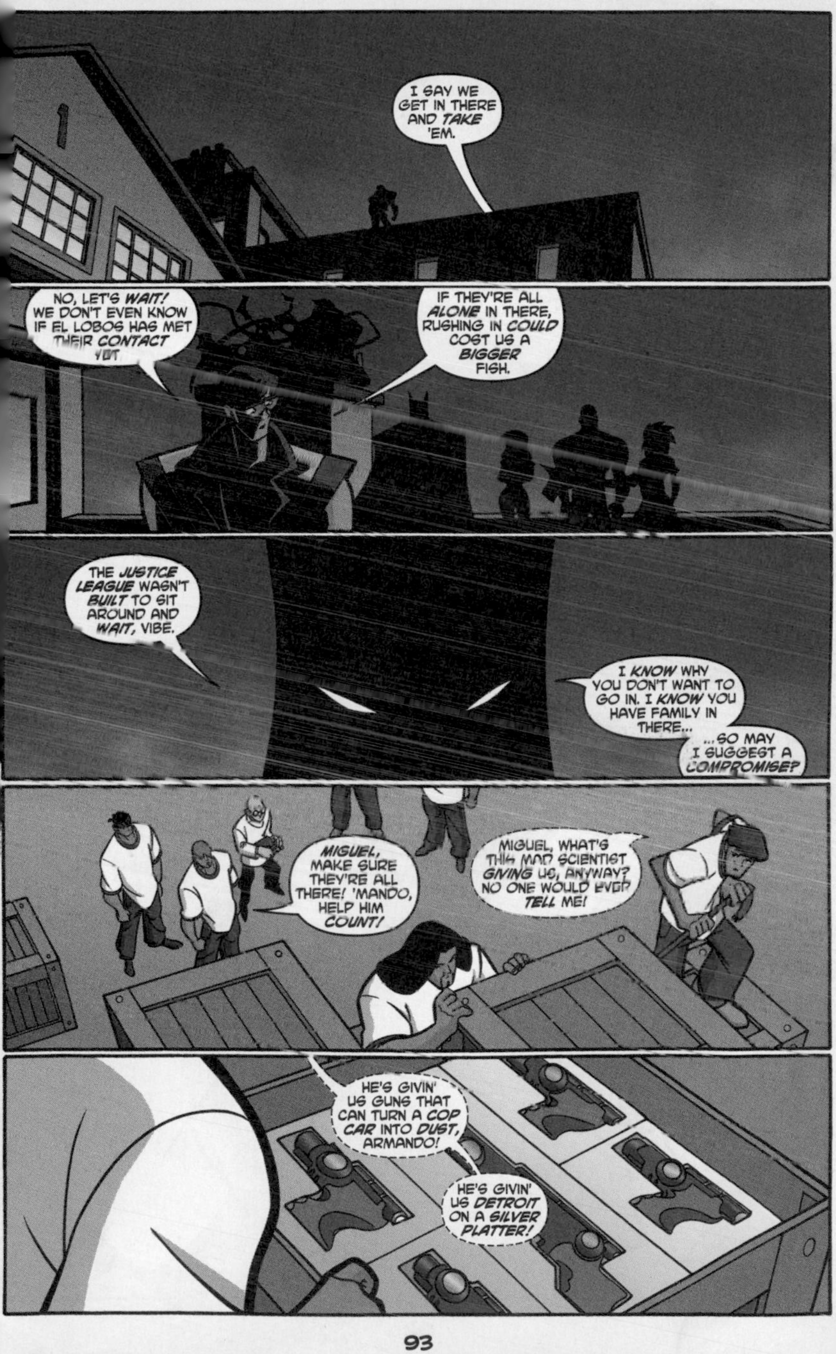
I SAY WE GET IN THERE AND TAKE 'EM.
NO, LET'S WAIT! WE DON'T EVEN KNOW IF EL LOBOS HAS MET THEIR CONTACT YET
IF THEY'RE ALL ALONE IN THERE, RUSHING IN COULD COST US A BIGGER FISH.
THE JUSTICE LEAGUE WASN'T BUILT TO SIT AROUND AND WAIT, VIBE.
I KNOW WHY YOU DON'T WANT TO GO IN. I KNOW YOU HAVE FAMILY IN THERE...
...SO MAY I SUGGEST A COMPROMISE?
MIGUEL, MAKE SURE THEY'RE ALL THERE! 'MANDO, HELP HIM COUNT!
MIGUEL, WHAT'S THIS MAD SCIENTIST GIVING US, ANYWAY? NO ONE WOULD EVER TELL ME!
HE'S GIVIN' US GUNS THAT CAN TURN A COP CAR INTO DUST, ARMANDO!
HE'S GIVIN' US DETROIT ON A SILVER PLATTER!

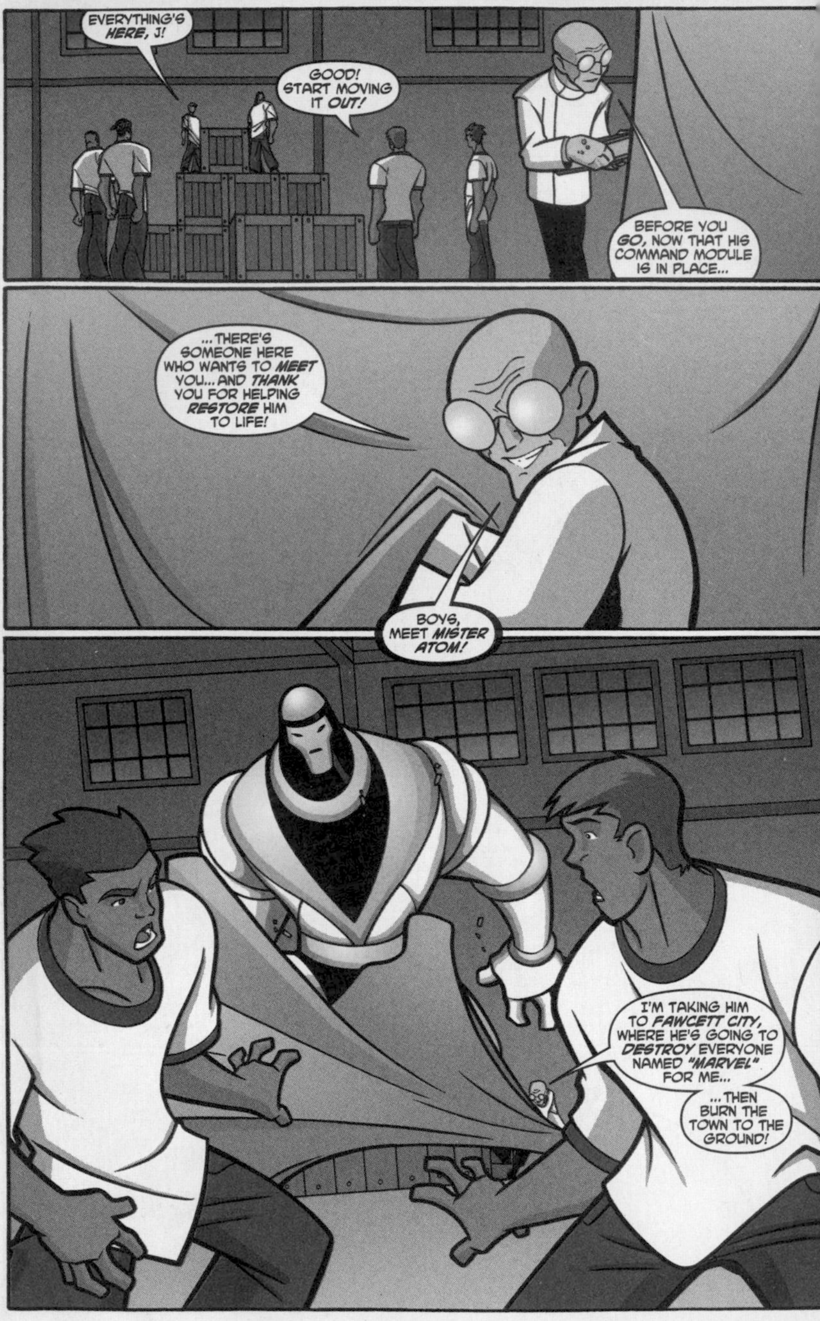
EVERYTHING'S *HERE*, J!
GOOD! START MOVING IT *OUT!*
BEFORE YOU *GO*, NOW THAT HIS COMMAND MODULE IS IN PLACE...
...THERE'S SOMEONE HERE WHO WANTS TO *MEET* YOU...AND *THANK* YOU FOR HELPING *RESTORE* HIM TO LIFE!
BOYS, MEET *MISTER ATOM!*
I'M TAKING HIM TO *FAWCETT CITY*, WHERE HE'S GOING TO *DESTROY* EVERYONE NAMED *"MARVEL"* FOR ME...
...THEN BURN THE TOWN TO THE GROUND!

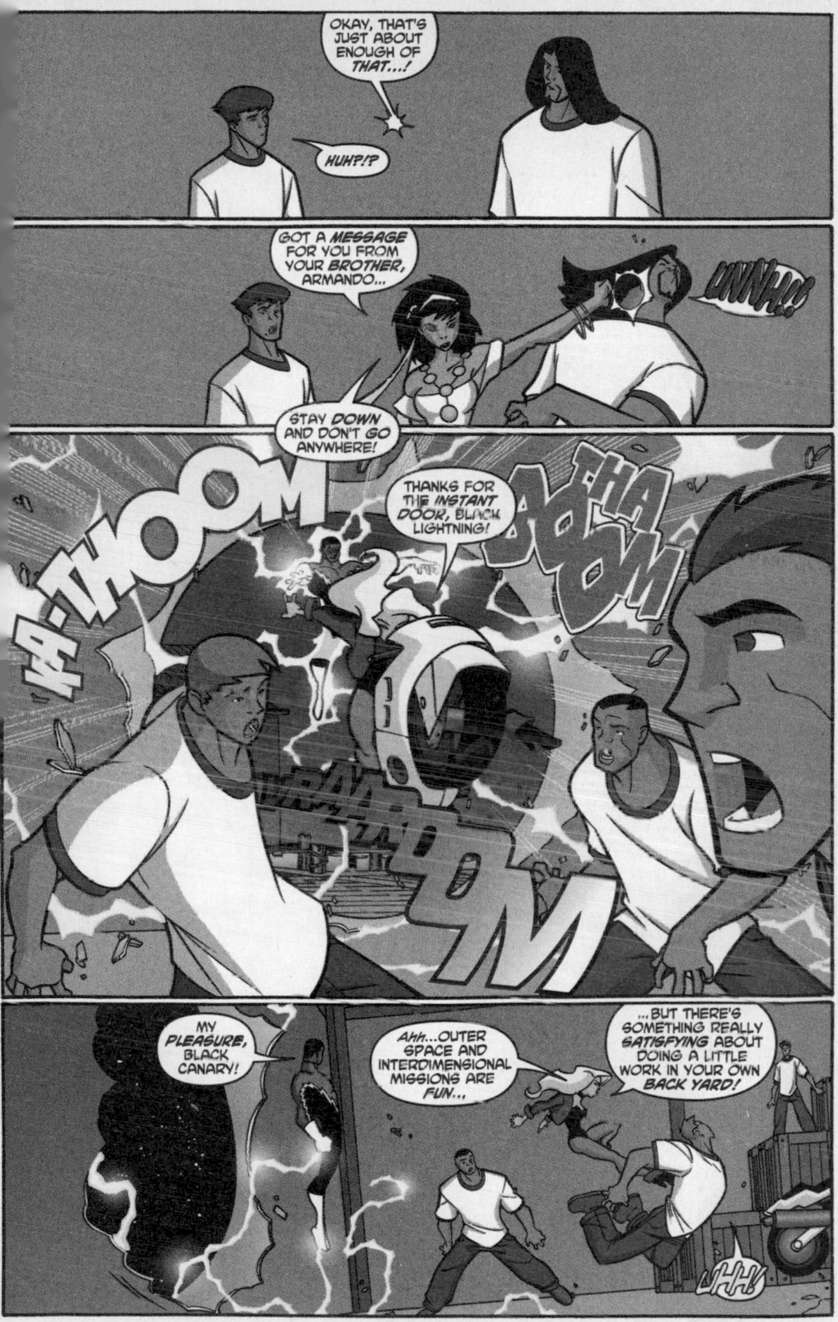
OKAY, THAT'S JUST ABOUT ENOUGH OF THAT...!
HUH?!?
GOT A MESSAGE FOR YOU FROM YOUR BROTHER, ARMANDO...
UNNH!!
STAY DOWN AND DON'T GO ANYWHERE!
KA-THOOM
THANKS FOR THE INSTANT DOOR, BLACK LIGHTNING!
THA DOOM
MY PLEASURE, BLACK CANARY!
Ahh...OUTER SPACE AND INTERDIMENSIONAL MISSIONS ARE FUN...
...BUT THERE'S SOMETHING REALLY SATISFYING ABOUT DOING A LITTLE WORK IN YOUR OWN BACK YARD!
UHH!

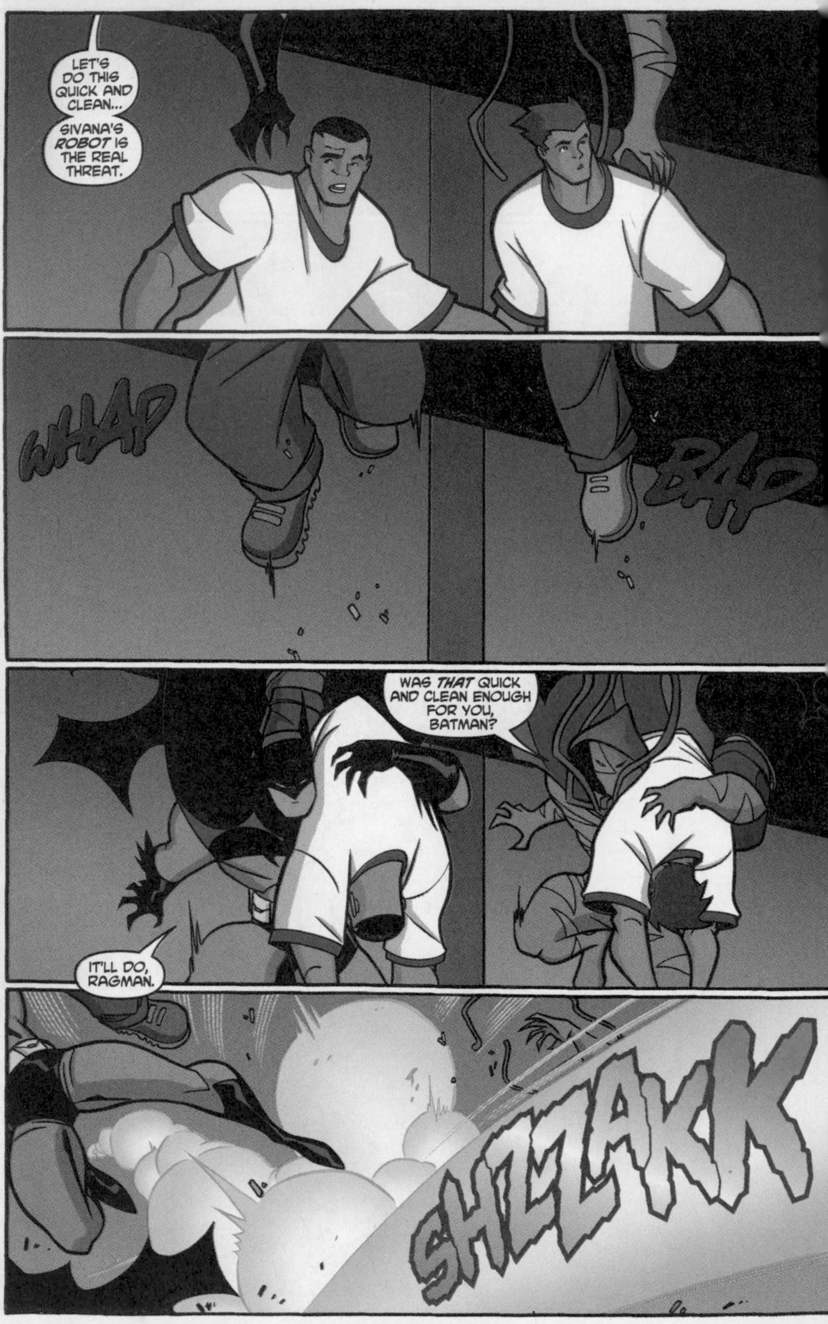
LET'S DO THIS QUICK AND CLEAN...
SIVANA'S *ROBOT* IS THE REAL THREAT.
WHAP
BAP
WAS *THAT* QUICK AND CLEAN ENOUGH FOR YOU, BATMAN?
IT'LL DO, RAGMAN.
SHZZAKK

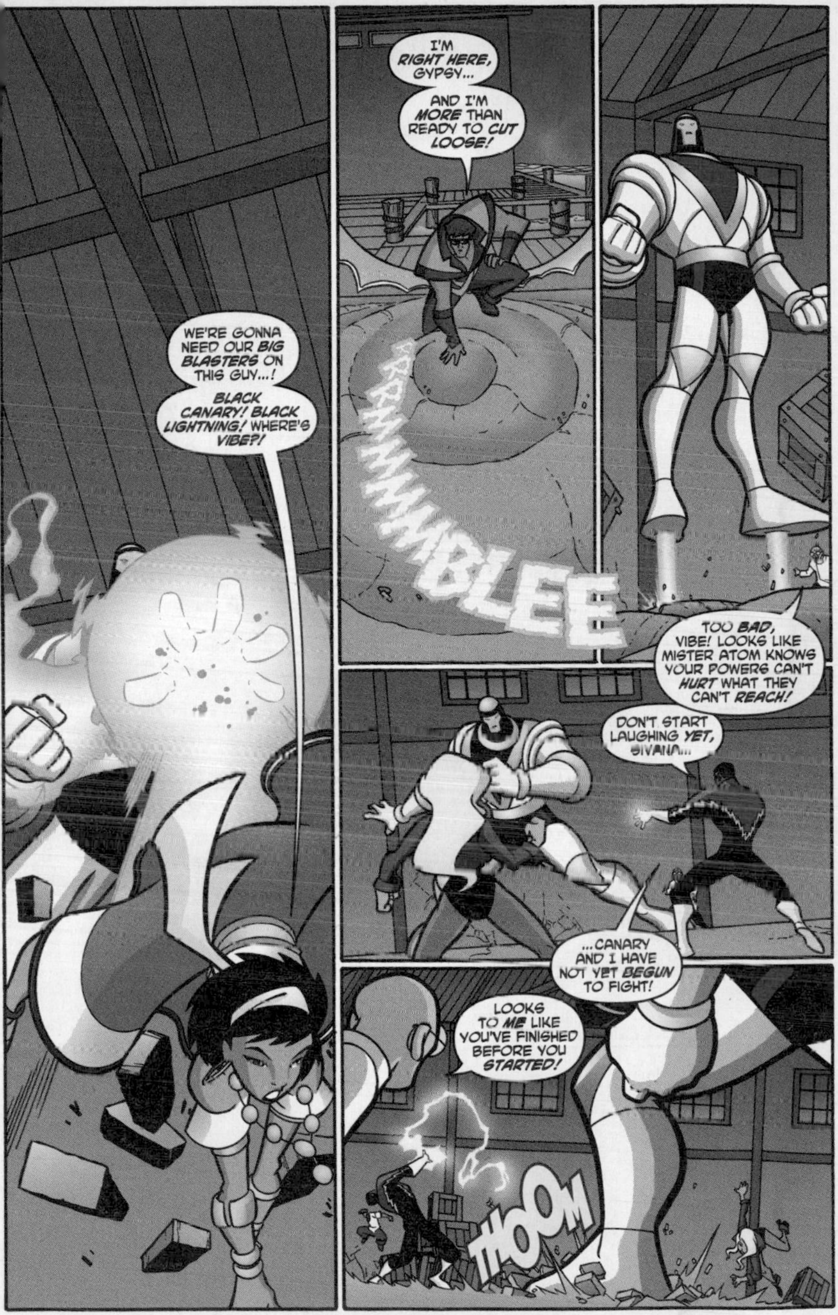

WE'RE GONNA NEED OUR BIG BLASTERS ON THIS GUY...!
BLACK CANARY! BLACK LIGHTNING! WHERE'S VIBE?!
I'M RIGHT HERE, GYPSY...
AND I'M MORE THAN READY TO CUT LOOSE!
BRRMMMMMMBLEE
TOO BAD, VIBE! LOOKS LIKE MISTER ATOM KNOWS YOUR POWERS CAN'T HURT WHAT THEY CAN'T REACH!
DON'T START LAUGHING YET, SIVANA...
...CANARY AND I HAVE NOT YET BEGUN TO FIGHT!
LOOKS TO ME LIKE YOU'VE FINISHED BEFORE YOU STARTED!
THOOM

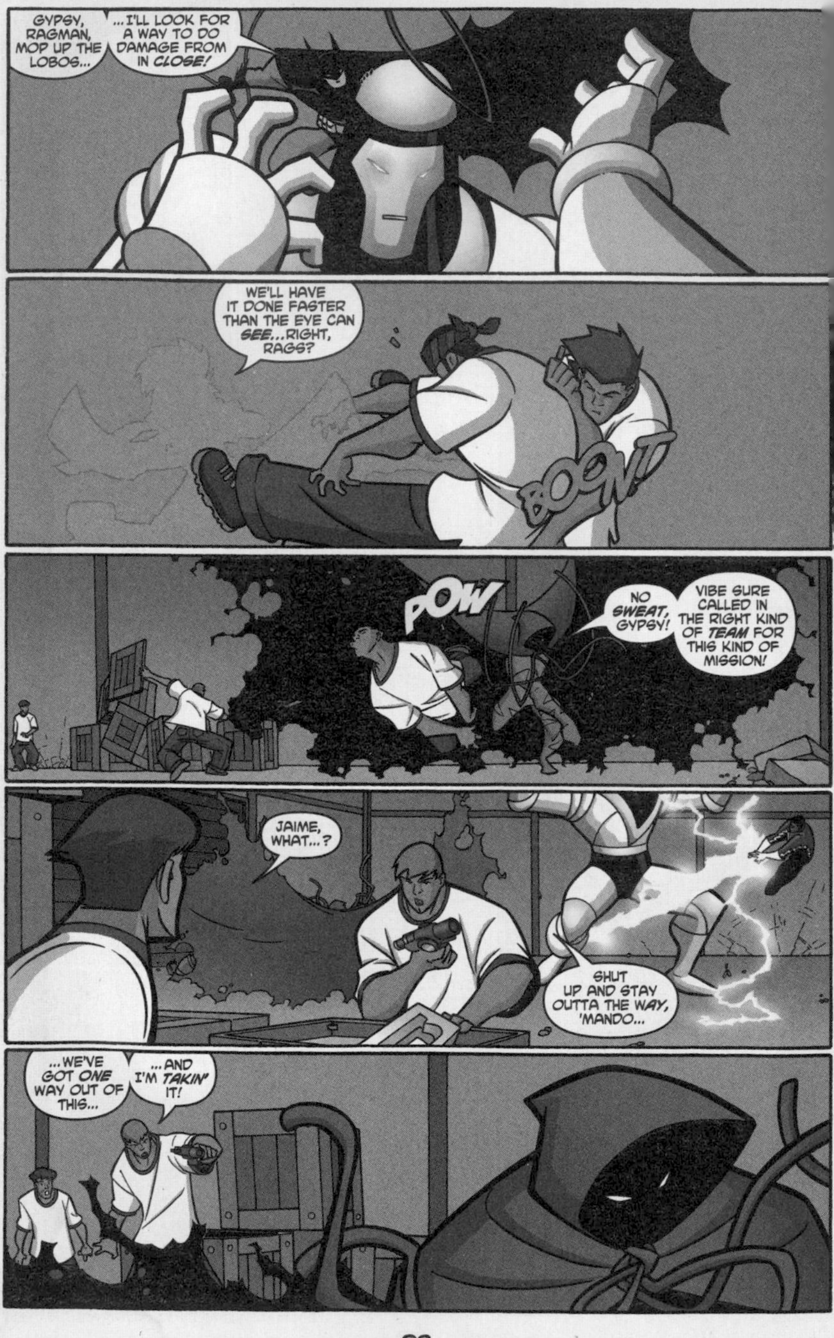
GYPSY, RAGMAN, MOP UP THE LOBOS...
...I'LL LOOK FOR A WAY TO DO DAMAGE FROM IN CLOSE!
WE'LL HAVE IT DONE FASTER THAN THE EYE CAN SEE...RIGHT, RAGS?
BOONT!
POW
NO SWEAT, GYPSY!
VIBE SURE CALLED IN THE RIGHT KIND OF TEAM FOR THIS KIND OF MISSION!
JAIME, WHAT...?
SHUT UP AND STAY OUTTA THE WAY, 'MANDO...
...WE'VE GOT ONE WAY OUT OF THIS...
...AND I'M TAKIN' IT!

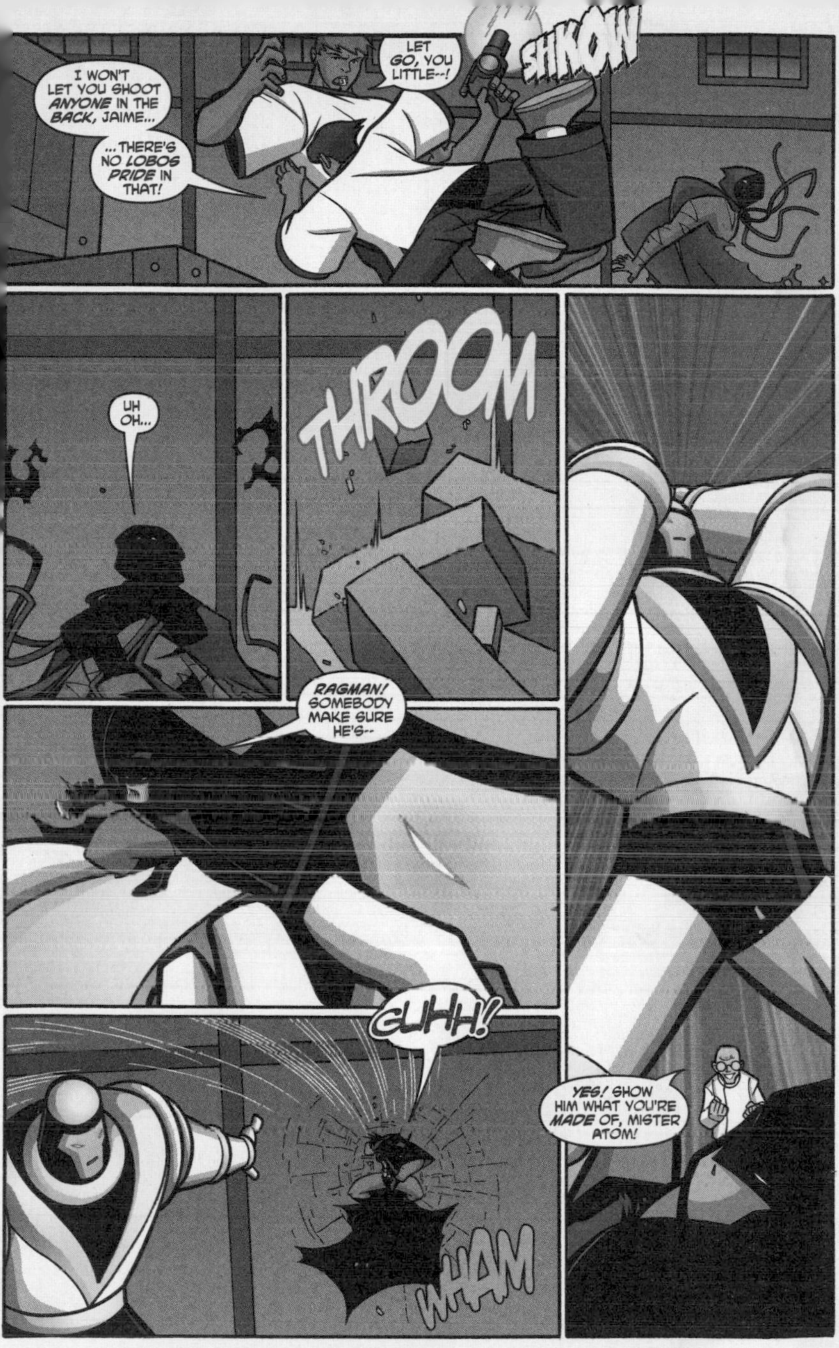
I WON'T LET YOU SHOOT ANYONE IN THE BACK, JAIME...
...THERE'S NO LOBOS PRIDE IN THAT!
LET GO, YOU LITTLE--!
SHKOW
UH OH...
THROOM
RAGMAN! SOMEBODY MAKE SURE HE'S--
GUHH!
WHAM
YES! SHOW HIM WHAT YOU'RE MADE OF, MISTER ATOM!

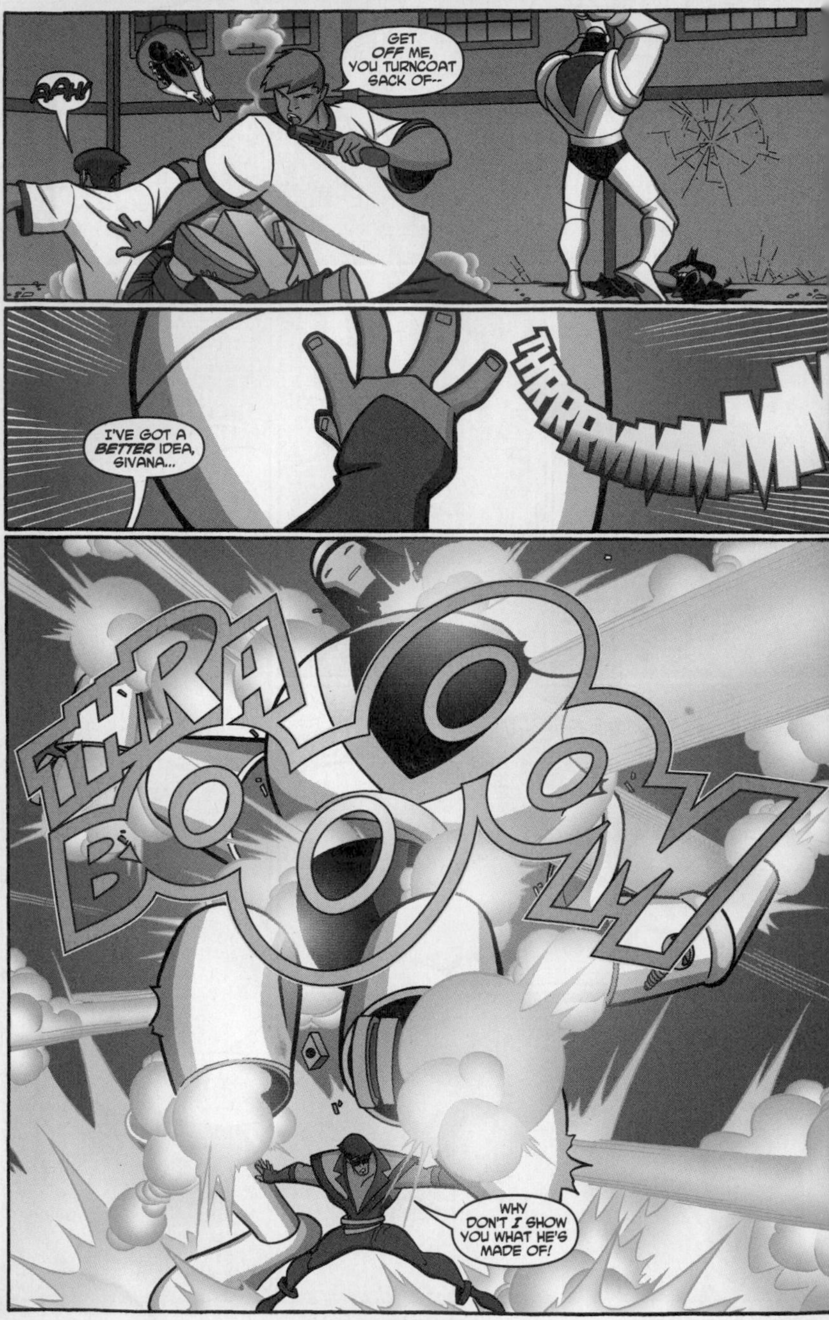
AAH!
GET OFF ME, YOU TURNCOAT SACK OF--
I'VE GOT A BETTER IDEA, SIVANA...
THRRMMMMN
THRAOOOW
BOOOOM
WHY DON'T I SHOW YOU WHAT HE'S MADE OF!

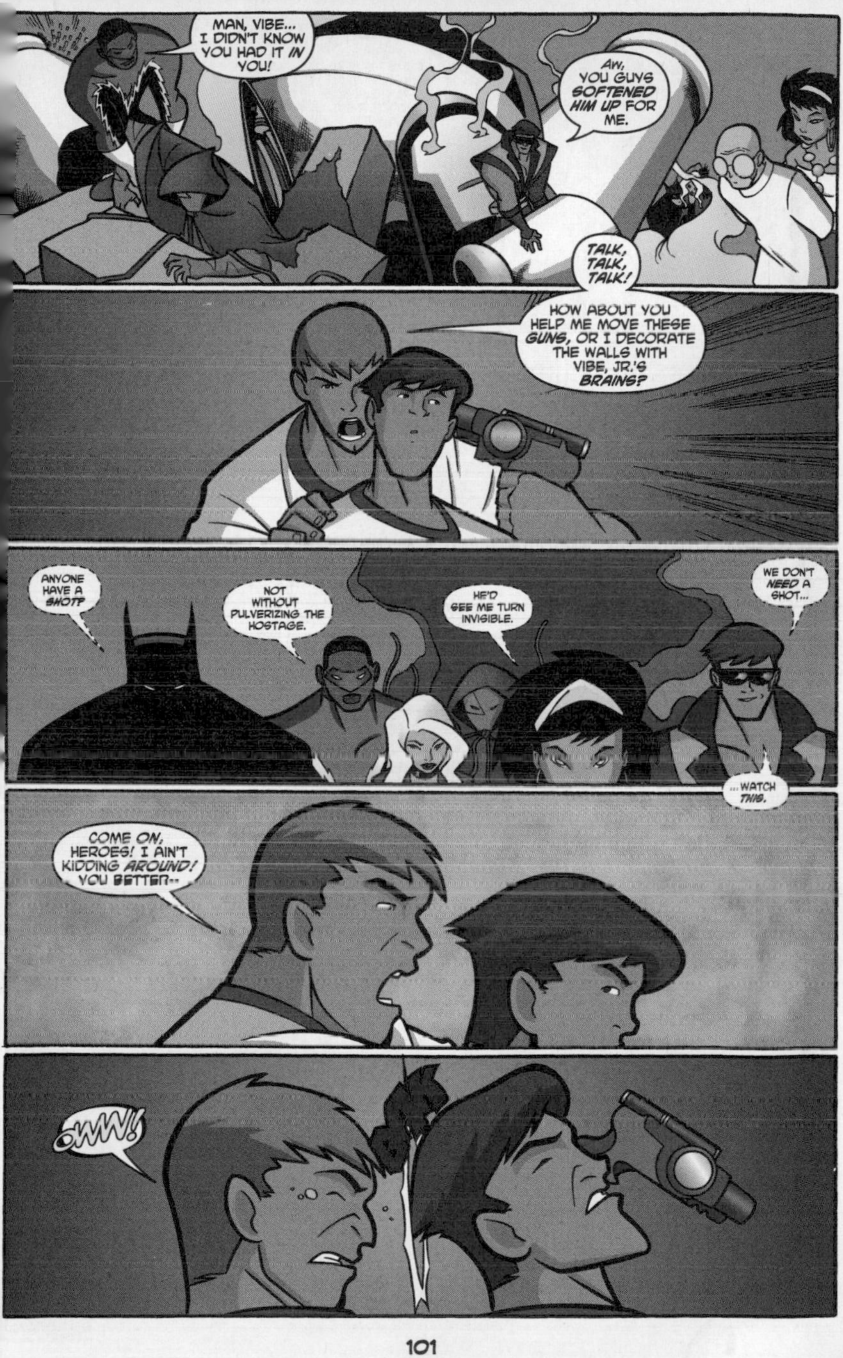
MAN, VIBE... I DIDN'T KNOW YOU HAD IT IN YOU!
AW, YOU GUYS SOFTENED HIM UP FOR ME.
TALK, TALK, TALK!
HOW ABOUT YOU HELP ME MOVE THESE GUNS, OR I DECORATE THE WALLS WITH VIBE, JR.'S BRAINS?
ANYONE HAVE A SHOT?
NOT WITHOUT PULVERIZING THE HOSTAGE.
HE'D SEE ME TURN INVISIBLE.
WE DON'T NEED A SHOT...
...WATCH THIS.
COME ON, HEROES! I AIN'T KIDDING AROUND! YOU BETTER--
OWW!!

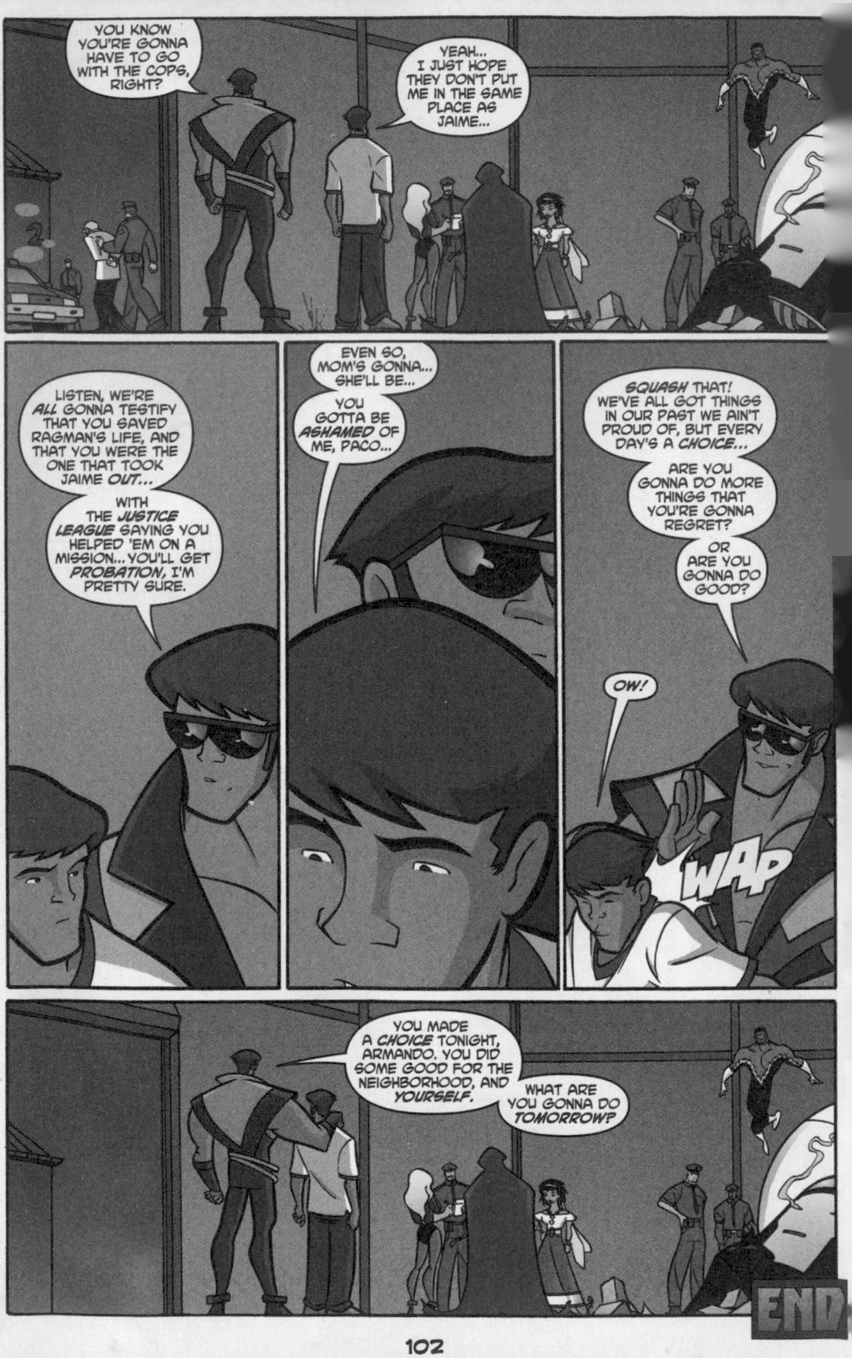
YOU KNOW YOU'RE GONNA HAVE TO GO WITH THE COPS, RIGHT?
YEAH... I JUST HOPE THEY DON'T PUT ME IN THE SAME PLACE AS JAIME...
LISTEN, WE'RE ALL GONNA TESTIFY THAT YOU SAVED RAGMAN'S LIFE, AND THAT YOU WERE THE ONE THAT TOOK JAIME OUT...
WITH THE JUSTICE LEAGUE SAYING YOU HELPED 'EM ON A MISSION... YOU'LL GET PROBATION, I'M PRETTY SURE.
EVEN SO, MOM'S GONNA... SHE'LL BE...
YOU GOTTA BE ASHAMED OF ME, PACO...
SQUASH THAT! WE'VE ALL GOT THINGS IN OUR PAST WE AIN'T PROUD OF, BUT EVERY DAY'S A CHOICE...
ARE YOU GONNA DO MORE THINGS THAT YOU'RE GONNA REGRET?
OR ARE YOU GONNA DO GOOD?
OW!
WAP
YOU MADE A CHOICE TONIGHT, ARMANDO. YOU DID SOME GOOD FOR THE NEIGHBORHOOD, AND YOURSELF.
WHAT ARE YOU GONNA DO TOMORROW?
END